Kismetwali
and
Other Stories

Reetika Khanna Nijhawan

OM
Om Books International

First published in 2015 by

OM

Om Books International

Corporate & Editorial Office
A-12, Sector 64, Noida 201 301
Uttar Pradesh, India
Phone: +91 120 477 4100
Email: editorial@ombooks.com
Website: www.ombooksinternational.com

Sales Office
107, Darya Ganj, New Delhi 110 002, India
Phone: +91 11 4000 9000, 2326 3363, 2326 5303
Fax: +91 11 2327 8091
Email: sales@ombooks.com
Website: www.ombooks.com

ISBN: 978-93-85031-72-4

Printed in India

10 9 8 7 6 5 4 3 2 1

For my father, Vimal Khanna, the intrepid sailor and spinner of yarns.

Contents

Acknowledgements

I would like to thank...

Jahaan and Keya, my children, for reminding me never to give up;

My friends across continents who read these stories in their unpolished state and offered feedback and words of encouragement;

Suman Khanna, my mother, for reminding me to keep my promise;

Arun, my husband, and Rajat, my brother—for your unwavering support;

Ipshita Mitra at Om Books International, for bringing this book to life;

Sylvester Monroe, my dear friend and mentor—for always answering your phone and

Frank Weaver, editor extraordinaire—you weave magic with words. I am forever indebted to you. This book is yours as much as it is mine.

Finally, I am grateful to all the *walas* and *walis*—the indispensable providers of service and peddlers of goods—who occupy the lowest rungs of Indian society. I claim no intimate familiarity with the true weight of their toil or the details of their exacting lives, but I recognise and salute their industriousness, invincible grit, and dogged sense of purpose.

~

The sea shanty sung in 'Shavewala' is from 'The Lass That Loves a Sailor,' one of the most popular patriotic songs written by British actor and composer Charles Dibdin (1740-1814).

The epigraph from Dante's *Inferno* in 'Kismetwali' may be translated as—

Fear not, for one's fate is something
that cannot be taken away. It is a gift.

The long snippet of poetry quoted in 'The Woman of Fortune' is from 'The Naini Tal Catastrophe of 18th September 1880' by Hannah S. Battersby, published in 1887 in the book *Home Lyrics* (Toronto: Hunter, Rose & Co.). The snippet of Latin poetry quoted in that same story is from *Carmina Burana*, a cantata of medieval poems set to music by Carl Orff (1895-1982). It may be translated as—

The wheel of Fortune turns:
I sink, debased,
while another is raised up.

Foreword

I did not know much about India before I met Reetika Khanna Nijhawan. In fact, our first meeting in 2004—to talk about her initial assignment as a freelance writer for the *Atlanta Journal-Constitution*, where I was an editor—showed just how little.

I do not know what I expected when I met her at the newspaper security desk. But it certainly was not the attractive young woman I initially looked right past as she stood there waiting in the lobby. Except for a few newsroom colleagues at work, the extent of my experience with Indians had been extremely limited—mainly brief, stereotypical encounters with highly skilled information technologists at one extreme; and taxi drivers, convenience store workers, and motel managers at the other.

Getting to know Reetika and her family over the past decade greatly expanded my understanding and appreciation of India and Indians. Reading Reetika's prose has opened a whole new world. And with *Kismetwali and Other Stories*, she has taken me even deeper into a part of that world few outsiders ever get to see. It is the world of the Indian underclass, born and reared into the service of others. And her stories speak eloquently and honestly about the ancient caste system in India, which still assigns individuals to rigid, socio-economic status based solely on pedigree. These are people who make their presence felt primarily by attending to the routine necessities of daily life that their employers and customers cannot or choose not to manage for themselves. Their only acknowledgment is the suffix *wala* or *wali* attached to the name of the job by which they earn their meagre livelihood. They are the barbers (*shavewalas*), the cab drivers (*taxiwalas*), the cleaning ladies (*safaiwalis*), the kebab vendors (*kebabwalas*), and others who toil in oblivion, while enriching the lives of those they serve.

A child of India's more privileged class, Reetika has shared stories about growing up in a house in northern India, where she and her family routinely received the sundry services of such people she called 'the invisibles.'

"Early every morning, before the *newspaperwala* had tossed that day's neatly folded edition of the *Times of India* onto our front lawn, my arthritic grandmother would shuffle from room to room to unlock all eight doors to the house, opening my childhood home to the invisibles," she told me. "Each of them was allowed to enter the house by one specially designated threshold, and each for a specific purpose."

In the opening story, 'Shavewala', Reetika introduces us to Hari, a hardworking, honest man of humble origins, thrust into heart-rending circumstances. Hari is summoned regularly into an upper-class home to groom a dying sailor. Over time, he comes to admire the valiant efforts of the man's devoted wife to prolong her husband's life with dignity. And in the end, Hari makes a heroic contribution to their remarkable love story.

Though India is an unfamiliar country to me, through Reetika's prose, I now see that its people are not so different from people I have known. 'Phoolwali' is the young girl selling flowers in Mumbai. Only geography sets her apart from the nameless little girl with a bucketful of roses standing at a traffic light near my old apartment in downtown Los Angeles.

In 'Taxiwala', Reetika shows us that the strict lines of social demarcation that separate people are just that—lines, not insuperable stone walls. We may know nothing of the privations or the dreams of these indigent men, women, and children who serve, but across those artificial lines we all share the same joys, sorrows, hopes, and fears.

In this remarkable collection of stories, the author puts names and faces to the anonymous individuals without whom the countless small amenities of civil society would simply disappear. India's iconic leader Mohandas Gandhi, and Rev. Martin Luther King Jr. understood this better than most. "We cannot all be famous because we cannot all be well known," Dr. King said. "But we can all be great because we can all serve."

The author's grandmother would often remind her that the servants were not lesser beings. "And she was right. In all the ways that matter, I am no different from them," Reetika once told me, explaining how she thinks of herself as a *kahaniwali*, "the humble teller of tales."

I knew nothing about this India before I read these stories. But they resonated with a remarkable relevance to my own humble beginnings as a poor inner city kid from the housing projects of Chicago, where many members of my family worked in the service industry. The stories are well told and engaging. And they strike a universal chord about how connected we are to each other, even across the fault lines of class and race. You do not have to be Indian to understand and appreciate these stories. You just have to be human.

–*Sylvester Monroe*
Washington DC
March, 2015

Shavewala

The Moving Finger writes; and, having writ,
Moves on: nor all thy Piety nor Wit
Shall lure it back to cancel half a Line,
Nor all thy Tears wash out a Word of it.
                    —*The Rubáiyát of Omar Khayyám*
                        (tr. by Edward FitzGerald)

DI-DI-DAH-DIT.

There. He had done it again. The letter *F*, tapped out by a trembling finger against his thigh in unmistakable Morse code, could mean anything. *Or nothing—mere muscle memory, a habit of nerves.* Kaveri hoped he was trying to relay their old secret signal of endearment, though just as likely it could be something ridiculously profane, and who could blame him? By the expression on his face, it was difficult to say. She had seen it many times before. She remembered that one night finding him on the bridge deck, hunched against the railing, with the same faraway look in his eyes. The ship had been delayed by weather, and now it lay anchored off Bremerhaven, rocked gently by the calm, cold Atlantic, until a berth opened on the jetty the next day, or perhaps the day after. With what longing had Vinay stared at the distant lights of the city, twinkling lustily in the frigid night air. And oh, how well she knew him. More than anything, on this night of all nights, he wished he were on shore taking part in the festivities. In no time at all he would have sniffed out a party, or got one up himself, and by the wee hours he would have made fast friends of everyone he met. Of course, come the morn, he would be itching to get back to sea. A most complex man—such was her husband as she knew him, had known him, once upon a time.

Lost in thought, he had remained unaware of his wife's presence on the deck until she called out to him.

"Hey, Sparks."

"Ah, Kaveri. I was just about to come looking for you." He gave her an affectionate peck on the cheek and then glanced at his watch. "It's almost midnight."

Somewhere along the harbour a symphony orchestra began playing, and the faint strains of music, borne by a gentle land breeze, wafted toward the ship across the cold, black expanse of water.

"What do you know, we're being serenaded," she quipped. "It's Beethoven's Fifth."

"And a perfect night it is for it," he said. "Though to be honest, the only fifth I'm fit for right now is a bourbon."

She reached up with both hands and began stroking his temples. "How's that headache?"

"The aspirin helped. At least it's not throbbing now." A pensive expression suddenly clouded his features. "You know, I've never made a mistake like that before. It's worrisome."

"Don't beat yourself up over it, Vinay. We all make mistakes and that was such a small one. Leaving out just one letter can't make that much of a difference."

"In my line of work it does. A garbled message can kill a man or sink a ship."

"You're just tired. Maybe it's a lucky thing we can't celebrate in town. A good night's sleep will work wonders for you."

They listened to the rest of the symphony in silence. The captain and a few of the other officers, some with wives, meandered out to join them, and at the finale a thunderous salvo of fireworks lit up the night sky. Vinay clasped Kaveri in his arms and kissed her on the lips. "Happy new year, my darling," he said. "This one will be even better than the last, I promise." Someone popped the cork on a bottle of champagne, and while the bottle was passed around everybody shook hands and toasted one another's health in half-a-dozen languages.

Finally, Vinay shouted gleefully to no one in particular, "Damn, it's colder than a witch's teat out here." He grabbed Kaveri by the arm. "Let's go inside and get warm." Then he nuzzled her ear and whispered softly, "I can show you some real fireworks if you want."

True-blue and tenacious, Vinay took his promises very seriously. That was the only one he ever broke to her. The year did not get better. The headaches became more frequent, the forgetfulness less random. And when Kaveri found him wandering around their house in a daze, with one shoe on and the other off, she knew they had a problem.

So here they were again, anchored and waiting and missing their chance. But it was different now. There would be no berth for him on the jetty, no safe harbour to sail into, no celebration, no thunder of fireworks convulsing the air. Kaveri would have dragged her husband back out to sea if she could, but she possessed no such power.

Like a record skipping, the finger continued to tap out the letter F, over and over. Alert for the smallest sign of recognition or distress, she watched him intently now, the once muscular, vital man shrivelled up and sagging in the wheelchair as though he had straw for bones. The faraway look had become a permanent feature. He always used to relish sitting out here on the veranda for his Saturday morning shave, luxuriating under a froth of foam and sunshine while he listened to his favourite music. She hoped that some conscious part of him still enjoyed it.

Flipping open the straight razor with an alacrity that can come only from years of practice, Hari quickly stropped the edge and then began circumscribing her husband's French-style beard with careful strokes of the long blade. No longer lost in thought, but simply lost, Vinay was incapable of critical inspection in the hand-held mirror, yet the *shavewala* pruned for perfection. He gently pushed his client's head further back and stretched the folds on his neck, going over previously concealed sections.

Kaveri liked that about Hari. He never rushed a job. And so she stood watching, not to scrutinise, but finding in the simple act of observing a peaceful respite. Vinay was in someone else's hands, and for these few minutes she no longer had to be in charge. She imagined that this was how mothers must feel when their children were away at school.

Wiping away the last remaining flecks of lather with a clean washcloth, Hari wheeled Vinay back into the bedroom, and together he and Kaveri easily lifted her husband, who weighed practically nothing, onto the bed. Then she covered him with a thin blanket, replaced the cushions along his hips and shoulders, and adjusted the pillow under his head. There was no after-shave glow in his dark skin, which had the appearance and texture of old, dried-out animal hide. She rubbed a few blobs of face cream between her hands and spread it evenly on Vinay's face. The expensive imported moisturiser, which she used sparingly on her own skin to keep it looking youthful, merely left a synthetic sheen on his sunken features. It was like smearing cream on the face of a gaunt, plastic mannequin. She was not even sure why she did it—whether to alleviate his unarticulated agony or to mask the evidence of atrophy, she could not say. It did not matter. Her ingenious attempts to disguise the signs of impending death on her 46-year-old husband's face failed repeatedly, but Kaveri was not quite ready to give up.

As she performed her futile ministrations, Hari remained standing by the foot of the bed, his hands folded together at his waist. She could sense his eyes on her, and she remembered the day some 15 years ago when Vinay had brought him home and introduced him as though he were an old high school buddy. "This young man here is Hari, the *shavewala*. He recently set up shop under that old *peepal* tree near the entrance to Landour Bazaar. You know which tree I'm talking about? Anyway, Hari is going to come to the house on Saturday mornings to give me a proper shave, right here on the veranda. I will close my eyes and listen to Johnny Cash, while he does all the work!"

The prospect of allowing a stranger into her home would normally make her feel uncomfortable, but Hari seemed safe and familiar, even though they had never met before. Something about this *shavewala*, perhaps the warmth in his large, eager eyes or the kindness in his smile, convinced Kaveri to trust him.

She could tell that he was dismayed to see a little less of Vinay with each passing Saturday, as if every week another small piece of his longtime client had gone missing.

"Vinay *sahib* was always full of life," Hari said sadly, shaking his head. "I still remember all the jokes he used to tell. The Ajit jokes were my favourite. He did a really good villain voice."

Vinay's impersonations of Ajit Khan, a popular actor who made a career out of playing scoundrels in Hindi films, had been delightfully flawless. Kaveri could still hear the echoes of her husband's diabolical intonations and the demonic laugh that rose from deep in his belly.

"Tell me an Ajit joke, Hari."

"A joke that *sahib* told me?"

"Yes. A joke Vinay told you."

It took him a few seconds to shake off the despondence that had seeped into his soul. It was a vague feeling, ominous and without form. He could not describe it in words, but it touched him with the icy fingers of some ghastly *churel* clutching greedily at his marrowbones.

"Okay. So, Ajit turns to his assistant Mona and says...." Hari cleared his throat and made a half-hearted attempt to mimic the actor, but he played his character with a painfully self-conscious demeanour and very little in the way of vocal inflection. "Mona darling, put this guy in the liquid oxygen. The liquid won't let him live—and the oxygen won't let him die. Ha, ha, ha."

Kaveri managed a shallow laugh from pursed lips and turned to look at Vinay. Would Hari's lacklustre delivery spur the irrepressible entertainer to sit up, unassisted, and show the *shavewala* how it really ought to be done? "You've got it all wrong, Hari!" he would have said. "You have to say it in a deeper, raspier voice, like you're choking on gravel. And by the way, Mona isn't in that movie. It's Robert who's supposed to put the police officer in the liquid oxygen."

Vinay the master farceur lay motionless, oblivious now to all jokes, gazing fixedly on the ceiling fan spinning overhead.

"Thank you. I liked that. Tell me another one next time." Kaveri handed Hari his payment, which he accepted with a customary bow.

"Hari, can you come on Wednesday mornings as well? I think *sahib* prefers your skilled hands to my impatient razor work. Oh, and the night nurse can no longer stay over on Tuesdays. Perhaps you can help me get him to the bathroom after the shave? I like to bathe him in the mornings."

"Kaveri madam, I have two assistants at my shop now. I can come whenever you wish. Just call me on my cell—I always keep it with me." Hari extracted a small black phone from his pocket and held it out for her inspection. She smiled at the *shavewala*'s guileless enthusiasm.

"You are like family, Hari. We have known you for so many years and now, these past few months since *sahib* fell sick, you have been a big help. I want you to know how very grateful I am."

Her gratitude was genuine. She could still count on Hari. Old friends who once sought out the couple—the dashing mariner and his stylish wife—had gradually drifted away, until almost none were left. It seemed like only yesterday that Vinay stood tall in a navy sports jacket and scarf, holding a whisky in one hand and gesturing wildly with the other. "And then the sailor comes home and says to his wife, 'Why is his belaying pin where my belaying pin should be?'" He was the cynosure at every social gathering, the proverbial swashbuckler regaling his audience with off-colour humour and an impressive repertoire of seafaring tales that were as unbelievable as they were true.

Employed as a radio officer for an international shipping company, trained for the job and duly certified at St. Xavier's Technical Institute in Mumbai, Vinay had journeyed like a modern-day Odysseus, venturing into countless foreign lands where, invariably, he stumbled headlong into one adventure after another. And he always returned home with a sea-bag full of stories, made all the more thrilling in the way he told them. A favourite escapade of his—and one that warranted frequent retelling—involved incarceration for a day in a Cuban prison.

"So, I fly to Havana to join my ship, and the customs guys open my suitcase. They find the 900 *beedis* I had packed, enough to last me through the six-month voyage. I try to explain to these fellows that a *beedi* is a poor man's smoke in India. Just some cheap tobacco wrapped in a *tendu* leaf. I'm not ferrying drugs, I tell them! Then I have to explain that even though I work in the merchant navy, and that I can afford all the Marlboros I want—after all, I earn my salary in U.S. dollars—my wife made me quit cigarettes. That made them laugh. I suppose being henpecked is a universal phenomenon, but they still put me in jail, and kept me there until a supervisor came to test one of the *beedis*. He liked it so much, I gave him a packet!"

Even though he was finished for the day, Hari could not take his eyes off the figure on the bed, staring at him as if in a trance. Kaveri knew the look. Watching the piecemeal disintegration of a human being, especially someone as young, strong, and vivacious as Vinay, left him feeling helpless and scared.

"Hari, don't forget to have your *lassi* in the kitchen before you leave," Kaveri said. The concern in her words nudged him back from the edge of a deep, dark chasm of despair. Several times before, she had slipped into that netherworld herself. Yet, impelled by the sheer determination to live for Vinay and take care of him till her last breath, she would claw her way back into the light.

"Thank you, Kaveri madam. You are very kind," Hari said, slowly drawing his gaze away from the sinking sailor.

Like her mother, Kaveri never let anybody leave the house with an empty stomach. To her younger self, such unrelenting hospitality evidenced a compulsion to reign supreme in one's domain. As soon as she had taken the helm of her own home, however, she had to admit that her mother's sensibilities made perfect sense.

"Everyone must leave our house full and happy," Mama would declare. "That goes double for the servants. Our relationship with them is deeper than most are willing to admit. My tax lawyer may save me money, but it is the *ayah* who helps me nurse you when you fall sick. It is the gardener who tends to the roses that make me smile. These people do so much more than just their jobs."

Vinay shared his mother-in-law's views about the hired help, though he did not insist on feeding them quite as much. Instead, he engaged them as though they were his bridge partners. Not once had Kaveri been for a taxi ride where her husband failed to chat up the driver. And contrary to custom, he always surprised the *taxiwala* with a tip. They would thank him profusely and call him a good man.

Kaveri remained standing by the bed, transfixed by what little was left of the 'good man'—this modest, amusing man. *And clever too.* She had never seen anybody beat him at *Scrabble.* He forged words like *quixotic* and *zaftig* with remarkable ease, giving the definition when challenged and accepting gracefully the ensuing applause, even when it was tinged with envy. Now he would never play that game again. Once the malevolent tumour had taken root, spreading its sinuous tentacles throughout his brain, Vinay could not even tell the difference between mouthwash and chicken soup.

The cancer knew no pity. Not content to subjugate his mind, it had begun to assail his other vital organs as well. Death was invading his body one cell at a time, forcing him to endure the microscopic massacre in excruciating increments without giving him the merciful *coup de grâce* that would put an end to every misery. She knew he was in pain because she saw him wince, soundlessly, when the doctor pinched him to check for responsiveness. Yet, in his more lucid moments he often attempted to work his lips into a smile, lest his own suffering afflict her as well.

She remembered how he had winked at her when the nurses wheeled him into the recovery room after an unsuccessful surgery. Weeks later, when the theoretical prospect of a slow, painful death had become an almost inevitable reality hurtling toward them, he ignored the proximity warnings and distracted her with dirty sailor jokes. In the holding room where he awaited his turn for radiation therapy—a last-ditch effort to effect a cure, with both of them praying that a slim beam of photons might spark a lifesaving miracle—he stood up on a chair and captivated his hapless audience of dying patients and their forlorn kin. From his perch he emptied his arsenal of jokes, and at the end he even got them to join in the chorus of an old sea shanty. They all sang along—

> But the standing toast
> That pleased the most,
> Was...'The wind that blows,
> The ship that goes,
> And the lass that loves a sailor'.

And thus, for just a few minutes, his infectious mirth transformed all those in attendance into amnesiacs, forgetful of their personal tragedies.

Yes, he was–is–a good man.

She wondered if any untold dirty sailor jokes still lay buried in some crevice of his brain untouched by the malignancy, like a forgotten pirate treasure waiting to be discovered. *God must have a perverse sense of humour to steal laughter from such a jester.*

Kaveri extracted an Elvis cassette from Vinay's extensive music collection and fed it into the mouth of an antiquated player. "Please don't throw them away," he had implored. "These tapes will be vintage some day." Was his music to become her crutch when widowhood finally knocked the legs out from under her?

She waited patiently for the empty hiss of the tape to pass before 'Hound Dog' began booming out of the small speaker with the force of a caged animal seeking release. Kaveri knew the lyrics by heart, like a multiplication table learned at school, but she could not bring herself to sing along.

~

The doorbell rang in two long tones, announcing the arrival of her next-door neighbour, Sonia. Having been housebound for months, Kaveri had become acutely aware of the nuance of noises, both loud and soft. Hari always rang once, a short staccato chirp. The night nurse glued her finger to the bell, unmindful of the racket it created.

She had become familiar too with the hum of the refrigerator, with its periodic jolts in pitch, like a lover's snore; the squeaking of the ceiling fan that ceased only when it was allowed to run at full throttle; the unevenness of Vinay's breath when his lungs failed a full inhalation, and he compensated for the resulting lack of oxygen by taking short, sharp gulps of air, like an inept swimmer floundering at the deep end of a pool.

"I hope I didn't disturb you. I just saw the *shavewala* leave, so I thought Vinay must be awake." Kaveri was happy to see Sonia, who visited less frequently since her husband had become bedridden. She handed Kaveri a bowl of cold rice pudding. "It's for the patient," she said with a smile. "I know how much he likes it."

"Thank you. He'll appreciate it. Where's Chetan?"

"Away at sea, as usual. There's no lack of work for a chief engineer these days. He sends his regards." Like Kaveri, Sonia was a merchant navy officer's wife. They had sailed together twice. "Do you remember the time we made *kheer* on that ship? The name escapes me. Oh yes, the *Iran Ekram*." Sonia chuckled at the memory. They were the only two officers' wives aboard. It was Sonia's first voyage, and she was grateful for the female companionship.

"Of course. How can I ever forget that grumpy head chef? He wouldn't allow women anywhere near his precious galley." Kaveri had been able to cook in the ship's galley on previous voyages, sometimes preparing Indian food for the entire crew.

"What an ass. I think he was just afraid of the competition. He wanted to make sure that R/O Vinay liked his birthday cake better than the *kheer* you had planned on preparing instead."

"But we beat him, didn't we!" They laughed in unison, reminding each other of how they made *kheer* after all—boiling milk and rice in an electric kettle in Sonia's cabin, flipping the switch on and off, again and again. The kettle of course was destroyed, hissing and spitting all the way to the end.

"But wasn't that the best *kheer* ever?" Sonia said, looking into Kaveri's eyes. She was saddened by her friend's misfortune, but secretly grateful to be the one doing the consoling. "This one is almost as good, though. Promise me you'll eat some too. Don't let that naughty sailor boy polish it all off." Sonia hugged her friend and headed for the door. "Call me if you need anything."

Kaveri did not know if she was relieved or angry that Sonia had failed to ask how Vinay was doing. She had not even wanted to see him. Sometimes, when people inquired about her husband, she wanted to scream at them, "He's dying, you jerk! How the fuck do you think he's doing?"

Then again, if they neglected to ask about him, or chose not to visit at all, she construed it as callous indifference. Either way, she was mad at the whole world.

~

Kaveri inserted another cassette in the tape deck and played one of Vinay's favourite songs, 'Oh, Pretty Woman.' Roy Orbison's soulful voice filled the bedroom, exorcising the demons of despair from their sanctum.

Would the familiar lyrics stir him into remembrance?

You used to sing this to me, my love.

Nothing. Not a sound, not a movement. Even his finger had stopped its nervous, repetitive tapping, *F, F, F, F,* over and over.

That was the trouble. She remembered everything, every little detail. The lessons he gave her in Morse code during their idle moments together on the sun-splashed deck of the ship, the surprisingly cosy cabin next to the radio room, with the twin bed that was never too small for the two of them, the portholes that framed such haunting views of an ever-changing ocean and that, when opened, filled the room with the clean scent of salt air. Or those times when the torrential rain pounded against the glass and she felt as though she were encased in a submarine about to submerge. It never frightened her as long as Vinay was around.

He might be gone for six months at a stretch, sometimes longer. As often as possible, she accompanied him on his voyages, and their life became one long riotous adventure at sea. But even when she stayed behind, they were never far apart. He wrote her letters in longhand, one every day, and they would arrive at the door in bunches, each with its own exotic stamp and postmark, like a bouquet of flowers sent from afar. And once a week he sent her a telegram. Because even a radio officer must pay for personal messages by the word, he had devised an economical acronym—*F.L.A.S.K.*— to let her know that all was well. Only she knew what it meant—"Flying love and sweet kisses."

Enough! Kaveri wiped her tears and got to work. She turned Vinay over and surveyed his frail body for bedsores, acknowledging the irony in searching for something she hoped never to find. She tried to think of nothing else—their wondrous past together, her uncharted future—but just the simple, mechanical job at hand. It was how she coped with the tragedy now—by stripping away raw emotion from the reflexive task of keeping her husband's body alive.

Kaveri folded his left ear lobe up to get a better view of the skin behind the ear.

All clear. Moving on to the other ear.

Suddenly, Vinay's eyes flew open.

"Sparks!" Kaveri exclaimed, overjoyed at the prospect of reaching out to him through the prison bars of sickness, even for a brief moment. She had so many questions to ask. *How are you feeling? Do you still remember the happy years we spent together? Do you even remember who I am?*

But to her utter disappointment, Vinay could not focus. His eyes darted about the room and then, just as suddenly, the eyelids dropped shut as though that fleeting moment of cognizance, or something nearly like it, had never occurred at all. Kaveri pressed her fingers against the side of his neck and, with relief, detected a faint pulse. Yet feeling that sign of life was like touching the invisible noose around his throat as it tightened slightly, day by day, squeezing out a few more ounces of life with each beat of his heart.

Ever since she heard the diagnosis of the malignant brain tumour with a vainglorious name she could neither spell nor pronounce, Kaveri had experienced a dizzying gamut of emotions. Denial was the first, and the strongest. She once kicked and punched the neurosurgeon treating her husband after an unsuccessful surgery, holding him personally accountable for the inefficacy of his operating instruments. "I sure hope you can do more with your dick than with your stupid scalpel," she had bellowed like an inebriated sailor hankering for a bar fight. The nurses pulled her away from the shaken doctor and struggled to prevent her from attacking again.

Once she moved past denial, she began behaving in ways that called her very sanity into question. She paid the family astrologer in gold, handing over her entire trove of wedding jewellery to realign the stars into a favourable configuration. With obsessive persistence, she accumulated an impressive library of grief-management books, each one filled with more metaphysical babble than the last one. As soon as she realised that they offered neither solace nor a solution to her predicament, she promptly made a bonfire of them in the yard.

In a fit of existential rage, one day Kaveri tossed away all the deities that stood guard atop her household shrine, flinging each shining idol into the large and now unkempt flower garden behind the house. Hours later, fearing the divine repercussions of her impulsive act, she leaped out of bed and, stealthily as a grave robber, scoured the field with a flashlight to retrieve the idols. Once she had collected all the silver statuettes strewn among the weeds—Ganesh, Lakshmi, Krishna, Hanuman, and the Shivling—she washed them with milk and water and rearranged them on the chest of drawers, a space sequestered for sacred purposes. With hands folded in prayer and her head lowered in deference, Kaveri let her tears fall directly onto the floor. She begged for forgiveness, offering her own beating heart in exchange for her husband's life.

Hindus have so many Gods, she thought, but not one would answer her prayers. Still, she had to admit that fate had fashioned for her a husband from a swatch of perfection, cut to her exact specifications, and she was grateful for that. Perhaps it was only a matter of time before fate came knocking at the door to ask that she give him back.

They met for the first time on a spouse hunt. Kaveri's father had placed an advertisement in the matrimonial section of the *Times of India*, describing her qualities in succinct telegraphese—

> Beautiful Khatri girl, fair-complexioned,
> 5ft 6in, convent-educated, B.A. (English),
> seeking suitable Khatri boy

Vinay's mother had shortlisted her based on just those qualities, her height in particular, which would complement her son's six-foot frame.

Her father's only criteria were that the groom have a well-paying job and belong to the Khatri class.

"So why did you say yes?" she asked Vinay several months into their marriage, when the new union had matured into a comfortable alliance of passionate equals.

"I liked the way your round bottom moved." He stood up to demonstrate, holding a pillow against his hips and wrapping himself in a *sari*. "I was standing right behind you, and this is how you walked." Vinay strutted across the room with an exaggerated sway.

"I do *not* walk like that," Kaveri countered, laughing uncontrollably, a hand over her mouth.

"Maybe not quite like that," he agreed. "But very, very sexy," he whispered, pulling her close.

Later, when he lay spent beside her, he confessed to being attracted by her confident yet feminine poise. "My mother wanted a traditional girl who would fit well into the family," he told her. "But I wanted someone bolder, a woman who would accompany me on my voyages. Somebody who could get used to living for months on a ship full of sweaty seamen, eating whatever was served—and most of all, enjoying the adventure of discovering new places."

Kaveri admitted to having no reservations whatsoever on that score. On the contrary, her biggest fear was to be left behind, stuck with the in-laws while her husband was away at sea.

"Nah, I'd rather have you along," he said. "Just thinking about making love to you and not being able to do it for months at a stretch would drive me crazy." He reached for her again. "Come here, my pretty woman."

Many years and countless voyages later, they always laughed while recounting their misadventures that stood out as mile markers along their seemingly endless journey together.

"I will never forget the face you made when the waiter accidentally served you frog leg soup in Bangkok!"

"Remember how you tripped over your *sari* and fell ass over teakettle on the gangway?"

"The worst was when we had to ride that crowded, smelly bus in Karachi."

"And how we searched like crazy through all our luggage when we misplaced our passports in Hamburg."

"Oh, but the scariest was when I landed in Bandar Abbas to join you on the *Iran Ekram*, and I couldn't find you at the airport!"

~

"It is very sad, Beena, very sad," Hari informed his wife over dinner. "Vinay *sahib* was such a nice man, always telling funny jokes. And now, he can't even say two words." His children, a boy and a girl, sat beside him on the floor that had been covered with old newspapers to serve as a clean space for dining. The only table in their tiny brick hut served as a makeshift television stand. He would have preferred to use the money for a small refrigerator, but Beena had insisted on buying a television.

"Kaveri madam looks after him all day. She promised *sahib* she wouldn't let him die in a hospital." Hari scooped up the remaining lentils and rice with his fingers, licking them in satisfaction. "I think he is going to die soon."

"Good for you. When *sahib* dies, she'll call you to warm her bed. That's what these lonely rich women do." Hari reflected glumly that his wife had the mouth and mind of a street rat.

"Don't you ever shut up?" he said. "Always attacking people. What has that woman done to you, huh? Have you forgotten how she got our kids admission to the big school? They would be in that useless government school had it not been for her. She pays the fee, buys them books and uniforms. And remember the time you got malaria—didn't she take care of all the medical expenses?"

"Yes, yes, I know all that. These rich people do such things just to make themselves happy. To get *wah-wah* from their friends. It's all an act."

Hari was in no mood to argue. He stepped outside their hut to smoke a *beedi*. He remembered sharing his smokes with Vinay *sahib* secretly, after madam made him quit cigarettes. It occurred to him then that he loved his *sahib* like a brother.

~

"Tell me, Mannat, tell me what is going to happen?" Kaveri cried into the phone. Her friend at the other end let the sobbing pass before she spoke.

"First of all, promise me that you won't give any more money to the *pandits*," Mannat said. "That's not going to help."

"Then what will help, Mannat? You tell me. Of all people in the world, only you would know."

Kaveri had met Mannat Jogi a few years before, quite by accident, at a flower show in Mumbai, while Vinay attended a refresher course at the Institute to maintain his certification. Drawn to each other by their mutual interest in rose hybrids and foreign travel, they struck up a conversation and had remained long-distance friends ever since. Mannat enjoyed a reputation in Mumbai as a gifted clairvoyant. Kaveri had never had an occasion to call upon those abilities—until now.

"Tell me what is going to happen?" She yelled the last few words into the receiver, and then caught herself. "I'm sorry, I didn't mean to raise my voice. It's just that...."

"You're upset, that's only natural," Mannat reassured her. "You already know what's going to happen. It's inevitable."

"I can't just stand here and watch him die every single day. I have to help him, Mannat. I have to do something."

"You will, Kaveri. You will find a way."

~

Hari instructed one of his assistants, an ambidextrous young lad who had quite a way with shears, to close up for the night—an easy task, given that the *shavewala*'s establishment consisted of nothing more than two chairs under a *peepal* tree. All the boy had to do was run a metal chain through the legs of the chairs and around the tree, and then click the lock to fasten the ends together. Hari did not need much more than that, since the bulk of his income came from making house calls. It all started several years ago when Vinay *sahib* had asked Hari to come over to his home and give him a shave there. Immensely pleased with the service and attention to detail, he recommended the *shavewala* to all his friends at the bridge club. Now, with a full roster of regular clients who called him on his cell phone, he enjoyed a steady income. And Hari had the good *sahib* to thank.

He looked forward to his weekly visit to the Hanuman temple on his way home. An ardent *bhakt*, Hari never failed to pay his respects to the stalwart monkey God, whom he admired for his loyalty to Lord Rama and for his remarkable strength.

Standing barefoot before the decorated idol, his palms held together in prayer, Hari recited all 40 verses of the *Hanuman Chalisa* from memory. Then, in silent meditation, he petitioned the deity to look kindly upon his client and friend, poor Vinay *sahib*, who was battling a severe sickness. Devotions done, he greeted the *pandit* as he exited the temple and humbly accepted the *boondi prasad* offering.

Once outside, he looked for his worn-out sandals among the pile of shoes that belonged to other temple visitors. As it was Tuesday, the day designated for Hanuman *puja*, there were many to sift through until he found his own. As he began to walk away, a horrific sight shocked Hari to the core. A few feet from the temple entrance, a boy no more than seven or eight years old lay shivering on the ground, in a pool of his own faeces and vomit. Not a shred of clothing covered the nakedness of his sickly, emaciated body. He did not even have the strength to crawl or roll away out of the noxious muck. No one dared approach the child for fear of dire contagion.

It saddened Hari to see such suffering in one so young. He asked the beggars flanking the entrance of the temple if they knew who the boy was or where he came from. His mother had left him there, they said; nobody knew if she would return. Someone had gone inside the temple to find a doctor among the devotees, but clearly, the poor child had little chance of surviving. "*Is bechare ko mauth aa jaye to acha hoga,*" they all said, nodding in unison. It would be best for him to die.

~

Kaveri stepped out of the bath and wrapped her hair in a towel. Even though Vinay had fallen asleep, she felt guilty about spending a few extra minutes under the shower. When the seizures, like devastating earthquakes, became more intense the week before, the doctor had increased his steroid dosage, which helped him sleep. Not that it would do much good beyond that. The damage to the man's body, though imperceptible to the naked eye, became evident in his laboured breathing and reduced motor function. The left arm was now about as useless as an appendix.

She removed the towel from her head and noted the strands of damp hair adhering to the cloth. Ever since Vinay's diagnosis, she had been steadily losing hair. She tried to imagine what he would have said. "Don't worry, my darling, it's just stress. Radiation therapy will leave me completely bald. And no matter how much hair you lose, you'll still have more than I!"

In an act of defiance against no one in particular, but against the world at large and the Gods above, Kaveri picked out a shimmering peacock-blue *kurti* to wear, with pink rosebuds embroidered around the neckline. She refused to dress in the pale shades more befitting a widow-to-be. *I'm not there yet*, she told herself, uncapping a magenta lipstick for the first time in months. She twisted the bottom of the tube and rubbed the lipstick on the back of her hand a few times until she was satisfied with the smoothness of the tip. She was determined to look beautiful for her husband, even if he could not fully appreciate it.

Kaveri stepped into the bedroom, hoping for one coherent moment with him. *Please let today be different*, she prayed.

She saw a pillow covering Vinay's face and rushed to the bed to lift it off.

His eyes were open. Summoning all his last remaining strength, Vinay pulled the pillow back over his face with his right hand. Kaveri yanked it away again, hurling it to the floor, then tossed aside all the other cushions she used to support his frail body.

"Please," he whispered.

"No. No. No." She yelled at him and slapped him hard across his face. "Absolutely not. What were you thinking?" She slapped him again, harder. And then she kissed him. Vinay's ashen lips turned an ugly shade of purple.

"Kiss me," Kaveri said, shaking him roughly by the shoulders. "Kiss me back, do you hear me?"

She saw the tears trickling down his sunken cheeks and along his grey temples.

Kaveri collapsed next to him, drenching his T-shirt with tears of her own. The shirt—his favourite, or so he claimed, purchased by him in Recife on a roguish whim—was inscribed with the words *Sex Instructor, First Lesson Free.* Kaveri had never let him wear it until this morning, when she had dressed him.

She lay there crying beside him when suddenly she felt a warm wetness spread across her thighs. She had forgotten to give Vinay the bedpan at 11:00 A.M., as she always did every morning after her shower.

Today turned out to be different after all.

~

"Thank you for coming, Hari." Kaveri's tone was impassive. "Let's take him straight to the tub. You can shave him there." She undressed Vinay with Hari's help, unfazed by the awkwardness of the *shavewala*'s presence.

They stood there together for a moment, watching Vinay float naked under a mantle of flower-scented bubbles. Just as Hari was about to begin his work, Kaveri stopped him and took the blade from the *shavewala*'s hand. She turned her husband's head to expose his jugular, then brought the blade to his neck with a trembling hand.

Hari stepped back and waited respectfully, his arms locked together and head facing down. He wished to give the couple their privacy, as if they were making love right in front of him.

"I can't do it, Hari. I can't." Snapping the blade closed, she returned it to its owner and left the bathroom. Kaveri had no more tears to shed. Her grief was an arid, horizonless expanse where no life stirred.

Afterward, Hari stepped out of the bathroom and shut the door behind him. He found Kaveri sitting on the floor in the living room. Vinay's entire cassette collection lay scattered all around her. He watched her as she peeled the tape off the spools, one after another, her hands moving in a swift, mechanical rhythm.

She looked up at Hari, her dull, lifeless eyes studying him slowly. Her forlorn gaze came to rest on the open blade in his hand.

"It's done, Mona darling," he said, wiping the straight razor with a clean washcloth. "There is no oxygen in the liquid now."

Phoolwali

Keep love in your heart. A life without it is like a sunless
garden when the flowers are dead.
                                                    –Oscar Wilde

Sita, the *kudewali*, sauntered contentedly round and
round the majestic *peepal* tree before finally settling into
a clean, shady spot on the wrap-around cement bench.
The ample girth of the massive bole was decorated with
countless encircling strands of *mauli*, the red and yellow
thread of Hindu prayer rituals performed by those in
need of miracles, however small. She felt drawn to the
sacred tree not for its spiritual attributes but for its
astonishing beauty. The heart-shaped foliage formed a
colossal yet delicate canopy that shook with the slightest
breeze. Dwarfed by the tree's ancient, green immensity,
Sita breathed deeply, inhaling the scent of its fragrant
sap, delighting in its umbra of peace, even though the
smell of death hung all around her.

The sound of the iron gates being pushed open on rusty hinges disrupted her *dhyan*, the way the tranquillity of a still pond is disturbed by the splash of a pebble thrown upon its waters. She opened her eyes and saw a girl and a grey-haired man, both dressed in white, enter the grounds of the funeral home where she sat waiting. Sita recognised the Parekhs immediately. After all, she had been collecting the garbage from their palatial building for years. She did not expect them to acknowledge her presence, of course. Fortune had endowed them with remarkable wealth, while she was just the neighbourhood trash collector. As far as they were concerned, she might as well have been invisible.

A gentle breeze dislodged a few *peepal* leaves, which fell on and around Sita like sprinkles of holy water dispersed by a priest during a prayer ceremony. Hastily, she gathered up the leaves and placed them carefully inside a soiled calico satchel that never left her side. *Blessings from above*, she thought. Later she would weave them into something beautiful for her mother. Right now, though, she had work to do.

The owner of the funeral home was a large, domineering man whom Sita boldly addressed as *Yamdoot*—the 'messenger of death'. The little *kudewali*'s impertinence should have vexed him; instead, it made him smile inside. He greeted the grieving father and daughter at the gate and led them to the ash pit near the *peepal* tree, where the older of the two Parekh girls had been cremated the day before.

Mr. Parekh sprinkled water and milk over the ashes and then inhaled deeply before stepping into the shallow pit. Rolling up the sleeves of his *kurta*, he resolutely began culling bone fragments of his dead child from among the blanket of ashes, dropping each piece that he found, large and small, into a simple clay pot. He wept openly and without shame; and a trail of tears in the ash marked his circuitous trek through the pit, which was no bigger than a billiard table. He ricocheted aimlessly from one side to the other, like an animal trapped in a cage, forcing himself to continue the arduous task. His daughter, whom Sita supposed to be about 18, watched impassively from one corner.

It surprised Sita to see the girl accompanying her father on his doleful mission. The business of death is a long and complicated one in India, with specific rules and a string of requisite ceremonies orchestrated by a trusted *pandit* exercising his priestly authority for the well-being of the departed soul on its journey. According to Hindu custom, the women of a family in mourning rarely entered the precincts of the crematorium, and only the male members gathered the ashes of the deceased.

Sita worked part-time at the crematorium, arriving at mid-morning after she had finished collecting trash from people's homes. Here she assisted grief-stricken men with the exacting task of sifting through ash for the unconsumed remains of their loved ones. This practical modification of tradition, one that permitted the assistance of an 'outsider,' albeit a woman, suited Mr. Parekh just fine. He wiped his face with a white handkerchief and gestured to the crematorium owner. He was done.

Yamdoot barked at Sita. "*Ayree*, why are you still sitting under that tree like a *maharani*? Can't you see Parekh *sahib* is finished? Get off your throne and find the rest of the bones. Then sweep up the ash."

"Yes, yes, I know, *Yamdootji*," Sita said with a hint of mock deference. "I have been doing this for years. Don't worry."

"Vinati, what the devil do you think you're doing?" Mr. Parekh suddenly called out. His surviving daughter was about to step into the ash pit with Sita, but her father stopped her with a firm hand on the shoulder.

"Why can't I help?" Vinati asked in a defiant tone.

"Vinati, girls are not supposed to do this," her father responded impatiently.

"But *she* is a girl," Vinati objected, pointing an accusing finger at Sita.

"Yes, of course she is. But it is her job to do these things. According to tradition, you shouldn't even be here. You should have stayed home with your mother."

"Since when do you care about tradition? You were drowning yourself in whisky before Vandana's body was cold. Or do the scriptures dictate that you must get drunk on the occasion of your child's death?"

"Vinati, that's enough. I know this is difficult for you. It is unbearable for me. Please don't argue. Let's just get this over with. We've been through enough already."

They had witnessed the deliberate destruction of Vandana's body the day before, heard her cartilage crackle under hungry flames, and watched 19 years of an unfinished life go up in smoke. What little remained of her would now be unceremoniously consigned to a clay pot.

"Parekh *sahib*, why don't you come to my office and sit down for a few minutes. Catch your breath. Sita will finish up here." Better than most men, *Yamdoot* recognised death's insidious way of enkindling controversy over the most mundane matters. He had seen people squabble over the quality of wood used to build the pyre, the number of shawls that must be placed over the dead body, the arrangement of flowers, the type of urn that would be worthy of holding the ashes of the deceased, on and on. There was no end to death's mindless malice.

Sita too was intimately familiar with the discord and desperation that death could engender among its surviving victims. Yet she believed that a divine hand had given her employment at the crematorium to help bring some comfort to the grieving by performing these distasteful duties. *Yamdoot* did not have to tell her twice. Tucking up the long end of her *kameez*, she squatted on her haunches and began raking through the ashes with deft fingers. One by one she plucked out the last remaining fragments of bone and tossed them with unerring aim into the gaping mouth of the urn. Her face held an expression of concentration rather than a grimace, as one might expect. Not everyone could do this work. Rooting through the incinerated remains of the dead was enough to make anyone's gorge rise, and for that reason *Yamdoot* had come to value Sita's services. She recalled how her friend, Kanchan the *phoolwali*, had begun retching uncontrollably as soon as she touched a big chunk of thighbone, still warm from the fire. That had been Kanchan's first and last day on the job at the crematorium. After that, she went back to selling flowers, which smelled a lot better anyway.

Since the charred stench of death clings tenaciously to the inner lining of one's nostrils long after the culling is done, Sita was fortunate in having mastered the ability to breathe through her mouth early in life. As a child, she had accompanied her mother to work, gathering bags of waste from the rich people's flats for a small but precious fee. Together, they carted the collection of trash from the luxurious apartment complex to a large ditch nearby and dumped it, whereupon they proceeded to comb through the fetid, rat-infested refuse for whatever paltry treasures they might lay hands on—empty bottles, outmoded electronics, broken toys, worn-out shoes—which they subsequently sold for a pittance, if they could, or saved for themselves. Discarded women's sanitary napkins, when only slightly soiled, were especially in demand among their female customers.

Sita's most precious find by far had been a chipped sandalwood statuette of Lord Buddha seated on a lotus throne. The intricate carving fascinated her, especially the swirls of the figure's hair mounted high on his head and the delicate fingers held in what she learned was called the *dhyana mudra*, the gesture of meditation. The serene look of rapture on Buddha's face and the slight, all-knowing smile captivated her imagination. Sita wondered—*What is he thinking?* Perhaps he was not thinking of anything, because he was free. Sita's mother had let her keep the Buddha, even though it would have fetched a good price.

After collecting all the bone fragments from the ash pit, Sita stood up and shook her flip-flops to expunge the fine powder that had accumulated on the soles of her feet and clumped up between her toes. Then she reached for a broom fashioned from palm leaves and began sweeping the ashes into a tidy little pile, starting at the outer edge of the pit and circling her way around toward the centre.

Vinati watched in silence while the *kudewali* worked, her arms folded across a boyishly flat chest, inching closer until she stood at the very edge of the ash pit. From the corner of her eye, Sita saw the Parekh girl reach surreptitiously into the urn and pull something out.

The girl gazed briefly at the shard of bone in her hand, as though it were something familiar that she handled often, like a favourite piece of jewellery; and then, with the furtiveness of a shoplifter, she slipped the shard into her purse.

Sita laid down the broom and, using just her bare hands as a scoop, carefully gathered up all the ashes and deposited them in the urn. Then she covered the opening with a cloth, so that none of the contents would spill out. The pit was now ready for the next funeral.

Yamdoot returned with Mr. Parekh in tow. Sita handed over the urn and turned away, leaving the men to settle accounts. She approached Vinati. Was that a flicker of recognition in the rich girl's restless, bloodshot eyes? *Perhaps she recognises me by my scar*, Sita thought, touching the angry red blemish bisecting her cheek. It was the only distinguishing feature of an otherwise unremarkable face.

"I am sorry about your sister," Sita said kindly. "I used to see her sometimes when I came to collect the trash from your building—President Park. We are neighbours, you know, sort of. I live in the colony right behind the garbage dump near Cuffe Parade."

Sanitation trucks made sporadic pick-ups at the dump to haul away whatever they could carry, always leaving behind about a third of the ever-growing pile of reeking waste. The noxious mound had become a landmark of sorts. "Hang a right at the garbage hill," the residents of the district would say if anyone asked for directions to the Afghan Church or the navy residences. "You can't miss it. Just follow your nose."

Dusting the ash off her hands with the hem of her *kameez*, Sita reached into her bag for a string of *mogra* flowers and offered it to the rich girl. Though slightly wilted—they had travelled in Sita's bag all morning—they were still saturated with a sweet smell. Sita always had a few garlands left over from the previous night, when she and Kanchan sold flowers together on Marine Drive.

Cupping her hands, Vinati silently accepted the garland. She recalled her sister's fondness for the tiny white blooms, and knew that Vandana would have hung the floral string in the car, just over the air-conditioning vent on the dashboard.

In Vinati's cool reserve, Sita could sense a mix of grief and high-handedness. Although they lived cheek by jowl and appeared to coexist amicably enough, the divide between their respective classes remained unbridgeable, as evidenced, amongst other things, by their garbage. *In my whole life I may not own a single empty perfume bottle to throw away, but in death her ashes and mine will be indistinguishable,* Sita thought. Born into privation, she delighted in drawing such parallels with the upper class, but never with animosity. Such was the state of the world, and there was nothing to be done about it.

Without a parting word, Vinati turned and joined her father, and together they left the crematorium as a black Mercedes pulled up to the gate. An impeccably uniformed chauffer hopped out to hold the door open for them.

"Thank you, Manjit," Sita heard the girl say as she stepped into her chariot.

~

The grieving family's pilgrimage to the city of Haridwar was a long and gruelling one. It took several hours by air, and several more by road, to reach the riverbank of the Ganges and hire a *pandit*—there were hundreds to choose from—to perform the last rites. Standing at the lowest step of the *ghat* along the edge of the river, Vinati watched her father intently as he followed the instructions of the priest and dispersed the contents of the urn over the sacred waters, tapping the bottom a few times to ensure that not a speck of his dead daughter's remains was left inside. Like a tired parent humouring his little girl with a quick piggyback ride at bedtime, the wind in fitful gusts carried the ashes only a short distance before releasing them into the murky currents. Mrs. Parekh, weeping silently beside her living daughter, let out an anguished sob.

The elaborate hour-long ritual, punctuated by the droning recitation of Sanskrit *mantras*, gave Vinati no solace. Instead, she took comfort from the small fragment of bone that she had secretly snatched from the urn the day before and now clutched in her pocket. She could not bring herself to relinquish this last little piece of her sister by tossing it into the polluted river, and so she kept it hidden from view.

The days after their return to Mumbai never measured the same. Some were lengthened by insomnia. Others flashed by as if experienced in a state of hypnosis. But they all began with a deceptive ordinariness that involved crisp buttered toast, diced mangoes, freshly squeezed orange juice, and German-made vitamin supplements.

That the three of them now habitually found themselves sitting around the breakfast table at the same time was in itself notable. In the past, they had almost never eaten together as a family. With Vinati and Vandana enrolled in an erratic schedule of classes at a local college, Mrs. Parekh rarely rose out of bed before 10 A.M.; and Mr. Parekh would usually return from his morning workout at the gym long after his daughters had left for the day. Now, with one of the daughters permanently absent, a new regimen had been established, and the uncustomary family communion made the tragedy even more palpable. It was seated among them in a vacant dining chair. It overflowed from their juice glasses and coffee cups. It came served on an invisible platter placed precisely between the mangoes and the toast.

Yet, nobody ever spoke about Vandana.

Conversations between Vinati and her parents remained desultory at best, though invariably polite, skimming indifferently over inconsequent topics such as the escalating price of real estate and the outcome of the latest election. Their temperate dialogues now stood in stark contrast to the volatile exchanges of recent years, when the girls had grown more in spirit than in inches.

As longtime members of Mumbai's affluent entrepreneurial class, the Parekhs' social calendar overflowed with glamorous engagements. For years, the hobnobbing couple had left Vinati and Vandana in safe hands, with their grandmother and a bevy of trusted maids. The little girls seldom saw their parents after seven o'clock in the evening. As children, they fell asleep while watching television. As young adults, privileged to attend college and pursue the pleasures of youth, they were granted unlimited freedom and funds. As with all good things, however—and surely many of their fellow citizens would consider an abundance of freedom and money to be very good indeed—there can be too much of it.

After the housemaid discovered Vandana's body drowned in the bathtub, along with a half-empty pouch of cocaine in the sink, the Parekhs labelled the tragedy an accident, thus exonerating themselves from any possible blame. The couple did not fling accusations at one another, nor did they seek succour in each other's company. Instead, they dealt with their grief by dividing it in equal parts—and then evading it the best they could. Mrs. Parekh spent her evenings at home, watching inane soap operas on the television; while Vinati's father attached himself to his smartphone, working his thumbs stiff over pointless business details that would otherwise have taken care of themselves. While comforted somewhat by Vinati's presence at home, they allowed the bright glow of their respective devices to mesmerise them to the point of heedlessness as their youngest—and now their only—child slipped slowly but surely into an abyss of darkness.

For Vinati, the absolute absence of her sister soon crystallised into an invisible companion, a tangible presence with physical dimensions, around which she could wrap her arms and hold onto for dear life. But sorrow remained insidiously amorphous, springing upon her in class like a ghost, whispering maliciously to her in bed at night, and surprising her with a choking grip around her throat whenever she passed by the Marine Drive promenade. That used to be one of their favourite haunts in Mumbai, a locus of enticements full of life and colour where they could laugh together and stare at boys and plan a hundred different futures. Even when they got into a little trouble—usually at Vandana's instigation—the adventure made the consequences worthwhile. One autumn evening, with the *Ramlila* festivities winding to a close, they had sneaked off to Chowpatty Beach to watch the towering figure of the demon-king Ravana as it was set alight at sunset and burned in effigy. The huge bonfire illuminated the entire beach, and even from a distance the heat from the flames warmed their faces while the pop of exploding firecrackers hidden inside the figure drew forth peals of startled laughter. Afterward, they mingled with the crowds, made up mostly of working-class families and boisterous teenagers, then dared to take a ride on an ancient human-powered Ferris wheel with attendants leaping from the metal struts and onto the crossbars, where they flailed wildly in mid-air until their weight swung the wheel down and around and the men climbed the struts again. The sisters held onto each other and screamed with excitement as the rickety wheel turned, faster and faster, and from their whirling, dizzying vantage point they took in all at once the sights and sounds of the *Dussehra* bazaar—the snack vendors serving up a savoury banquet of *bhelpuris* smothered in tangy chutneys and the *kulfi* sellers hawking their sweet, creamy wares, the trained monkeys performing comical tricks on the sand, acrobats and contortionists, musicians and snake charmers, colourfully dressed dancers and the astrologers casting fortunes for anyone willing to part with a few rupees to hear how their dreams might come true. That single night contained all the promise that life held for the sisters long after *Ramlila* and far beyond the Marine Drive promenade.

Now it all seemed only a desolate wasteland.

Over the next few weeks after the funeral, Vinati's mother and father gradually returned to the tranquillity of their routine schedules—Mr. Parekh at the helm of a lucrative real estate business, and Mrs. Parekh managing a high-end florist shop. Peace and purpose, however, remained completely out of Vinati's reach.

~

"You should come by the shop, Vinati. I could really use your help, now that...." Mrs. Parekh's voice trailed off. When she was alive, Vandana would often spend her afternoons at their mother's shop, *Boutique Blossoms*. Customers lingered to watch Vandana orchestrate stunning and original arrangements of flowers—carnations, orchids, anthuriums, whatever struck her fancy—like musical notes in a free-form jazz composition.

"I don't know, Mama. I'm not good with flowers—not the way Vandana was."

"You should come anyway. Maybe you can help at the register."

"What if I don't want to?" Vinati pushed back defiantly.

"Look, young lady, your uncle will inherit your father's business someday, and this is all you'll get. We'll find a good family for you to marry into, so you won't have to work if you don't want to. Let me tell you something, though—having your own business gives you independence."

"But I don't want to get married! I want to go to graduate school in the U.S. and get my degree. I want to get away."

"How can you even consider leaving us, after what happened to Vandana? You are all we have left. You are not going anywhere."

~

The small, carved sandalwood box lay hidden behind a pair of six-inch stilettos in the far corner of the walk-in closet. Vinati carried the wooden case from its dark sanctuary and laid it gently on a bed piled high with her sister's clothes. Mrs. Parekh had placed her in charge of disposing of Vandana's belongings.

"We have to give her things away, we have to let her go," she told Vinati before leaving for work that morning. "You don't have classes today. Why don't you empty her side of the closet? That way you'll have more space. Remember how the two of you grumbled about sharing the closet?" she added encouragingly.

Vinati could not decide whether she admired her mother's pragmatism or was appalled by her insensitivity. She picked up a scarf from the heap of clothes and pressed it to her face, inhaling the faint traces of Vandana's musky scent. The complex circular embroidery patterns on the scarf resembled wheels within wheels in motion. Staring at them, Vinati felt her head spin.

"Don't you dare wear that scarf!" she thought she heard Vandana say. They had often argued over wardrobe possessions, especially when Vandana waltzed over to Vinati's side of the closet without permission.

"Gosh, Vandana, you are so unfair. You always take my things without asking," she complained.

"Oh, take a chill pill. Remember, I'm your elder sister, I am allowed to do that. And in exchange—I will protect you from all the bad boys. Like a lioness." Vandana roared and lunged for Vinati's ticklish spots.

"Stop, you bossy beast! I don't need any protection."

The happy memory brought forth a rush of tears. She had no idea how she could continue living in a room filled with her sister's voice, her scent, her laughter, her stuff. *Why doesn't God give us an eviction notice and order us to pack our shit before we die?*

Picking up the carved box from the bed, she walked out to the expansive balcony overlooking the Arabian Sea, and eased the lid open to gaze at the one real piece of Vandana still with her. The bone looked dull against the red velvet lining of the box. She ran her fingers across the smooth surface, wondering which part of the body it belonged to. Was it from one of the knees that she kept bruising with her wild antics? The cheek that Vinati so often kissed, or the shoulder against which she rested her head for comfort? She would never know.

Though the actual death was self-inflicted, induced by a deadly white powder all too readily available to the reckless children of privilege, Vinati blamed herself for allowing Vandana to stay on her path of annihilation. Once she became aware of her sister's cocaine habit, she had threatened to tell their parents, which enraged Vandana. It was by far the worst argument they ever had. In the end, Vandana promised to stop snorting the stuff if Vinati would just keep silent. When she refused, Vandana swore to expose Vinati's relationship with Salem, a Muslim boy who lived on the sixth floor of their building.

Vinati never imagined fighting a crusade to be with Salem. She certainly did not love him. She simply enjoyed exploring her own sexuality by giving his hands and mouth free rein over her lips and body. But the prospect of sparring with her parents for messing with a Muslim boy exhausted her, and so she had backed down. She regretted that now. Standing on the balcony and staring out at the distant horizon, she felt as if she were drowning in the vastness of the sea, with no one to pull her out. Guilt festered in her like a grievous wound, and yet that very same guilt kept her from accepting the vulnerary remedies offered by her concerned friends. Just as she could not save her sister, no one could save her.

~

Lured by lofty tales of city life, most chauffeurs are migrants from outlying villages. Although they leave behind the plough and cattle, they cannot fully divest themselves of a rustic roughness that may take the form of a churlish demeanour, abrasive inflections, general scruffiness accompanied by an oppressive body odour—and sometimes, lewd glances in a strategically adjusted rear-view mirror.

For this reason, of the three chauffeurs—one for each car the Parekhs owned—Manjit was Vinati's favourite. Comfortable in the skin of a servant, he did his job with uncommon humility and grace. Manjit displayed no desire either to buy or to elbow his way into a higher class. His measure of success lay in living a decent life forged by honest labour. It amazed Vinati to see somebody like Manjit hanker for nothing beyond the necessary. Though perched high on a pedestal of familial wealth and status, she sometimes felt dwarfed by Manjit, as though he were a levitating guru and she but a poor, misguided soul.

"Good morning, Vinati madam," Manjit saluted, and held the car door open. "College?" he added, pushing in the long strap of her bag before closing the door.

"Not today, Manjit. Take me to the train station," Vinati instructed with a sense of purpose in her voice.

"Where do you need to go madam? I can take you," Manjit insisted. For a moment, she considered telling Manjit about the Dharmachakra Centre's *Art of Breathing* brochure that a friend had given her, and the class she would attend in Bandra later that morning. Instead, she resolved to make the journey alone and unassisted.

As he drove to the station, hands firmly gripping the steering wheel, Manjit urged Vinati to reconsider her decision to ride the rails by herself. "But madam, the trains are very full these days—even the ladies' coupe is always packed. It worries me for you to be travelling alone."

Vinati disregarded the driver's avuncular advice. She felt uncomfortable when Manjit treated her like a fragile China doll. Did he think she was incapable of successfully navigating the crowds and travelling without the comforts of air-conditioning? Besides, she was not alone at all. She would have Vandana for company—or at least a small part of her—tucked safely away inside the sandalwood box that Vinati carried in her bag.

"Be careful on the train, madam," he continued, "and keep your hands on your belongings at all times."

Vinati glanced out the window as they approached Victoria Terminus. The imposing colonial Gothic structure never failed to make an impression. The two pillars at the entrance, one crowned with a tiger to represent ancient India and the other with a lion emblematising British rule, celebrated an anomalous confluence of cultures. *They are like my sister and me*, Vinati thought—*always together and yet so different*. Vandana had surely been the lion of the family, fierce and imperious, and now she was gone. Vinati cursed under her breath as she stepped onto the curb and waved goodbye to Manjit. Would she never escape these constant reminders of her dead sibling?

Inside, the station bustled at a mid-morning pace, somewhere between fast and frantic. Caught amid a throng of sweaty commuters, she jostled her way to the platform and, by some miracle, onto the correct train.

Even at this hour the rail car was so crowded that she had no choice but to stand all the way to Bandra. The discomfort of the journey did little to strengthen her resolve to disengage somehow from her troubled reality. The *Art of Breathing* class had already commenced by the time she arrived, and she struggled to keep up. Barely able to follow the instructions of the guru, Vinati attempted to learn the rudiments of *ujjai*, of deep ocean breathing, but to little avail. Tumultuous thoughts endlessly intruded and swirled within her, reaching a frenzy by the end of class.

She experienced none of the benefits of balance and calm touted in the brochure. Rather, a feeling of utter hopelessness dogged her like a shadow as she made her way back to the Bandra train station.

She gave it another try on the ride back home. As instructed by the teacher in class, Vinati turned her gaze outward—to the destitute masses living along the tracks, the naked children playing in the debris of urban life, the overworked and underpaid commuters on passing trains hanging precariously from doorless exits. She studied the women around her. Here was a fishmonger balancing a basket on her head, there a quiet young girl with braids reeking of floral hair oil. She could not forge a connection with any of them. They all belonged to a different world from hers. The overpowering stench of dead fish, mingled with the fake floral smell of hair oil, churned the bile in Vinati's stomach.

The train ride seemed to last an eternity. When it finally pulled into Victoria Terminus, Vinati shoved her way through the crowd toward the exit, and alighted from the car with a wave of women more accomplished than her at making agile landings. Amid the crush of bodies, she lost her balance and fell to her knees, almost getting trampled in the process. Her fellow passengers scurried away, leaving her alone to dust herself off and lament her scuffed shoes and bruised knees. A little dazed, she tried to get her bearings and then headed toward the parking lot.

Vinati wearily climbed the steps to the footbridge. At the top, she could not help but notice the multitude of beggars ranged along the handrails. As she traversed the length of the bridge, she surveyed in mute shock the human detritus surrounding her, these wretched castaways of the city. Some stood hunched over, soliciting benefactions with outstretched arms. Others lay crumpled on the ground, like discarded balls of newspaper blown by an errant wind against the barrier. An old beggar, his bones visible under parchment-like skin and scant rags for clothing, was perched near the top of the steps at the opposite end. *A living carcass,* Vinati thought to herself as she approached him, forgetting for the moment her own ordeals. He clutched a battered tin can—his begging bowl—which he waved around in a figure-eight motion, rattling the few coins inside.

Already touched by the man's condition, she realised with a start, as soon as she knelt before him, that he was blind too. He sensed her presence but said nothing. Vinati extracted a 500-rupee note from a snakeskin wallet. It amounted to less than 10 euros. She did the math instinctively—for she and Vandana had vacationed together in France the previous summer. For this wretched man, it would be an exorbitant sum of money, *un grand pourboire.* Instead of dropping it in his tin, Vinati placed the note in the palm of his hand and closed his fingers around it.

"It is 500 rupees," she cordially informed him.

Setting his tin on the ground, the beggar suddenly grabbed her wrist with a surprisingly iron grip. He pulled her close and whispered, "Is there something else you can give me, something you don't need and want to get rid of?" His voice sounded strangely high-pitched, like that of a young girl.

Just as suddenly, the old man released her, and now in a deep baritone began thanking her loudly and profusely for her generosity. A tremor of fear or shame rippled through Vinati's body. She stood up and hastily retreated, gaining speed with every step as she descended to the bottom of the stairs.

The sounds of a scuffle arose behind Vinati, and she swivelled around to see what was happening. A young boy of about 15, shirtless and missing an arm, had lunged at the beggar, grabbing for the note in his hand. The boy pulled harder, prying the man from the ground. The beggar lurched forward and fell to his knees, but he refused to let go of the money. The boy, just as stubborn, began dragging him roughly down the flight of stairs toward Vinati. A deep gash appeared on the man's forehead, leaving behind a trail of blood on the steps and platform. The beggar's fingers uncurled, revealing the coveted note. The boy snatched the prize and vanished before Vinati could reprimand him. Just then, another train pulled into the station, releasing a flood of passengers that engulfed the beggar and Vinati. The passers-by remained steadfastly oblivious to the injured man in their midst, stepping on the beggar's fingers and tripping over his legs, but he did not stir. Within seconds there were bloody footprints everywhere.

My God, I've killed him. The words rattled in Vinati's head, like the coins in the beggar's tin can. Petrified of being held accountable for the disturbance she had inadvertently caused—and quite possibly, the death of a man—she fled the scene, shoving people out of her way with both hands.

She found Manjit waiting under a mammoth billboard in the parking lot. He handed her a bottle of ice-cold mineral water as he opened the door of the air-conditioned car.

"Ah, madamji! I am so relieved to see you. Did you have any trouble on the train?"

"It was okay, Manjit. No problem." With trembling hands, Vinati uncapped the water bottle and poured it over her shoes to wash away any traces of blood.

"My brother Gyan is a taxi driver in Delhi. He says the government is planning to make a train system there also. I hope it will be cleaner than Mumbai trains."

~

The eight-by-ten-foot tin-roofed hut that Sita shared with her parents and two brothers did not come equipped with running water on the inside, but there were community taps scattered around the settlement. By good fortune, a new spigot had recently been installed just outside their hut, though the water supply remained sporadic during the day.

Sita washed her hands vigorously, using the end of a bobby pin to loosen the stubborn build-up of grime under her fingernails. It was a laborious process, and she always made a point to turn off the tap in between rinses—an act of conservation best learned through deprivation. Water, after all, was too precious to be wasted. To purge the lingering smell of trash, Sita rubbed a lemon wedge over her short nails.

"Ayree, Sita, what is taking you so long? Come inside and help me, your highness."

To a stranger, the tone of her mother's voice might have sounded harsh, but Sita knew otherwise. Her mother's love more than made up for the injustices that fate had visited upon her. One in particular she would never forget. It had happened one night while they stood outside their hut, watching the spectacle of two men engaged in a drunken brawl (a not-uncommon entertainment of the street, for such is the nature of the diversions available to those who have barely enough for basic survival). One of the men seized a red-hot skewer from the *kebabwala*'s grill, brandishing it like a sword. He stumbled toward his opponent, but stepped on some dog shit and slipped. Flailing to keep his balance, he inadvertently slammed the skewer into Sita's face. Her small hand still in her mother's grasp, she felt the metal burn into her soft flesh with a searing sensation sharp as a thousand bee stings.

Sita's mother held her for many nights after that, intent upon healing the trauma inflicted upon her spirit along with the injury to the child's now mutilated face. "You are special, my darling," she consoled Sita. "You will always stand out in a crowd, like a white lotus among a bunch of red camellias." Her mother's words brought as much relief as the salve of herbs she smeared across the weeping wound every night.

And woe betide anyone, adult or child, who dared tease the child about her disfigurement. Then the woman became a veritable lioness, roaring ferociously to protect her maimed cub. During the weeks of Sita's recuperation, the mother tutored her daughter in the art of needlework. But instead of sewing buttons and darning socks, Sita preferred to string together the flowers that her friend Kanchan brought from the *phool* bazaar, fashioning the varicoloured blooms into marvellously intricate garlands and bracelets. Working with flowers had helped take the edge off her misfortune, and eventually the incident became a faint memory from a distant past. Yet even now, a sharp twinge of pain would sometimes knife through the skin around the scar, as if it were being seared all over again. Sita splashed cold water on her face to wash away the stinging, turned off the tap, and headed inside.

Her father and brothers would return home soon, and dinner was not quite ready. Tying the ends of the *dupatta* around her waist, Sita sat on the floor next to her mother, who had prepared a precise measure of lentils and spicy cauliflower for their meal. It had to be precise, because without refrigeration it was impossible to preserve leftovers for the next day. Sita kneaded the dough and rolled out eleven thick *chapattis*—two for everyone in the family and the customary third for her father.

"Oh ho, you are still making *chapattis!*" Her friend Kanchan had arrived with a full basket of flowers. "Hurry up, Sita. You have to help me string the *mogra* into garlands." Friday nights were good for business; Kanchan did not want to miss the evening strollers on Marine Drive.

"Done!" exclaimed Sita, sliding the last piece of puffy bread off the hot skillet. "From trash to ashes to a burning hot *tawa*—my fingers have touched everything unpleasant today," she said with a laugh. "Now this is my reward, these beautiful flowers. Let's go! I'll eat dinner later." On the way out, she scooped up a bunch and held them against her scarred cheek. More than anything, Sita longed to sell the flowers herself, but she considered herself too ugly to be a *phoolwali*.

Kanchan, on the other hand, with her soft features and comely figure, seemed to have been fashioned by the Gods expressly for this line of work. Encamped conspicuously at the intersection dominated by the Intercontinental Hotel, she sang Hindi film songs and twirled around and waved the sweet-smelling garlands in the air, drawing as much attention to herself as to her wares. Sita, meanwhile, sat behind her on the pavement with the basket of flowers, stringing together still more garlands to sell. Trade was brisk this evening, and it was all she could do to keep up with demand. Young girls wrapped the garlands around their wrists like bracelets, women fastened them into their hair like Bollywood starlets, and the taxi drivers hung them in their cabs as air fresheners. Sometimes, Sita used a thin wire to fashion the *mogra* flowers into cunning animal shapes, to the delight of the children passing by and the consternation of their parents, who were powerless to resist their young ones' pleas to adopt such clever and beautiful pets.

On cool evenings like this, even the rich folk enjoyed cruising up and down Marine Drive, their windows rolled all the way down to let in the fragrant ocean breeze, which thrilled both the well-heeled and unshod alike. *They may not see me, or wish to see me,* Sita thought to herself. *But I know the wind kisses my coarse, dark skin just as it does their creamy white faces.*

After the dinner hour, the pedestrian crowd began to thin out as they retreated into their homes and hotel rooms for the night. Restless couples quickly progressed from holding hands to something more daring, always keeping an eye out for meddlesome cops. Sita wondered if she would ever know the love of a man. Her father had promised that he would soon have a large enough dowry to compensate for her blemish. Yet she knew that while marriage was one thing, love itself—real love—could not so easily be arranged by human machination.

She heard a wet, smacking sound behind her and turned to see a teenage couple furiously making out, moaning loudly and groping one another. Resting her chin on her palm, Sita watched them, curious about how it must feel.

"*Oye*, what's your problem? Get lost or I'll give you another scar to match that one." The boy raised a threatening hand, his crotch bulging in skintight jeans. More embarrassed than frightened, Sita placed the basket of flowers on her head and walked away. She saw Kanchan talking to the *seenghwala*, helping herself to the peanuts from his basket while she flirted with the boy.

"I'm going over by the Oberoi," Sita called out, pointing to the hotel at the far end of the promenade. "There aren't enough customers here. Meet me when you are finished chatting and ready to get back to work." She knew that Kanchan liked the handsome *seenghwala* and would probably linger with him for a long while. That would give her time to make more garlands.

Sita crossed Marine Drive and headed at a brisk pace in the direction of Nariman Point, hugging the sea wall so she could smell the ocean, watch the moon reflected in its rippled surface, and hear how the waves lapped against the barrier rocks. Nearing her destination, she slowed abruptly when a familiar figure came into view.

~

Vinati stood on the ledge of the sea wall, at the exact spot where she and Vandana had spent so many Friday evenings, talking the way sisters like to do. It was different without her. Everything was different, and she hated it. Vinati uncurled her fingers. Moonlight illuminated the fragment of bone cradled in her hand. She raised her arm, ready to hurl it far out into the ocean. But it was impossible. She could not let go. Defeated, she sat down on the cement wall, her legs dangling over the edge.

"What are you thinking, just sitting there on the ledge?" Sita inquired, startling Vinati from her reverie. She glanced around to see who had spoken and recognised her immediately. It was the *kudewali* girl from the crematorium. Too embarrassed to answer, Vinati turned her sombre gaze back toward the ocean.

Undeterred, Sita continued her interrogation. "Were you trying to throw a rock into the water? I can throw pretty well. Want to see?" Sita clambered up next to Vinati and peered into her palm. This was no rock. She knew exactly what it was. Vinati pulled her hand away and started to get up. "Don't leave," said Sita. "I'll make a special *savari* for your sister."

From her bag Sita drew forth a stack of fresh *peepal* leaves. Vinati watched in fascination as the *kudewali*'s dexterous fingers punched tiny holes in the leaves and then wove them together with the wire from her basket into the shape of a boat with watertight hull and high gunwales. All the while, Sita talked about her life in the shadow of President Park, the special things she had picked out of the Parekhs' trash, how she got her scar and, above all, her desire to be a *phoolwali* like her friend Kanchan. When she had finished, she invited Vinati to lay her sister's bone shard on top of the profusion of jasmine petals with which she had lined the inside of the boat. Finally, together they covered it with a shroud of marigolds.

Leaning over the edge of the sea wall, Sita cast the boat off on the receding tide. The gently undulating waves became the palanquin bearers of Vandana's remains, carrying her out to sea along a moonlit path. In complete silence, Vinati and Sita watched the ornate vessel float farther and farther away, until it was finally lost from view.

After that, Sita bought a paper cone filled with peanuts from the *seenghwala*, and the two girls sat together and talked and shared the peanuts, still gazing out at the calm ocean but no longer searching. Vinati told Sita about her parents, about Salem, about her sister's drug habit, and how she may have killed a beggar that day.

"Beggars are tougher than you think," Sita assured her. "So are you. Your sister would want you to be happy."

~

Though very busy sketching ideas for a new line of zodiac-themed floral arrangements, Mrs. Parekh welcomed Vinati and Sita into the shop. It was her daughter's first visit to *Boutique Blossoms* since Vandana's death.

"So what brings you here today?" she asked, pushing aside a sheaf of rejected designs. She was surprised to see the *kudewali*, but she held her breath. The fact that Vinati had dropped in at all pleased her immensely.

"Do you still need help in the shop?" Vinati asked. "Sita here has quite a way with flowers," she added, an unusual cheeriness in her voice.

"Is that so?" Mrs. Parekh was not normally inclined to look down her nose at people of a lower caste; yet one could hardly blame her for being sceptical. *What is Vinati doing with this girl*, she wondered. And who had given this impertinent *kudewali* permission to leaf through her designs like that?

"Trust me, she is very talented," Vinati insisted.

"All right." Still dubious, Mrs. Parekh pointed to the array of flowers in the refrigeration case. "Let's see what she can do with those."

It did not take Sita long. After just a few minutes, she handed Mrs. Parekh an elaborate floral lion, complete with mane and tail.

Mrs. Parekh was stunned. "When can you start, my dear?"

~

Friday evenings have become special again. Vinati sits on the sea wall at the far end of Marine Drive, munching warm peanuts while she awaits the arrival of her new friend, Sita, the *phoolwali*.

Taxiwala

It must be understood that neither by word nor deed had I given Fortunato cause to doubt my good will. I continued, as was my wont, to smile in his face, and he did not perceive that my smile now was at the thought of his immolation.

—Edgar Allan Poe

A shrill, demonic cawing heralded the arrival of a new day. If omens were to be trusted, it promised to be a long and gruelling one. Eight pairs of black, malevolent eyes scrutinised the man suspiciously through the dust-specked windshield. Even in its groggy state, Gyan's brain instinctively fished about for the correct turn of phrase. *What was it called? Oh, yes. A murder of crows.* The *taxiwala* prided himself on his knowledge of interesting English expressions and colloquialisms, odds and ends acquired painstakingly over the years from his gabbier *firang* passengers. In that respect, Gyan's place of business doubled as his classroom. The American tourists and businessmen who drove with him were especially appreciative of his more than serviceable conversational skills. That, and the impeccable cleanliness of his taxi's interior, made all the difference between comfortably scraping by and a tipless fare. *A gaggle of geese. A parliament of owls. A siege of herons. A murder of crows.* He liked the last one best. It sounded so sinister.

The combined weight of the birds in front of him bent the overhanging branch on which they perched low enough that the leaves brushed against the glass. The malevolent eyes of the crows continued to glare at the *taxiwala*. As if to belabour the ominous point, one of them unceremoniously expelled a jet of excrement onto the windshield. *So that's the kind of day it's going to be. Okay, I get it.*

Gyan sat up slowly, massaging a stiff knee. There was no room to extend his legs in the back seat of the taxi, where he had spent yet another restless night. The forced constriction of his long, muscular frame for hours on end invariably resulted in an aching joint or two. On these cool November nights it was like sleeping in an icebox, and then he often woke up with a rash of goosebumps up and down his arms to complement the cramping of his limbs. He yawned and shivered and huddled deeper into his threadbare cotton jacket for what little warmth it offered, drawing the frayed lapels tighter around his shoulders. After dropping off his last fare many hours after midnight, he had parked at his usual spot, under a luxuriant *bael* tree that had somehow survived New Delhi's frenetic urban development. He favoured that particular tree because its spreading branches provided shade against the brutal sun in the summer months and some slight refuge from the noise of the city, not to mention a semblance of privacy. The *taxiwala* yawned again and stretched out his arms, cracking his hairy knuckles on the roof of the car as he reached across the seat to adjust the rear-view mirror. Angling his head to see as much of his reflection as possible, Gyan took stock of his appearance.

The sorry, apish mug staring back at him looked like it belonged to someone sorely bested in a fist fight. Fatigue had etched dark circles under a pair of bloodshot eyes; his cheeks and jowls, mottled with a stippling of black bristles that grew in uneven patches on the flesh, had gone all puffy; and his thick mop of hair, dishevelled by fitful bouts of dozing, desperately required the services of a comb. To make matters worse, his temples throbbed with the beating of a thousand gongs. On top of physical exhaustion, hunger and dehydration left him feeling sick to his stomach. It had been a long, unpleasant night.

Were it not for the gentle but insistent rapping on the window next to his ear, Gyan would have happily slumped back into a foetal position and succumbed to the sleep that his body demanded. It was too late for that now. Krishan, the *chaiwala*'s son, would not be deterred. His nose pressed against the glass, the boy peeked in with an intensity of purpose, using his free hand as a visor against the glare of the early-morning sun. The fingers of his other hand, seemingly made of asbestos, held up a small glass of scalding hot tea.

"*Baba* saw you waking up," Krishan yelled through the small gap in the window. "He sent *chai*." The boy's tone was all business. Though barely nine years old, he wore the solemn face of a grown man. It occurred to Gyan that he had never seen the lad smile, much less laugh with the heedless abandon that is the hallmark of childhood. Still, he knew that Krishan, unlike many of his compeers, could count himself fortunate to be working at his father's little tea shop, a makeshift establishment not far from where Gyan's taxi was parked. Indeed, having a father at all gave him an enviable edge in the struggle for survival in New Delhi.

The streets of that city are home to countless children, considered little better than feral dogs, who live their entire lives like earthquake victims. Born on society's fault lines and permanently displaced by circumstance, these outcasts among outcasts are disqualified at birth from enjoying even the most routine amenities of life. Nameless casualties of deep-rooted tradition, their numbers fill the ranks of a perennial, invisible, yet ubiquitous underclass. At busy traffic lights they flock around the lines of halted cars and knock on the resolutely rolled-up windows, eternal supplicants seeking alms, yet fated to receive only a universal moue of distaste. Patting distended bellies or gesturing toward parched mouths, they mime a desperate appeal to sympathy and cry out for pity before resuming their forlorn quest for benefactors. Every now and then, one of their fellow citizens may be moved to compassion toward them. More often than not, however, they are simply ignored, cursed at, or shooed away like an annoying but inconsequential swarm of flies.

For his part, Gyan found it impossible to remain entirely deaf to their urgent pleas for succour. He was a *sahib* to the beggars because he was fully clothed and even drove a motor vehicle—signs that fortune had bestowed upon him something akin to affluence. He wondered how anyone could ignore such misery, especially when even the smallest kindness could do so much to alleviate it. He never failed to be astonished at how eagerly the city's poorest of the poor would accept the proffered scrap of leftover kebab or a half-drained soft drink bottle, as if invited to partake of a royal feast. Sometimes his dreams were haunted by the murmurings of these wretched orphans of the street, entreating him for money to buy food. "*Sahib*, one rupee only, *sahib*. Please, I am so hungry...." What was to become of such creatures? Their grim outlook made him shudder, for he instinctively understood that those who have never known pity may one day themselves become pitiless.

Gyan rolled down the window, still smudged on the outside with tiny prints left behind by dirty, calloused hands, and held out two rupees for Krishan.

"No, no, *baba* said never to take payment from you because you are his good friend. He never forgets that you lent him money for my sister's wedding." Krishan spoke fast, reciting the words mechanically, like a rhyme he might have learned had he attended school. "I will bring more *chai* later," he promised, handing the glass to Gyan, and scurried off to the teashop. Business was always brisk in the mornings, and the boy had many customers to attend to. Across the square, Gyan could see steam wafting like a mountain mist over a giant pot of tea that formed part of the shop's sign above the door, an irresistible lure to the unceasing ebb and flow of passers-by. Even though the tea glass remained almost too hot to handle, he needed to put something in his stomach. He nestled back in the seat and took a grateful sip of the ambrosial brew, letting the sweet aroma of cardamom fill his nostrils. To most Indians, tea is a panacea, and in that regard Gyan was no exception. In short order he felt its effects seeping through his body, easing sore muscles the way fresh oil lubricates overworked gears.

Watching Krishan disappear into the shop, Gyan felt fortunate to have escaped such a lamentable childhood. He had grown up in a quiet village 300 km west of New Delhi, where the days began with plans for boyish mischief and ended with whispers about what adventures the next morning might bring. Extending his arms like an airplane—a far cry from holding them out for charity—Gyan hurtled from one escapade to the next, with his older brother Manjit always in the lead. Poor but carefree, they found their own pleasures, without charge, in chasing hordes of frolicsome butterflies through expansive mustard fields, golden-yellow as far as the eye could see. For a lark, they liked to deflate the bicycle tyres of the village scrooge. When they got hungry, they sneaked into the *zamindar*'s land to steal the juiciest mangoes they could find. For young Gyan and his brother, life was an exercise in practical joy, almost entirely uninterrupted by personal tragedy.

The strains of an unfamiliar melody suddenly filled the inside of the cab, yanking the *taxiwala* from his reverie. It took him a few seconds to identify the source of the music. *Of course! My cell phone.* He frantically pawed at his jacket pockets in search of the cursed device. He had almost forgotten that his daughter Rima had once again changed the ringtone on his phone, setting it this time to the chorus of the latest hit song out of Bollywood. He wished she would not do that. How many times had he attempted to reason with her? "I don't even know when someone is calling me, Rima *beta*," he had entreated. "I always think it's the radio. Why can't I just have it sound like a real phone? *Riiing-riiing.* That is how it should sound!"

"Oh Papa, don't be such a fuddy-duddy. It is a beautiful song. Just listen to the words. You can picture the heroine dancing in the rain, dreaming of her true love. She wants to marry him, but there are so many obstacles to overcome." Rima proceeded to recount for her father the general plot of the film, a musical saga of love thwarted but ultimately victorious—which aptly described the theme of virtually every other Bollywood love story with which Gyan was familiar. He rolled his eyes in exasperation.

"You should not let yourself be dazzled by fairy tales, Rima," he cautioned his spirited daughter. "Your mother and I have worked very hard to provide you with opportunities we never had. Please don't waste them. We sent you to college so you could make something of yourself, something real—not some fantasy."

"And for that I am thankful," she assured him, suddenly serious. "Don't worry, Papa. I'm not waiting for some film hero to sweep me off my feet with silly love songs. I have a job now, a good one. Wait and see. One day you will be very proud of me." With an affectionate hug and a peck on the cheek, she quickly quelled her father's fears, the way daughters always manage to do.

The chorus repeated itself, as it would continue to do until he answered. Glancing down at the small screen of his phone, Gyan recognised the number on the read-out. It was Mrs. Kapoor calling, one of his regulars. Although she owned a nice car and was perfectly capable of driving herself, the elderly, congenial lady preferred to be chauffeured around by Gyan rather than brave the congested city roads on her own.

"Good morning, madamji! What can I do for you on this delightful day?" Though he could almost guess what the call was about, he listened patiently to what she had to say, making polite noises into the mouthpiece during the infrequent pauses in her monologue. "The club? Mm-hmm. Yes. Of course." As expected, Mrs. Kapoor wanted to be driven to her weekly bridge session at the Delhi Gymkhana Club. Truth be told, right now he just wanted to go home to his wife, to lie in her embrace and regale her with his exploits of the day before.

Finally, he heard silence at the other end of the line. Gyan rubbed his weary eyes. He was tempted to turn down the job, but he needed the money. Also, Mrs. Kapoor tipped well. "Twenty-five minutes, madamji. I'll be there in 25 minutes."

Thoughtfully he stroked the coarse growth of stubble on his chin. One last fare—then he could return home to the arms of his beloved. The trip would not be too far out of his way. Gyan consulted his watch. He had just enough time for another cup of tea and a quick visit to the public lavatory to make himself look more or less presentable before leaving to fetch Mrs. Kapoor. As if on cue, Krishan reappeared at the window, this time with a large aluminium kettle in hand to refill the glass. Gyan thanked the boy and leaned forward in the seat, sipping the steaming tea as fast as he could.

~

Gyan's reputation for punctuality was well deserved. Precisely 23 minutes after the phone call, he pulled into the driveway of his client's residence. Two minutes later, he climbed the short flight of steps to the front entrance. He always thought it impolite to honk the horn to announce his arrival. Instead, he rang the bell and waited patiently, listening for the sound of slow footsteps approaching the door. When Mrs. Kapoor stepped outside, he offered his arm for support as they made their way to the taxi.

Thanks to the morning rush hour traffic, it was a long, slow ride from her home to the Delhi Gymkhana Club. Unlike many of his other passengers, Mrs. Kapoor preferred to pass the time in conversation rather than listening to popular radio music or be subjected to inane disc jockey chatter. They made small talk about this and that, and then she inquired about Gyan's family. When he told her about Rima's new job with the bank, madamji congratulated him.

"My wife Savitri and I are very happy. As soon as she finished college, I told Rima she could work anywhere she wanted. Anywhere, that is, except with the airlines. You know, I drive many air hostesses from the airport. You would not believe some of the things I have seen them do. It would sicken you." Gyan snorted his disapproval. "Living without limits can corrupt anyone, even girls from good families."

He knew whereof he spoke. The new boutique airlines, as well as the international carriers, were now offering young, single girls the enticement of lavish pay checks to fly with them. Straight out of school, the new entrants earned more than their fathers, radically shifting the balance of familial power. The combination of youthful imprudence and financial independence, in Gyan's opinion, formed an intoxicating mix that could only lead to trouble.

"Yes, it's dreadful what is happening to our young people," Mrs. Kapoor agreed. "Too much freedom, too soon, is dangerous. Tell me Gyan, does Rima have to travel far for work?"

Gyan brooded over the question before answering. Being a parent, he had learned, meant living under a constant fog of fear. "That is the only problem, madam*ji*. The bank where she works is a long distance from our home. She has no choice but to ride the bus every day. It scares me."

"Far be it for me to alarm you, but you have ample reason to be scared." It was true. They both knew that a recent influx of unlicensed bus drivers from neighbouring states had rendered the streets of New Delhi quite unsafe. One could not open a *Times of India* or *Hindustan Times* without reading about the latest horrific incident. Pedestrians, cyclists, and stray animals took to the public thoroughfares at their peril.

Worse yet, Gyan had also heard grim tales about how some of those rough village folk preyed on women travelling alone—young, educated working girls in particular, for the very notion of a self-reliant Indian female securing her own way to material prosperity was known to arouse in the provincial mind a sense of resentment so extreme that it unleashed the savage animal within. Masses of indignant men from backwater towns suffered the affront of seeing attractive, successful women flout time-honoured mores by talking freely, wearing western clothes, and working in comfortable air-conditioned offices, where they earned prodigious salaries far greater than anything that an unskilled male could ever hope to command. Yet such men, traditionally exalted in their native communities merely by virtue of the gender into which they were born, found themselves compelled to fight for their very survival in this city, earning their bread—and never any butter—by toiling at the most menial and degrading jobs available. Drudgery was their profession and poverty their daily wage. This upside-down state of affairs stood as a perpetual reminder of their inadequacy as family providers and a constant, drumming reproach to their very manhood.

And to answer that reproach, these men did not hesitate to commit heinous crimes of sexual abuse and violence. The barbarity of their acts shocked even the collective sensibilities of a country that dismissed the practice of female infanticide as a trifling lapse in communal probity. For these self-appointed custodians of morality, violating a woman's dignity served as a method to show the 'arrogant' *mahila* her proper place in society.

While Gyan understood the anger and frustration of these proud men with punctured egos, he could never find a rationale behind such atrocious methods of 'justice.' He was aware that his own daughter might fall prey to such brutes. In light of his conversation with Mrs. Kapoor, he found it difficult to keep from dwelling on that unnerving possibility.

"You will worry about your daughter until the day you die, Gyan," she sighed knowingly. "And perhaps even long after that. Such is the price one pays for the joys of having children."

"You are right about that, madam*ji*. But I wish she did not have to ride the bus."

"Why don't you buy Rima a cell phone?" Mrs. Kapoor suggested. "That way she will be able to call you if she finds herself in trouble."

"She already has one, but it's not very good. I've been saving up to buy one of the fancy new models for her birthday."

Driver and passenger talked non-stop for half an hour, devising strategies to keep Rima safe from reckless bus drivers and felonious yokels, until they finally arrived at the entrance of the Delhi Gymkhana Club. Leaving the motor running, Gyan helped Mrs. Kapoor out of the taxi and up the steps.

"Can you be so good as to wait for me?" she asked, a hopeful smile carved into the mesh of wrinkles on her face. "I shan't be long."

"Of course, madam*ji*. I'll park the car in the lot and get something to eat in the meantime. Call me on my cell whenever you are ready to go."

As soon as he parked, Gyan marched directly to the very first street food vendor that came into view. He could not remember the last meal he had eaten. Was it lunch yesterday? In any case, he was famished. The rumblings of his stomach became suddenly clamorous. Something cheap and quick would suffice for now. But what he really yearned for at this moment, more than anything in the world, was a home-cooked meal. He imagined himself sitting down to Savitri's *poori aloo*, perhaps the tastiest dish in her impressive culinary repertoire. *Yes, that would certainly hit the spot.* His mouth watered at the very thought.

Gyan purchased two *bun samosas* and wolfed them down. Greasy and filling, they sated his hunger while simultaneously whetting his appetite for some delicacy from his wife's kitchen. If Mrs. Kapoor wrapped up quickly, he would have time to go back home for a bite of something more satisfying and a short nap before his scheduled pickups later that day.

A naturally reserved and contemplative man, Gyan had long cultivated the habit of turning inward and chewing the cud, as it were. He leaned against the side of his taxi and closed his eyes, relishing the warmth of the November sun against his dark skin. Though the pounding in his head had abated, he still felt bone-tired. His thoughts wandered to the events of the previous night.

The Lufthansa flight from Frankfurt had arrived at Indira Gandhi International Airport a little later than usual. As previously arranged, he had parked in the crew pickup area and, unruffled by the delay, waited patiently to pick up Miss Kumar after her long flight. She exited the terminal well past 1:00 A.M., chortling indecorously about something with her fellow crew members. He expected she might be travel-weary and would just want to be driven home. Instead, she directed him to Gurgaon, to an address to which he had taken her several times before.

A young flight attendant whom he regularly ferried to and from the airport, Tanya Kumar represented everything that Gyan himself disliked about the new generation of spoiled, emancipated girls. She dressed provocatively, complained constantly, talked and texted incessantly on her cell phone, and showed little respect toward anyone of any class. Once, after dropping her off at home, he discovered her phone wedged in the back seat of his taxi. He drove 25 km out of his way to return it, free of charge, only to be reprimanded.

"Idiot! Why didn't you bring it sooner? I've been tearing my place apart looking for this thing." Though her grooming was impeccable and she dressed in stylish, costly clothes, Tanya proceeded to swear at him like some common *paan*-chewing *kaamwali*. At the time, Gyan had felt the urge to slap her. Of course, he would never do any such thing. Instead, he reminded himself that she was little more than a child who clearly did not know any better, reckoning that her immaturity was reason enough to overlook such insolence. He held his tongue and simply walked away, without reward or gratitude.

As he navigated through the deserted streets of Gurgaon, he wondered what her parents, who lived in Meerut, would have thought about such nocturnal excursions. No doubt she had friends in this section of the city with whom she stayed up late. *Or lovers perhaps.* Watching her in the rear-view mirror, he had to admit that an attractive young woman like Tanya would not lack for suitors. She was blessed with fair skin and an alluring, heart-shaped face worthy of public adulation on a movie poster. A pair of large bovine eyes fringed by long thick lashes gave her a beguiling if not bewitching expression, and her raven hair—a lustrous silky plumage—fell in exuberant cascades around her narrow shoulders and down almost to her waist. Preening herself in a compact mirror, she puckered her full red lips and kissed the air. Then she slipped off the canary-yellow Lufthansa neck scarf and undid two more buttons of her uniform blouse. Not completely satisfied just yet, she cupped her generously proportioned breasts from underneath and pushed them upward to form an even more enticing cleavage.

All the primping in the world would not change Gyan's mind about her. The woman was crude, inconsiderate, and quite detestable, not even worth thinking about. The *taxiwala* turned his attention back to the road ahead, vigilant for stray mongrels and meandering cows.

"No, no, you incompetent fool, don't turn here. Don't you remember the way? Take the next left." Tanya ordered him to stop in front of one of the newer buildings on the street and to wait for her. "Don't go anywhere. I'll be back in 20 minutes." The building appeared to be constructed entirely of windows, and its gleaming façade reflected bright moonlight directly onto the street below. Though it was distinctively modern in its appearance and undeniably lovely to look at, Gyan did not understand how anybody would dare to inhabit such a fragile-seeming structure. Were an earthquake to strike, even a small one, he was certain the building would shatter instantly, collapsing with a hellish sound into a heap of splintered glass.

He knew from past experience that Tanya's 20 minutes could very easily stretch into an hour. But when two hours ticked by, he began to grow a little concerned about the safety of his charge. Wondering what might be keeping her, Gyan happened to glance up at the building and caught a glimpse of her on the second floor. The glass-walled apartment had no curtains to conceal the goings-on within, and he could see her dancing naked between two men, gyrating lewdly to music he could not hear. Embarrassed for the girl and shamed by what he had just seen, Gyan looked away. For the first time, he had witnessed Tanya doing what he had thus far only imagined.

At around four o'clock in the morning, an infernal tapping at the window rousted Gyan from his seat, where he had begun to nod off. It was Tanya. Stepping quickly out of the car to open the rear passenger door, he could smell alcohol on her breath, and he saw that she held a considerable wad of cash fastened into a bundle with a pair of yellow lace panties. Her flight crew lapel pin—a pair of gilded wings—kept the lace from unravelling. She teetered precariously on the points of her stiletto heels, then suddenly pitched forward. If he had not caught her, she would have slammed into the concrete pavement. He helped her into the back seat, mindful to place the money in her purse so she would not lose it. As soon as he drove off, she fell asleep. For the entire ride, the *taxiwala* kept a watchful eye on his inebriated passenger.

Once they arrived in front of the apartment building where she lived, Gyan was not sure what to do next. Fearful that his intentions might be misinterpreted if he carried the sleeping girl into her bedroom, he gently and repeatedly nudged her elbow in hopes of rousing Tanya from her drunken stupor. His persistent prodding finally paid off.

"*Chutiya!* Why did you wake me? I was having such a wonderful dream." Gyan ignored the insult and assisted

Tanya to her front door, then left as soon as she was safe inside. Too exhausted to drive all the way home, Gyan parked under the tree near his friend's tea shop, crawled into the back of the taxi and fell asleep.

He had missed seeing Savitri's face first thing in the morning when he woke up. He would like to have told her about Tanya Kumar, and to ask her why on earth a beautiful young girl with such a well-paying job would choose to make still more money by selling her body. Now, waiting for Mrs. Kapoor, he was convinced that his wife would say something insightful about the situation, words without judgement or rancour.

Unafraid to bare his most intimate thoughts and fears, Gyan shared everything with Savitri. He did not pretend to be strong with her, for she was his strength. Her opinions helped him make sense of a world that at times felt unjust, uncaring, and quite possibly insane. How that good woman could tolerate waking up to *his* poor muzzle of a face was quite beyond Gyan's understanding.

They had been decreed a couple nearly 25 years ago—two strangers, neither of them adults, when they circled seven times the sacred fire of matrimony. Gyan often wondered if the village matchmaker, a meddlesome old woman who had arranged the alliance for a generous fee, could possibly have foreseen the success of their union.

As a husband and father, Gyan had long ago renounced a coercive attitude toward women that he once shared with many of his peers. His wife was chosen for him to serve as little more than a consort, and an inferior one at that, fit only to bear him children and perform menial household chores. And like his peers, he expected to continue his visits to the village brothel—a cluster of small brick houses near the government hospital—even after marriage.

His older, more experienced sibling Manjit first introduced him to Halla Gully, as the brothel area was called. After that, though rather shy, he became a frequent visitor to the place. True to its name, the street was loud and boisterous, a locus for revelry and carousing in stark contrast to the more reserved streets surrounding it. Music blared from the brightly coloured houses as a lure to attract customers, each one louder than the last, with the intent of drowning out the competition. The staff at the hospital often complained about the noise, but the village authorities had neither the resources nor the willingness to remedy the situation.

The younger girls of Halla Gully, bedecked in all their cheap finery, trilled raucously together as Gyan wended his way past them. The older, greying courtesans, with only immense sagging breasts and layers of gaudy make-up to offer as blandishment, simply thrust thumb and forefinger into their painted mouths and whistled boorishly in his direction.

Bridling at their unwanted attentions, he always ignored them all. Fixing his gaze firmly ahead, Gyan made a beeline for the last house on the street, the one with the grey and yellow façade, where he invariably asked for the girl who went by the name of Hema. Among her other customers, she was considered tolerably pretty, but that was not the reason he chose her. For one thing, she did not chew *paan*, a habit that revolted him. Nor did she talk during intercourse, and said very little before or after, which suited him just fine. He stared at the austere walls of the room until he was satisfied, then paid her wordlessly and left.

Gyan did not want to know anything about the adversities of this woman's past or her future aspirations, if she had any. The heavy smudges of kohl around her eyes and the scarlet lipstick she wore could not mask the insensate creature that dwelt within. When he touched her, he did not feel as though he were touching a person, but a thing. Gyan possessed an innate capacity for sympathy toward others. Had she exhibited even a hint of genuine charm or vulnerability, he would have been unable to purchase pleasure from her so callously.

Right up until the day he was joined with Savitri, he wondered if married life would be any different.

To say that it *was* different would be an understatement.

For the duration of the two-hour-long wedding ceremony, he remembered sitting beside the unfamiliar woman he had just met, this Savitri, musing nervously over what she might look like. Was she bucktoothed? Was her skin pockmarked? Were her eyes crooked? Her face had remained a veiled mystery until the moment the priest instructed Gyan to line the parting in her hair with red *sindoor* powder, at which juncture he declared them married and the veil was removed.

What he saw could only be described as a revelation. His once betrothed, now his wife, was more beautiful than any man could have hoped.

Matrimony brought everything Gyan had thought impossible, and everything Savitri had imagined. That they became lovers goes without saying. They also became friends and partners, co-conspirators in their own future. In their bed—the narrow cot that creaked like the joints of an old woman—they would talk late into the night, about nothing and everything. Manjit, unable to sleep in the next room because of their amorous, incessant chatter, would yell at them to please shut the hell up. Then they whispered softly to each other, little people nurturing big dreams of living in the capital city.

Sometimes on sultry nights, when the stars appeared close enough to touch, they walked arm in arm down to the riverbank. As they drew near to the water, Savitri would break away and run from her husband, flirtatiously lifting her *sari* around her bare, golden-brown legs. Gyan gave her a head start, letting her take flight, and then he chased her, the way he used to chase butterflies in the mustard fields. When he caught her by the hips, they tumbled to the ground in a tangle of limbs and fabric, breathless with laughter.

Then, on the softest patch of grass they could find, they made love. They always started gently, almost cautiously, seducing each other by exquisite degrees. Every sense, from the tactile to the auditory, was conscripted into the earnest, joyful task of bestowing mutual pleasure. Warm mouths and caressing hands explored familiar territory with virgin curiosity, and the sounds of Savitri's arousal further fuelled her husband's passion. Often they climaxed in unison, falling together in a crescendo of ardent moans from the steeps of passion into a deep, delicious abyss of fulfilment. As they lay there on the ground, physically spent, Gyan would clinch her in his arms, burrowing his face between her soft breasts to listen to the pounding heart of his beloved.

And then she would ask the question.

"Do you think we just made a baby?" she quizzed him, her voice gravid with hope. "Do you think it will be a boy?"

From the very beginning, Savitri had been eager to conceive. Eventually she did, and nine months later she gave birth to a healthy baby girl, their first and only child. Sometimes she fretted over her failure to produce a son, even years into their marriage. "To give your husband a son, that is your first duty as a wife," her mother-in-law had never tired of reminding her.

"I don't understand," Gyan gently admonished her. "My mother is dead and gone. Why does it still bother you? We have a child. We are blessed. What more can I ask?"

"Perhaps you secretly regret not having a son, Gyan. You would tell me if you did, right? I know you are too nice a man to beat me, the way other husbands beat their wives. Don't you hear the neighbours next door? Sheela's husband keeps demanding a son, as if it will just pop out of her if he hits her hard enough with his fists. Oh, and did I tell you? She's pregnant again!"

"Then for her sake, let's hope it's a boy this time." Much about Gyan differentiated him from his peers. Punjabi men are a rambunctious lot. Their hands serve as essential tools of communication, useful for clapping, for backslapping, and—not least of all—for signalling hostile intent and, if provoked, following through on it. Gyan preferred rational persuasion to gladiatorial exchanges. In his view, physical confrontation was the first resort of a feeble mind. "Poor Sheela. Any man who hits a woman is no man at all," he declared forthrightly.

"Still, I sometimes wish...."

Cupping his wife's delicate face in his thick hands, Gyan looked into her grey eyes with all the love in his heart. "*Jaanu*, please believe me, I am truly happy. Why on earth do you torment yourself? Don't mistake me for some *maharaja*. I have no kingdom to pass on."

"It's not that."

"Then what? Are you worried about our old age? We don't need a son to look after us. We will save money for ourselves." Gyan clasped her around the waist and began nuzzling on her ear. "Once we have enough in the bank, we can leave New Delhi for good and grow old together without worries. Now please put down that broom and give me a kiss."

"What about our daughter?" Savitri persisted.

"Rima will always be our daughter," Gyan said. "But once she is settled in her job, we should encourage her to choose a husband. Then we'll be free to go back to our village, where we will climb trees and eat mangoes all day long."

She pushed him away. "Silly man! By then we'll be too old to climb trees! We'll both be like this." Hunching over and using the broom as a crutch, she hobbled around the kitchen like a toothless crone, lisping complaints about her bent, aching back.

Gyan laughed and applauded with childlike delight at her performance. Standing barefoot in their kitchen, he realised that he was a *maharaja*, this modest little home was his palace, and she was his *rani*, the queen of their domain. Gazing at her, his eyes grew wistful with desire and adoration, and she returned his look, beloved to lover.

"Oh Gyan, I cannot wait for that day. You work so hard. It would be wonderful to lead a simpler life."

"And a quieter one!" Gyan reminded her. "Don't forget that. My poor head hurts with all the honking. Why is everybody so impatient these days? Even at the intersections, as soon as the light turns green, the drivers behind me immediately blast their horns, even if the traffic is moving."

"*Ayree*, that's the way it is in this city. Nobody pays attention unless you make a lot of noise."

"Do you know what's even worse, Savitri? The crows. Nobody makes more noise than those bloody crows. How peaceful it will be to wake up instead to the sound of the koels singing in the trees. *Koo-Ooo, koo-Ooo!*"

"*Kik-kik-kik, kik-kik-kik,*" she sang back to him, dancing in circles and flapping her arms like a pair of wings. Then she threw down the broom and ran into his embrace.

Standing outside the Delhi Gymkhana Club, with the noonday sun warming his limbs, Gyan smiled at the remembrance of their conversation from the day before. Afterward, they had made love.

To give Rima a decent dowry and to afford a comfortable living in their village, complete with running water and electricity, they would need a substantial saving. He massaged the back of his knee, which still felt a little stiff. Difficult as it was, he did not mind working such long hours. In the end, it would be worth it. He glanced at his watch again. He hoped there would still be time for him to go home and see his wife.

Fortunately, Mrs. Kapoor proved true to her word. She did not keep him waiting for long. His phone was singing.

~

Soon after he pulled out of Mrs. Kapoor's driveway, his phone began singing again. He was stopped at a traffic light, anxious to get home, and hoped it was not another job. He did not recognise the number on the screen, but answered the phone anyway. As his wife had often advised him, "Never turn a deaf ear to Lakshmi when she calls." Now, more than ever, Gyan wanted to stay on good terms with the Goddess of wealth.

The traffic light turned green just as he brought the phone to his ear. A chorus of honking horns behind him made it impossible to hear the voice at the other end of the line. "Give me a moment, I can't understand you." Gyan pulled over to the side of the road, stopping right in front of a *fruitwala* arranging a display of pomegranates into a precarious heap on a cart, and rolled up his window to block out the noise. "Okay, I'm back. Who is this?"

It was their neighbour, Sheela. He heard her crying hysterically into the phone. Had her husband beaten her up again? With all her sobbing, it was hard to comprehend the words. She needed to calm down. *And come to think of it, why is she calling me?*

"Gyan, you must come quickly. I'm at Rudra Hospital, near the house."

"What's that? Did you say the hospital?"

"Yes! I brought her here in an autorickshaw," Sheela yelled into the phone. "The doctor hasn't seen her yet. There is so much blood, and I can't stop it. Hello? Gyan, are you still there?"

Oh no. Something has happened to my daughter. His worst fears had finally come to pass. One of those ignorant bus drivers had run her over. Or maybe some thug had attacked her on the way to the bank. He clenched his fist in anger. *When I get my hands on that....*

"I don't understand. Look, it is afternoon already. I thought Rima was at work. You must tell me, Sheela. How badly is she hurt? Is her mother there with you? Please put her on."

"No, no, it's not Rima. I'm talking about Savitri."

"*What?* What's going on? What happened?"

"She must have heard my rotten husband hitting me, and she came over to see what was going on. He was drunk, as usual. He told me he had a dream that we would have another baby girl—then swore that he would cut it out of me. He grabbed a knife from the table and swung it at me. That's when Savitri walked in. She just wanted to help. He never even saw her. It was an accident, Gyan. He didn't mean to stab her."

"Stay with her, Sheela. I'll be right there."

Cold, black rage clawed at his heart, while an inexpressible dread filled his veins and spread to every part of his body. Even his fingertips tingled with it. *Savitri!* The phone began singing again in his hand, but he let it play on without answering. Clients could wait. In his mind he charted the quickest route to the hospital, then hastily threw the taxi into reverse. The rear bumper nicked a corner of the vendor's cart, upsetting the stand and spilling the entire load of pomegranates onto the street. As he peeled out into the traffic to make an illegal U-turn, his tyres crushed some of the fruit into a bloody pulp, leaving behind twin tracks of red and a cloud of burnt rubber. In his blind urgency, all he perceived was the path ahead that would lead him to his destination without delay. He was oblivious to everything else—the sudden overture of screeching brakes, the symphony of honking horns, the piccolo-pitched whistles of a traffic cop, and the fruit vendor's melodic string of vehement curses.

~

"Hello? Anybody around? I'm looking for a patient. *Hello!*" The nurse's station located at the far end of the chaotic emergency ward remained obstinately deserted. He pounded the desk in vexation, then turned in a slow circle, scanning the room in search of his wife. Sheela, who had heard his booming voice above all the pandemonium, leapt up from amid a cluster of triage beds and called out to him. "Gyan, over here!"

Even from a distance, he recognised Savitri by her *sari*—yellow georgette with a pattern of pink roses—that he had given her as an anniversary present the year before. How she had admired the softness of the fabric, the detail of the embroidered flowers. Now two new blossoms of crimson, where the knife had punctured her abdomen, had unfolded and spread across the front of the delicate garment. The gold bangle gleaming on her wrist, a wedding gift from his mother, only confirmed what he already knew. She had never once removed the precious jewellery in all their years together. Otherwise, he barely recognised her. It shocked him to see the flesh on her face so wan and sunken. Sheela and the attending physician intercepted him as he approached his wife's bedside.

"Let me talk to her!"

"You can't," Sheela whispered. "She's sleeping now, Gyan."

"I gave her something for the pain, and to keep her calm," the doctor interjected. "She'll be out like a light for a while."

"Can't you just stitch her up?"

"No, we can't just 'stitch her up'! It's much more serious than that. We've managed to control the bleeding for now. But with two deep stab wounds like these to the stomach, she will need surgery."

"Then what are you waiting for?"

"Mister, this is a private hospital. First you have to pay for the operation. I have an opening in the O.R. at four. If you can deposit Rs. 25,000 by three, we can squeeze her in. Otherwise, I doubt she'll make it through the night."

"Did you say 25,000? I can't come up with such a huge amount so quickly!"

"In that case, I suggest you take your wife to a government hospital. Transporting her in this condition is a big risk—but go ahead and check her out if you like." Without any further explanation or pretence of concern, the doctor moved on to his next patient, deftly deflecting Gyan's pleas for time, for credit, for sympathy, for his wife's survival.

At last the *taxiwala* gave up and turned to Sheela in a daze. "If only we had medical insurance, like the rich people."

"I'm so sorry, Gyan. How does he expect you to lay your hands on that kind of money without any notice?"

"I don't know. I'll think of something." He squeezed his eyes shut and rubbed his temples, which had begun throbbing again.

"It's not much, but I have about Rs. 400 stashed under my bed," she rambled on. "It's the least I can do. Just walk right in and take it."

"Thank you, Sheela. I'll need a lot more than that, though." He willed himself to think logically, clearly, undismayed by catastrophe. It was his turn to be strong for his wife.

"Maybe you should do what the doctor suggested and take her to the government hospital," said Sheela.

"No, I'm not doing that. I want the best possible care for my wife," Gyan said decisively. "Okay, listen. You stay with Savitri. Promise me you won't leave her. And call Rima. Let her know what has happened. I'll be back as soon as I can."

By the time he climbed behind the wheel of his taxi, Gyan had puzzled out an itinerary in his head. He began working the phone while he drove. First he visited the bank to make a substantial withdrawal, but that was not enough. Then he raced to his neighbour's home and ran inside. Passing through the kitchen, he was shocked at the amount of blood he saw spattered across the kitchen floor. He found Sheela's few rupees exactly where she said they would be, loose coins and some notes tied up with string in a cloth purse tucked under the mattress. But he still needed more, much more.

The next few hours became a blur of desperate begging and lunatic driving, and only by a miracle did he avoid getting into any collisions along the way. After each stop, he would mentally tally up the rupees accumulating in his pocket. A salary advance from the taxi company, a small loan from his friend, the *chaiwala*, a larger loan from the kindly Mrs. Kapoor and several more from faithful clients who he knew would be willing to help. *Almost there*, he thought, daring at last to indulge in the luxury of hope.

His final stop would be the residence of Tanya Kumar. He needed just Rs. 1,500 more, and he was confident that he could get them from her. He would not be asking for a loan either, simply his due. She had lately failed to pay him for several late-night jaunts, so that was money owed to him. He even knew she had it on hand. The wad of cash he had so prudently placed in her purse the night before must have totalled that amount three times over.

The drive to Tanya's place took somewhat longer than anticipated. A bullock cart had overturned ahead of him on the Noida Bridge, blocking two lanes of traffic. Gyan could not move an inch, and he feared that his engine might overheat under the merciless midday sun. He was close enough to get a clear view of the accident, could hear the animal wailing on the pavement, and watched as the lone, elderly driver struggled in vain to tip the heavy cart upright again. *This can't be happening.* Exasperated almost to the point of madness, he threw open the door and charged on foot past the line of idling cars. Roughly pushing the old man aside, he took the entire weight of the cart in his hands and lifted it up and over. Then back behind the wheel of his taxi, he snaked his way through the hole he had just created in the traffic jam and sped away.

~

Anticipating that Tanya might still be asleep after the previous night's excursion, Gyan held his finger insistently on her doorbell until he heard a pair of feet shuffling toward the entrance, and the door opened. Her hair and clothing were a tousled wreck, her cheeks besmeared with the kohl and lipstick she had never bothered to wash off before flopping into bed. The look of speechless indignation on her face convinced him that he had indeed awakened her from a deep slumber. Without giving Tanya the opportunity to let loose with her usual volley of curses and insults, he folded his hands together and explained his predicament as quickly and politely as he could.

"And so, madamji, please pay me what you owe me," he begged. "As you can see, I need it urgently."

"Oh yaar, you people and your daily dramas. Just yesterday the maid wanted some extra pay for her sick baby. What kind of fool do you take me for to believe such stories? You people are such parasites; leeching off my kindness. Besides, I don't have any money in the house."

"But madamji...."

"Now go away," Tanya ordered, dismissing him with a flick of her hand. She slammed the door in his face.

A moment later, she opened the door.

"Okay, taxiwala, listen. I have to go back to Gurgaon tomorrow night. You can swing by at around eleven. I might have the money for you then." With that, she shut the door again. He could hear the deadbolt turn and her footsteps recede down the hall.

Though tempted to continue ringing the doorbell until she gave him what he wanted, he knew that such persistence would simply result in her making a frenzied call to the police, who would then haul him away to prison somewhere and make him wait to explain his motives before some bored magistrate. He did not have time for that *bakwas*. Crestfallen, he walked slowly back to the taxi and sat frozen, staring at the steering wheel. He had just wasted his time coming all the way out here—so much precious time. He had failed. Paralysed with outrage, fear, and frustration, he wondered what to do next. Time had almost run out. *Think, Gyan, think!* His wife was very smart. If she could talk to him, she would know what to do. He conjured up the image of his poor Savitri lying helpless and dying on the hospital bed in her blood-soaked *sari*, the spark of life sustained only by the rubber I.V. tube fastened to her slender wrist.

Gyan slammed an open palm against his forehead. *Her wrist.... That's it! How could I be so stupid?* He dialled Sheela's number, and thankfully she picked up immediately.

"Where are you, Gyan?"

"I'm heading back to the hospital right now. But I need you to do something. Remove the gold bangle that Savitri is wearing and bring it to the front entrance. I'll meet you there in 20 minutes."

~

Gyan rushed into the pawnshop conveniently located next door to the pharmacy just outside the hospital. It took some persuasion on his part—not all of it gentle—but the proprietor of the shop eventually agreed to give the full amount demanded in exchange for the delicate golden bracelet. No doubt, the pawnshop got the better end of the deal. The proprietor could have done even better, of course. He had seen that harried look in the eyes of his customers before, and those were the ones who were usually more than willing to part with their belongings, even the most precious ones, at any price. This *taxiwala* was different, however. As they haggled over the value of the trinket, the proprietor had felt a little afraid of the man and was glad to see him dash out the door with his fifteen hundred rupees.

~

The *taxiwala* dashed into the emergency room at exactly 3:30 P.M. He found Sheela sitting next to Savitri's bed, comforting his daughter. The doctor stood nearby, impassively rattling off instructions to a hospital orderly. The scruffy-looking attendant kept his eyes averted and listened to the instructions with a deferential air. "And once this bed is vacated...."

Gyan pushed his way between them.

"I have the money, doctor *sahib*. All of it. Can you do the operation now?"

"You are too late," the doctor replied firmly, glaring at him with undisguised disdain. "I told you three o'clock, and no later. There is no O.R. available now." He turned away to continue his rounds.

Undaunted, Gyan followed the doctor at a respectful distance, addressing the back of his head. "That is not right. You have such a big hospital. There must be more than one operation room. Please do something to save my wife." With each sentence, his voice rose several decibels higher than usual, taking on an increasing tone of distress.

The doctor was not accustomed to having the finality of his decisions called into question. He swung around and hissed at the impudent man dogging his steps. "*Oye*, we have many O.R.s. But those are already booked for our special patients, okay? Not for the *aam janta* like you."

With a few quick strides, Gyan closed the distance between them, until he was near enough to hear the doctor's panicky intake of breath. "You think she is *common*? There is nothing—do you hear me?—*nothing* common about my wife," he shouted, delivering each word like a thunderous blow. "She is a queen. My queen!"

Taller than most men and broader at the shoulders, Gyan cut an imposing figure that could intimidate without effort anyone inclined to challenge him. The doctor had no such inclination. His mouth had gone a little dry, in fact, and he decided on the spot—quite wisely—that continuing to butt heads with this persistent and possibly dangerous man might not be the better part of valour. Gulping nervously, he adopted a much more accommodating tone. "Very well. Why don't you go to the accounts department over there, sir, and deposit the fee. In the meantime, I will personally check to see if an O.R. has opened up. Okay?"

His eyes round with wonder and admiration, the orderly dropped any pretence of minding his own business and stared at the *taxiwala*. It was exceedingly rare to see anyone from the lower class, from *his* class, dare to besiege the venerable fortress of India's elites.

~

Gyan lifted Savitri off the gurney and laid her gently, ever so gently, in the back seat of his taxi. Rima cradled her mother's head in her lap, stroking the greying hair and gazing into the ashen face. Sheela, slumped over in the passenger seat, was the only one crying.

After the surgery, they had all assembled in the recovery room to hear the prognosis. Although the room was crowded with other patients and their families, the orderly had managed to snag a bed for Savitri next to a window. The light from the setting sun filtering through the glass cast a deceptively cheerful glow over the scene.

It was simply a matter of too little, too late, the doctor told them. "Even a few minutes might have made a difference. She was in very grave condition by the time we got to her. The internal damage was more than I had expected, and the significant blood loss only weakened her further. It doesn't look good. I'm sorry. I did the best I could, under the circumstances."

Gyan believed him. There was nothing left to do but wait. They all kept vigil throughout the night, listening to the shallow, laboured breathing of the dying patient. Savitri never regained consciousness. Toward morning, Gyan fell asleep in a chair that he had positioned next to the bed, her hand still grasped in his, as if that alone would suffice to keep her tethered to this world. By the time he awoke at first light, she was gone. The cawing of crows outside the window welcomed the day.

On the way home, a bus rear-ended Gyan's taxi at a traffic light. The sudden clang of metal on metal amid the din of habitually blaring horns went unnoticed by the herd of pedestrians going about their daily business, for they were long accustomed to the city's non-stop cacophony. The force of the collision sent Savitri's body flying forward, and it landed with an unceremonious thud on the floor between the seats. Gyan pulled over and gently lifted her back up. He instructed Sheela to sit with Rima in the back and hold the body by the feet to prevent it from falling again. He did not bother to inspect the damage to his taxi.

It is a peculiarity of temporal human affairs that glad tidings must be content to crawl on all fours whereas tragedy takes flight on the wings of doves. The news of Savitri's death spread fast throughout Gyan's little corner of New Delhi, and even well beyond it. By the time he pulled up in front of his home, neighbours and friends had already begun to gather in and around the couple's modest dwelling. Manjit, who had just arrived that morning from Mumbai, greeted his brother tearfully at the door. A white bed sheet had been placed on the floor to receive Savitri's body. Gyan laid her down on the linen with the loving hands of a parent tucking in a sleeping child for the night.

The *chaiwala* sidled up to him and placed a sympathetic hand on his shoulder. "Sheela's husband has run off," he whispered. "But don't worry, they'll find the bastard." Gyan nodded his head listlessly. It did not matter to him one iota what happened to Sheela's husband. He glanced down at the *chaiwala*'s son, who tugged at his sleeve.

"Sorry about Savitri *auntie*," Krishan said, his voice calm and controlled. "She was always very nice to me. She made the best *poori aloo*."

Savitri had always been fond of the boy. "If we had had a son," she once told her husband, "I would have wanted him to be like Krishan."

Gyan gave him an affectionate pat on the head. "That was my favourite dish too." He knew he was supposed to respond with words intended to sound deep and reassuring, something about the soul living on. But he could not. The notion that Savitri's invisible spirit might be indestructible gave him no comfort. All he knew was that her body had been destroyed. Never more would he gaze lovingly upon her face, never more embrace her, never more listen to the wild beating of her heart.

All day and until well after dark, a steady stream of mourners visited the house to offer condolences. But the soft babble of voices surrounding him could not quiet the clangour of grief ringing in his ears.

It was true what he had told the *chaiwala*—he really did not care what happened to Sheela's lout of a husband. The worst that could be said of him was that he acted like the drunken, clumsy oaf he had always been. The knife in his hand may have cut Savitri, but that is not what killed her. Over and over again Gyan replayed in his mind's eye the events of the day before, anxious to ascertain where things had gone so terribly wrong, and what could have been done differently to save the life of his beloved. And always he arrived at the same inescapable conclusion.

It was almost time for him to leave. Searching the room for his daughter, he saw her surrounded by a sea of friends and relatives. He knew that Rima would be comforted and stay safe with them for the next few hours.

He slipped out of the house, unnoticed.

~

At 11 o'clock sharp, Gyan honked the horn outside Tanya Kumar's residence. No one saw her drive away with the *taxiwala*. No one saw her get dropped off in front of the glistening glass building in Gurgaon. And no one saw her stumble back into Gyan's taxi three hours later, reeking of alcohol. The car sped away into the dark and disappeared. Safe in the care of her diligent driver, she promptly fell asleep.

Despite its reputation as a den of iniquity, G.B. Road at that late hour bore no resemblance whatsoever to Halla Gully. Once the ground-floor shops and businesses were shuttered for the night, this area of the city took on a distinctively sombre aspect. Indeed, without any garish lighting or wall-to-wall music to enliven it, the place seemed almost joyless. From the upper windows and balconies, the bare arms of women beckoned their clientele wandering furtively on the street below. At every corner, *paan*-chewing whores and tattooed pimps jostled for attention with catcalls and whistles. Slowly, Gyan cruised the length of the thoroughfare and came to a halt in front of a man leaning against a lamp post, the base of which was glazed with betel juice and bird droppings. He wore a fake leather jacket, black as the night, and a band-aid covered the top of his long beak of a nose where it had been broken in a recent fist fight. A half-consumed cigarette dangled from the man's lips.

"Keep driving, *dost*," he advised with a nasal twang, sizing up Gyan's potential as a customer. "If you're shopping for bargains, they're down the other end of the street. Around here everything is strictly first class."

"I'm not buying, I'm selling. It's high-quality *maal*." Gyan jerked his chin toward the back seat. "Are you interested? If not, I'll find someone who is."

The cold, matter-of-fact tone of the *taxiwala*'s voice, not to mention his physical size, made the man slightly uneasy. Still, he could not resist glancing into the car. The sight of the young, shapely beauty sleeping it off in the rear greatly excited him, for he was always on the lookout for new blood. The tight, black skirt hiked up around the girl's hips revealed perfectly unblemished thighs, and one could not fail to notice the faint scent of expensive perfume wafting out into the night air through the open window. He hastily stubbed out his cigarette against the lamppost and approached the passenger-side window, rubbing his hands together. Gyan interpreted the sound of swishing palms as a sign of interest.

"Is anybody going to come looking for her?" the man inquired.

"Not for a while. She lives alone."

"Okay, this is top-of-the-line stuff, I grant you. The best I can do is Rs. 20,000."

"Make it 25,000 and we have a deal."

As a prudent businessman, the pimp was not inclined to push his luck more than necessary. He knew a bargain when he saw it. Why, he would earn back twice that amount with this high-class *maal* in a single night, and lots more to come after that. Although he made a strict rule of not dipping into the merchandise, hell, in this one case he might even take her for a quick trot himself before putting her on the market.

The transaction was made swiftly and without fuss. The pimp yanked out a thick bundle of cash from somewhere deep inside his jacket, carefully counted out the bills, and tossed them onto the front seat. Then he gave a shrill whistle, and two burly men emerged from the surrounding labyrinth of shadows. Together the pair extracted Tanya Kumar from the taxi.

The woman, still lost in the oblivion of sleep, moaned softly, and then her eyes flew open.

"*Oye*, who are you guys? Let me go." She looked back toward Gyan in confusion and terror, screaming, "*Taxiwala!*"

The men harnessed her thrashing limbs with vice-like grips around her ankles and wrists, and muzzled her screams with a decisive hand over her small mouth. They disappeared swiftly with their prize down a trash-filled alleyway.

The pimp leaned down by the open window of the vehicle. "*Oye*, before you go, does she have a name?"

"Hema," the *taxiwala* replied without emotion. "You can just call her Hema."

Malishwali

Looking at these stars suddenly dwarfed my own troubles and all the gravities of terrestrial life. I thought of their unfathomable distance, and the slow inevitable drift of their movements out of the unknown past into the unknown future.

–H.G. Wells

The end is near, she thought.

The pill bottles arrayed on the nightstand in neat rows were almost empty. Soon they would not be needed. Though very sick, the woman wasting away under the light coverlet did not look sick. With her white silk headscarf and pale skin, she looked quite radiant, in fact, almost beautiful. She had refused to leave this world from a public hospital, crowded amongst other patients, and insisted on being brought home instead, where she could die in peace amid familiar surroundings. On her orders, the prized Nataraj statue had been moved from the drawing room into the bedchamber, and there it stood now, perched atop the polished teak vanity, presiding over the final dissolution of mortal flesh into memory or spirit. After that, the other servants had been dismissed for the day, perhaps forever. Their services were no longer required.

Only one remained to keep vigil at the bedside of her mistress. Ever devoted, she had followed the doctor's orders to the letter to make the dying woman's final days or hours comfortable. Before lapsing into unconsciousness, *memsahib* had asked that the indigo silk *sari* be taken from the armoire and laid out on the bed so that she could stroke the fine, soft fabric for the last time. It was her favourite, and the one that she wished to be dressed in after she was gone and her remains consigned to the fire.

Except for a faint pulse and the slight rise and fall of her chest, barely discernible, one would have thought her weakened body had already given up the ghost. She stirred suddenly, and opened her eyes, fixing her gaze on the sole witness to her journey's end.

"Are you thirsty, *memsahib*? Could I get you something?"

"Nothing for me. But for her, yes," the dying woman said. Her hand fumbled around under the coverlet for a moment, and then she drew out a silver foliated key ring, with eight keys attached, gleaming in the mute light of the room. "Please take this. Give it to Maya when you see her. Everything is hers now. And tell her I'm sorry."

~

"Papa, I cannot see anything inside!" A look of consternation mantling her face, the little girl pointed at the train as it pulled into the station and rumbled to a halt. "Why are the windows so dark?"

"Well, Maya, the windows are dark because the railroad workers cover them with a special kind of black plastic film."

"Why do they do that? It makes the glass look dirty."

"Why? Because they don't want you to see the elephants inside, of course. Everyone knows that elephants don't like to be stared at."

"Elephants! Really?" Maya cast a quick glance in Ashmita's direction, as if seeking confirmation of the extraordinary piece of intelligence she had just received, but her mother seemed preoccupied—for the umpteenth time that morning—with studying the schedule board mounted on the grey cement column in front of her. At that moment the doors of the train swung open to release its freight of passengers onto the crowded platform. Maya scanned the length of the station, hoping to catch a glimpse of disembarking pachyderms. "I don't see any elephants getting off the train."

"Oh, the doors on this side are much too small for elephants. The bigger doors are on the other side. That's where you would see them." Prem struggled to maintain a solemn expression in front of his daughter, but the mischievous glint in his eyes betrayed him. Giggling, Maya gently slapped his leg in mock exasperation.

"You are so silly, Papa," she scolded. "There are no elephants on the train."

"And you are so correct, my clever little child. Sadly, there are no elephants on this train. The real reason the windows are covered with black film is to block out the sunlight, which helps keep the interior cool and comfortable for the passengers."

"You mean like a curtain?"

"Yes, very good. Just like a curtain."

"Too bad they don't use real curtains, like ours," Maya said. "Nice, soft cloth curtains would look prettier."

"Are the two of you just going to talk nonsense all day?" Ashmita cut in petulantly. "We are never going to reach Bombay just standing here."

"My dear, please," Prem implored his wife. "We're on holiday, after all. Let us have a bit of fun."

"Fighting sweaty mobs has never struck me as fun." Maya's mother gestured toward the entrance to the air-conditioned car that was already clogged with boarding passengers. "This was your idea, so let's go," she added, gathering up her bag.

The physical size of any structure in India is never a reliable metric of how many people it may actually contain. The Dehradun Railway Station may be small, but the crowds that it accommodates are often impossibly large. Nevertheless, people find a way to squeeze in where a zephyr would fail to find passage. Grimly determined, Ashmita waded into the throng, the fingers of her right hand wrapped tightly around her thumb, like twine on a spindle. Prem and Maya dutifully followed, silent as a couple of unruly schoolchildren on a field trip who had just been admonished by their chaperone.

Maya felt lost amid the thick forest of legs surrounding her. Instinctively, she reached for her father's hand. Though not as soft as her mother's hand, his was at least open and available. Eventually, the trio wended their way inside the train and found their assigned seats.

Claiming the spot closest to the window, Maya was surprised to discover that the translucent black film allowed her to peer outside, though everything looked several shades darker than normal. All the bright, colourful *saris* of the women still standing on the platform now looked drab and undistinguished. She turned to her parents, eager to seek answers to a new set of questions bubbling inside her curious head, but they seemed to be embroiled in an argument.

"I wish you would have let me bring Radha along," her mother complained, a sullen tone in her voice. "She would have helped take care of Maya—you know your daughter can be a handful sometimes."

"Ashmita! She's your daughter too. We are a family. I think between the two of us we can take care of Maya ourselves just fine." Prem unfolded that morning's edition of *The Pioneer*. "Besides, I do not see the need for a servant on a family vacation. I'm sure you'll find that Bombay is full of perfectly capable *malishwalis*. The hotel will recommend a good one."

"Radha is like family to *me*," Ashmita riposted. "Next time, I will insist that she be included on excursions like this."

~

The dark, slight woman sitting cross-legged on the floor held the delicate teacup between her hands and contentedly sipped the steaming liquid. Her eyes scanned the spacious drawing room with curiosity, pausing here and there to admire particular features of the well-appointed interior.

As a professional masseuse who customarily plied her trade at the homes of her clients, Radha Chowdhury had often been granted a glimpse inside the palatial residences of many upper-class families, but this *haveli* outshone the rest. The lavish bungalow of the Talwars was a real *mahal*, a treat to Radha's eyes.

Plush red silk drapes, resembling a *malika*'s robes, hung on either side of the open windows facing the interior courtyard, abloom now in midsummer with roses and jasmine. A series of intricately carved wooden lattice shutters on the south wall provided both privacy and sunlight. The sofas and divans, arranged just so around the room, were deep and luxurious, with not a thread out of place on the rich upholstery. Ornate brass floor lamps around the room gleamed like pillars of gold. Finally, her eyes came to rest on the room's *pièce de résistance*—a two-foot-tall bronze statue of Nataraj—Lord Shiva in his depiction as Lord of Dance—holding court over the fireplace mantel. Framed in a gilt aureola, with his hair flying wildly in every direction, the left leg elevated gracefully in front of his torso, and the *kundalini* snake uncording itself from around the figure's slim waist, it was a remarkable representation of the deity performing his sacred *tandava*. Radha found herself mesmerised by the idol, as though it were enacting the cosmic dance of destruction and creation just for her personal delight. She clambered to her feet to get a closer look.

"I see you have an eye for lovely things," said a woman who at that moment appeared in the doorway. Striking, though not conventionally handsome, she was draped in a splendid indigo silk *sari*—worn the Gujarati way to cover the midriff—that shimmered in the sunlight as she entered the room. A pair of blue sapphire and diamond earrings dangled from her ears, and a bright vermilion *bindi* adorned the forehead. Though young and obviously very far along in her pregnancy, she nevertheless carried herself with an air of patrician stateliness and authority that belied her age, gender, and condition. Radha hastily stepped away from the mantel and approached the woman, bowing slightly and pressing her palms together in greeting. She knew that she was in the presence of the mistress of the *haveli*.

"*Namaste, memsahib.* Forgive me. I could not help but admire the statue. It is, as you say, quite lovely."

"That is why it is there, my dear—to be admired. So you are Radha, the *malishwali* who was referred to me?"

"Yes, *memsahib.* Your maid asked me to wait here for you."

Ashmita glanced down at the teacup abandoned on the floor. "I'm glad she thought to bring you some refreshment. Jyoti is not always so gracious toward our guests."

"Yes, she did. *Shukriya.*"

"Tell me a little about yourself. Are you married?"

"When I was very young, yes, but no longer. Just a few weeks after the ceremony, when we were still newly-weds, my husband raised his hand to strike me, but I would not allow him. And so he left."

Ashmita shook her head in sympathy. "Good for you for standing up for yourself."

"*Yeh to hota hai.* That is how it is where I come from. Women born in mud huts quickly learn to accept that any man can curse them, beat them, even violate their bodies.

I guess I must be stupid, because even as a child I could not learn that lesson."

"It is a man's world everywhere and always has been, I am sorry to say."

"So it seems," Radha said. "What I do not understand is why, in India, pious men build temples to our esteemed Goddesses—Maa Durga, Maa Kali, Maa Lakshmi—and then, when they have finished praying, they go home and mistreat their own women."

"It is a great irony, I agree. Yet, perhaps things are beginning to change. After all, we have just elected a woman to be our prime minister."

"I think it will take more than one woman, even one like Indira Gandhi, to change such an old country as ours."

"One can only hope. Whatever happens, it is never easy for any woman to live alone in our society. Do you miss being married?"

"Not at all. I like my freedom."

"Still, given your situation, surely you must worry for your own safety."

"Sometimes. But I do have help. No one bothers me while my *angrakshak* is around." Though she had no desire to be coupled to a man by marriage ever again, Radha had found the ideal bodyguard in her neighbour, Shyam, the *kebabwala*. For a small fee, he slept on her porch at night and kept an eye on things. He was a kind, broad-chested man who held an obvious fondness for the *malishwali*, but he respected her in equal measure. "I trust Shyam, and he never asks for special favours in return. He just protects me. Otherwise, I know how to take care of myself."

"Of course, your skills. We should discuss those. My friends tell me you are very good at what you do. Is this true?"

Radha considered the question for a moment before answering. "Your friends are kind for saying so. I was born with a gift. It would be wrong for me not to use it."

Her eyes fixed on this intriguing little *malishwali*, Ashmita stepped toward an incised teakwood loveseat that had the trimmings of a throne. "You may sit," the *memsahib* said in a voice turned suddenly deep and husky. Radha recognised that it was a command, not an invitation. The two women, separated not by age but by more than a few rungs on the social ladder, took their respective positions. Radha retreated to her still-warm spot on the otherwise cold mosaic floor, while Ashmita lowered herself onto the platform of soft, thick cushions. "You are younger than I had imagined you to be," she said. The negotiations had formally commenced.

"I may be young, *memsahib*, but I have a great deal of experience," Radha answered proudly. "These fingers have yet to meet the muscle they cannot ease or the knot they cannot loosen." It was not an idle boast. The *malishwali*, people said, had a singular knack for allaying the myriad distresses that oft afflict sinew, flesh, and bone. Her small, soft hands were deceptively cunning and strong. She could pummel and pull, knead and rub, twist and squeeze like no other. Lowering her eyes to Ashmita's swollen belly, she added, "And I am especially good with babies, who require a more tender touch." Radha concluded her opening pitch with a bright smile, warm as the kiss of the sun on a spring morning.

"What do you do differently with babies?" Ashmita asked. "Besides being tender, of course."

Radha inched closer to the *memsahib*'s feet, as if eager to reveal an exclusive secret that no one else should hear. "I can help put things right."

"'Right'? What do you mean?"

"It is easier for me to show you than to explain. May I?" Without waiting for Ashmita's nod of assent, she reached toward the embroidered hem of the petticoat. Momentarily taken aback by such boldness, Ashmita hesitated at first, but then extended her leg under the woman's hovering hands. Undraping the calf, Radha began to demonstrate her craft. "With long, strong strokes, I can coax bandy legs to unbend and lengthen. Like this. Do you feel that? It is very gentle, yet effective."

The sensation of the *malishwali*'s touch on her flesh was both soothing and electric. Ashmita leaned back and closed her eyes, luxuriating in every deft stroke and masterly caress. Winding up the demonstration with a rapid foot rub, Radha withdrew her hands, but the *memsahib* ordered her not to stop. "That feels exquisite," she said. "Carrying all this extra weight around pains my legs. Now, tell me what else can you do for the baby?"

Radha resumed the impromptu massage session, speaking confidently about her abilities as she unveiled yet more of her vast arsenal of techniques. "With a few gentle squeezes at the bridge of the nose every day, I can transform a pug protrusion into a thing of beauty. I can make a colicky newborn giggle with my special belly rubs. If it's a boy, I can help strengthen his muscles so he grows up strong. Or if it's a girl, I have a marvellous homemade mask to eliminate body hair—a secret formulation, very safe—that has been passed down through my family for generations. After all this pampering, of course, the little one will want to take a nice, long nap." Radha slid back into place and picked up her teacup, signalling the end of the session. She tilted her head to one side, a look of satisfaction beaming from her round face. "That helps the mother get some much-needed rest." As if to bring the point home, she added, "Happy baby, happy mother. And it goes without saying that I can fix those swollen ankles in no time at all."

From her perch on the loveseat, the *memsahib* had watched Radha with mild fascination as she spoke, observing how she relied as much on her hands and facial expressions as on her words to communicate. Though the *malishwali* was clearly of low birth—as evidenced by the plain cotton *sari* she wore, the absence of jewellery, and the hue of her skin—Ashmita found her to be rather endearing.

"The baby is due any day now," she said to Radha. "You can begin a week after the birth. Be here at 10 o'clock sharp every morning; I do not like to be kept waiting."

"I am never late. My rate is 45 rupees for the hour with *memsahib*, and 35 for the child, bath included. *Accha ji?*"

And now comes the haggling, thought Radha. She had, of necessity, become habituated to the process. She would state her price and, without a moment's hesitation, the prospective client would feign horror. "Too expensive," they always grumbled. It never ceased to amaze her how these *paisawalas*, with all their wealth, would bargain shamelessly over a few rupees. But the *memsahib* simply shook her head in agreement.

"*Accha*," Ashmita said, rising to her feet. "*Theek hai, hogaya.*" The meeting was over.

Radha stared in bafflement. *Okay? That's it?* Clearly, this Ashmita Talwar was not like the rest of them, she decided, now taking note of the *memsahib*'s appearance in greater detail. Her hair was cut unusually short, almost like a boy's. Other than the occasional western *firang* tourist traipsing about the city, Radha had never encountered a woman with such a hairstyle. Considering how flawlessly she dressed, it was surprising to see that the *bindi* was not perfectly round as it should be, as if it had been applied hastily and without care. And were it not for the lady's protruding tummy, Radha would never have guessed her to be pregnant. The rest of her body appeared remarkably slender. Most of the other *memsahibs* that Radha worked on were chubby, if not downright obese, with chins to spare, droopy flesh dangling from underworked triceps, tiers of doughy belly fat bulging from roly-poly paunches, and dimpled thighs as big as an elephant's shank. And who would know such intimate things better than Radha? After all, she had the rare privilege of seeing these well-heeled, overfed ladies in all their undisguised nakedness.

~

Maya left the quiet comfort of her mother's womb early on a Wednesday morning and entered the world wailing to beat the band. Lost in a cloud of anaesthesia, her mother remained practically oblivious to the infant's obstreperous arrival. She had chosen to deliver by caesarean section, preferring to live the rest of her life with a fine abdominal scar rather than suffer a few hours of physical agony. She never saw her child being born, or at least had no recollection of it.

At 10:00 A.M. exactly one week after the delivery, and every day after that, Radha arrived at the servants' entrance of the Talwar household, where she tended to the baby with as much devotion as if it were her own, humming and cooing the whole time she was in Maya's presence. Lovingly and with practiced hands, each morning she began by massaging the newborn's fragile little body with sesame oil. Within a month, Radha noticed that the delicate skin had begun to sprout a fine penumbra of hair. So twice a week Radha smeared a thick paste of gram flour mixed with yogurt, turmeric, and an assortment of natural herbs on Maya's face and limbs. While waiting for the mask to dry, she looked directly into the child's eyes and chanted the age-old nursery rhyme, 'Chanda Maama Door Ke...'. The lilting sound of Radha's voice helped keep the baby still. Thereafter, moving her fingertips in a circular motion, the *malishwali* gently rubbed off the hardened concoction, taking with it the dark, unwanted hair.

Next, she would settle into a low stool in the bathroom and stretch out her bare legs to form a cradle in which to bathe the infant. In the households of some of her other clients, anxious new mothers would often look on nervously as Radha soaped, rinsed, and dried the naked wiggling babies in her charge. "*Dhyan se!*" they cried out, urging her to be vigilant lest the precious, slippery cargo slide from her grasp. Yet nature had armed Radha with invaluable prescience, and she could perfectly anticipate every little movement these infants made. Not once had she lost her grip on the little ones entrusted to her care. Never had she dropped a baby on a hard, wet floor.

Radha was surprised to discover that Maya's mother showed little interest in standing guard over her in the bathroom, as her other clients often did, giving ineffectual orders and offering misguided advice about how best to handle a baby. In fact, the *malishwali* quite enjoyed the absence of scrutiny as she bathed Maya with the special homemade soap she never failed to bring with her to the Talwar home. The solitude, the sound of the baby's contented murmuring, and the delicious flowery scent of the soap lather made it a most agreeable time of day for her. *This is what my life would be like if I had a child of my own*, she often thought, not a little wistfully.

After the bath, she handed Maya over to the *memsahib* for a bottle-feed. Much to the dismay of her husband and family, Ashmita openly expressed her deep antipathy to the very idea of breastfeeding. "I was not born a cow," she declared defiantly. Ever loyal and not prone to judge, Radha knew better than to try to persuade the mistress of the house to nourish the baby in the manner that nature intended. Yet she could not help but feel a small twinge of envy. *Too bad these breasts of mine are as dry as the sand dunes of Rajasthan*, she mused more than once. *Otherwise, dear little Maya, I would gladly nurse you myself.*

Then the cook served Radha hot tea and glucose biscuits while she sat on the kitchen floor, waiting to be summoned by *memsahib* for her postpartum massage. True to her word, Radha's ministrations reduced the painful swelling in Ashmita's ankles within a matter of days. Prem was delighted. Never had he seen his wife so serene and content as in the hours immediately following a session with this latest addition to their household staff. He was somewhat less delighted by his wife's sudden decision that henceforth the couple should sleep in separate bedrooms, at least for the nonce, citing as the reason her profound reluctance to become pregnant again so soon after the birth of their daughter. While he struggled to mask his disappointment with this new domestic arrangement, he had to admit that Ashmita's reasoning possessed some merit—for Prem had become so enamoured of his first child that he could not imagine giving Maya anything less than the full measure of his fatherly affections by bestowing even a small part of them upon another.

~

By the time Maya turned four, the *malishwali* had become an integral part of the household, as evidenced by the mismatched cup and saucer set aside for her on the servants' crockery rack. Indeed, it was Radha who had heard Maya speak her first recognisable words, and it was she who had been the sole spectator to the toddler's initial tentative steps on wobbly legs. Although she adored the child and spent much time in her company, her duties were now centred primarily on meeting the demands of her employer. Thus, Radha arrived punctually at 10:00 A.M. three times a week to give *memsahib* her massage, and the dictates of custom had declared those hours to be sacrosanct. All who worked or resided under the Talwar roof, servants and family alike, were strictly forbidden to disturb the mistress and masseuse once they retired to Ashmita's bedroom.

Little Maya learned the hard way that to violate this unwritten rule meant inviting a thunderstorm of wrath upon her head. One morning she stood outside the locked door, knocking repeatedly, jiggling the knob, and crying for attention. "Please Mama, let me come in," the four-year-old begged, tears dangling from her long black eyelashes like melting snowflakes. "I promise to sit quietly in the corner." The ruckus continued in this manner for all of two minutes before she heard the click of the latch and saw the door swing open. Cocooned in a bed sheet, Ashmita towered ominously over her daughter, anger etched into the angular features of her face.

"This is *my* time to relax, Maya," she huffed through clenched teeth. "You must go away and sit by your grandmother until I am done."

"Can't I help?" Maya pleaded. "Radha and I will both relax you." Peering into the darkened room, she saw the *malishwali* sitting on the edge of the bed, her eyes brimming with love and sympathy for the child. She held a finger to her mouth, counselling silence.

"Leave now!" Ashmita commanded, almost shouting the words, oblivious to her daughter's wounded expression and trembling lower lip. She raised a menacing finger skyward. "And don't you dare get into mischief, young lady, or there will be hell to pay." Then the door slammed shut. Maya beat a hasty retreat down the hallway and, for the next hour, sat beside her grandmother, sucking her thumb and clutching her favourite doll.

"If you were a boy, I would have sent you to the *maidan* to play with the other boys," her grandmother said, shaking her head in disapproval. "But since you are a girl, someone always has to keep an eye on you."

Prem's mother never neglected to remind Maya at least once a day of the regrettable inconvenience of her gender. The old lady had always longed for a grandson, of course, a worthy male heir to the successful family business and considerable fortune that went with it. She would have taunted Ashmita mercilessly for failing to bear a son; but given that she herself had selected the pedigreed woman to be her daughter-in-law, what choice had she but to hold her tongue? Besides, Ashmita ruled the household now—in practice, if not in name—and she held the foliated key ring, with eight keys attached, to prove it. The silver accessory was a family heirloom, a symbol of female power over the purse strings, which Talwar tradition compelled the ageing dowager to entrust to her son's new wife on the day of marriage.

Glinting in the light as they jangled against Ashmita's hip, these keys were a constant source of fascination for Maya whenever she accompanied her mother on her daily circuits around the family's large bungalow and land. What secret portals did they open, what mysteries might they unlock? Gripping the free end of her mother's *sari*, as if it were a precious, inseverable lanyard securing child to parent, Maya trailed behind her mother and bombarded her with questions.

"What are all the keys for, Mama?" she asked. "Show me the doors." One in particular she found especially intriguing—for set inside the large, ornate metal bow was a polished ivory disc upon which the head of an elephant had been carved in cameo. "Why is there an elephant on that key?" She lunged for the ring to get a better look.

"Do not pull on my *sari*, May-*aa*!" Her mother always elongated the last syllable in Maya's name whenever the child annoyed her. "This is a very expensive *patola*."

"Sorry, Mama," the little girl squeaked contritely.

"Why don't you go and play with your dolls? You can see I have work to do."

One could not deny it—Ashmita had little free time left in her busy schedule to indulge a daughter's whims. Every morning, she hooked the key ring onto the waistband of her petticoat, and there it stayed until bedtime. It was the first task of many that would monopolise all her waking hours in the important business of running the large household for which she was responsible. Managing a sizable team of domestic help—two gardeners, two cooks, one cleaning lady, one washerwoman, two maids, one handyman, and two drivers—was a full-time job in itself, and overseeing them throughout the hectic day as they performed the chores she had assigned to them kept her fully occupied. But always the first order of business was to meet with her mother-in-law, the titular head of the family, to discuss that day's most pressing matters over several cups of Darjeeling tea—choosing the colour of the new curtains for the prayer room, deciding which mango trees in the yard had borne the best green fruit for that season's canning and, last but not least, wrangling over the menu for the day.

Sometimes they conferred over more troubling issues as well, such as the discovery one morning of a bundle of black sesame seeds near the back door, left there in the middle of the night by a jealous neighbour. Prem's mother had been inclined to fight fire with fire, but Ashmita preferred to take a more enlightened approach. Though this malicious act of *jadu tona* seemed but a minor vexation compared to others, still it had to be dealt with in the proper manner. First she instructed her maid to tie together some old, worn-out *saris* into a cordon to block off the porch, as if it were a crime scene. Then the family priest was summoned to recite a series of alexipharmic mantras to cleanse the area before finally disposing of the cursed seeds. Ashmita did not put much stock in black magic herself, but ordered the ritual to be performed anyway, more out of regard for the superstitions of the servants than from any real concern for the safety of her family. Her maid, Jyoti, who appeared especially anxious about the situation, murmured the phrase *jai Ganesh deva* over and over as she secured each end of the cordon to the wooden pillars, as if mere words would protect her from the insidious spell that had been invoked upon the house. Ashmita took great pains to assure her that she need not worry, that soon everything would be made safe and secure again.

Jyoti's fear must have been contagious, for little Maya had felt it too, gaping with growing apprehension as the morning's events unfolded before her. Years later, grown up and living in London, she would be reminded of the incident when the police taped off the area in front of her apartment building after a stabbing victim was found lying face down and bleeding on the pavement, the outline of a serpent spray-painted on the asphalt beside the man's head. Although it was clearly the handiwork of gangs and not sorcery, Maya nervously repeated to herself the same words, *jai Ganesh deva*, upon encountering the scene as she returned home from work. For like the maid, she had experienced a profound unease in the presence of such dark doings; and it was Ganesh, the Elephant God, to whom Maya always turned in times of trouble.

"Can you play with me now, Mama?" Maya asked in a small, hopeful voice. With his services successfully rendered and the modest fee discharged, the priest had finally left the grounds, and the affairs of the Talwar household were beginning to return to normal.

"No, May-*aa*," Ashmita answered curtly. A tone of peevishness crept into her voice. "I'm tired now. Can't you see how much I have had to deal with this morning?"

"I'm sorry, Mama." The little girl would have said no more, but a new thought popped into her head, like a bright red balloon released into a clear blue sky. She pointed to the cordon of old *saris* which had been tossed aside after the prayer ceremony and now lay coiled on the ground like a heap of snakes, waiting to be discarded. "Can I play with those?"

"Oh fine. Do that."

"Will you help me cut them up? I want to make new clothes for my dolls."

"No, Maya, I cannot help you right this instant. Look, here comes Radha. After my massage, I'm sure she would be happy to help you. Run along now and keep your grandmother company."

~

Sitting cross-legged in the courtyard under a canopy of sunshine, Radha undid the knots and freed all the *saris* from the improvised rope. Maya knelt beside her and watched as the *malishwali* deftly cut different-coloured pieces from the cloth. Then, with a needle and thread, together they fashioned several sets of perfectly fitted doll outfits. Finally, using the ragged remnants of the *saris*, the gardener's rake, and four chairs brought out from the dining room, Radha constructed a tent house where the little girl could play with her dolls.

"Thank you, Radha!" she exclaimed and crawled inside, a look of wonder in her eyes, as though she expected to encounter a performing circus under the billowing polychromatic roof. Radha followed her in, scrambling on hands and knees, and was herself struck by the loveliness of the sunlight filtering through the dyed silks overhead and mottling the interior with a rainbow of colours. It melted the *malishwali*'s heart to see the child take such pleasure in the magical world she had created.

"My own *mahal*...."

"Yes, little *malika*, your very own. So what should we do now?"

"Now," Maya said, seating her dolls beside her, "I think you should tell us all a story." The little girl loved the stories that the *malishwali* recounted on command—always fantastical tales of *rakshasas* and *apsaras*, Gods and Goddesses, fanged demons and bejewelled princesses—of which she possessed a seemingly inexhaustible supply, for Maya had never heard her repeat one story twice.

"Oh, very well." Radha thought a moment and then said, "I'll bet you have never heard the story of Shabari and Lord Rama."

"Never!"

"Then I shall tell it to you. *Bahut samay pehle*," Radha began (for that is how she began all her stories), "there was a poor old woman named Shabari who lived alone in the forest, but she never felt poor or lonely because she loved God so much. And because she loved god, her wise master had promised that one day Lord Rama would come to visit her. As you know, it is always important to make a guest feel welcome, but Shabari had no treasure or gifts to offer Lord Rama."

"Because she was poor?" Maya interrupted.

"Yes, exactly, because she was poor. So every day Shabari went out into the forest to gather up the most delicious berries she could find. That way, she would have something good for Lord Rama to eat when he arrived."

"Did he ever come to her house?"

"Not right away. Shabari waited for years and years, but Lord Rama never came. Every day she went out into the forest and gathered fresh berries—and still he never came. Yet Shabari was patient, and so she continued to wait, growing a little older with each passing year, until she grew so old that her eyesight began to fail."

"Do you mean Shabari was blind?"

"Almost. She could still see big things, like the mountain that rose into the clouds above her house and the wide, deep river that ran beside it. But even in the middle of the day, the world looked almost dark as night to her. That made it very hard for her to hunt for berries in the forest, so she used a walking stick to help guide her. And because she could not see very well, it was impossible for her to tell the difference between the unripe berries and the ripe ones. All she could do was bite into every berry she picked, keeping only those that tasted sweet and throwing away the sour ones. Then one day, it finally happened. Shabari heard a knock on the door, and when she opened it, there stood Lord Rama, disguised as a weary traveller."

"If Lord Rama was in disguise, how did Shabari know who it was?"

"Because the man's face shone like a thousand suns. He must be a God, even she could see that. Who else could it be but Lord Rama? She invited him in, along with his brother, Lakshman, and she gave them a seat at her lowly table and offered them a plate of freshly picked berries. When Lakshman saw that all the berries had bite marks, he felt insulted and pushed the plate away in disgust. But Lord Rama was so moved by Shabari's devotion to him that he declared them to be the most delicious berries he had ever tasted and devoured the whole plateful at once. Then, when it was time for him to leave, he rewarded Shabari by giving her a very special *darshan*. With a wave of his hand, he restored her eyesight."

"Shabari could see again?"

"Oh, yes! And not only was she able to see farther than she had ever seen before, but now she could see things that used to be hidden."

"'Hidden?' What do you mean?"

"She could see the birds flying above the mountain clouds and the fish swimming along the bottom of the river. She could see the shadow of a mouse sleeping in its hole on a dark night. She could see a gnat's breath and the stars on the other side of the moon. She could see the difference between truth and lies. She could even look into the hearts of men, which can be the darkest place of all. By the time Shabari breathed her last, she had seen everything there was to see in the world, and so she died happy."

Maya clapped her hands. "That's a good story! I wish I could see everything. Radha, do you think Lord Rama would ever visit our house?"

"He might, if you love him enough—or maybe he already has visited, but no one recognised him! Now it's your turn to tell *me* a story."

"But I'm little. I don't know any stories."

"My child, your whole life is a story, don't you realise that? I have an idea. You could tell me something about your school. That would be a good story."

"Okay, I'll try." She thought a moment and then said, "Mr. Marshall is a very funny man. Every time he sees me, he pats me on the head and asks me what I learned today. And then he bends down and looks inside my ear and says, 'Yes, I can see you know more today than you did yesterday.'"

Radha smiled at Maya's attempt to mimic the principal's gravelly voice. "That is funny. Mr. Marshall sounds like a nice man. And do you like all your other teachers?"

"They're nice too. But no one is as nice as you. You're my favourite teacher."

"I'm no teacher," Radha said. "I am just a simple *malishwali.*"

"Yes, you are a teacher. You taught me how to make clothes for my dolls."

Radha gathered Maya up in her arms and held her close. The child did not see the tears of happiness streaming down the servant's cheeks.

"Radha?"

"Yes, my child."

"Do you think Mama will let me use one of her nice silk *saris* to dress my dolls someday?"

"Yes, Maya, I think someday she will. Maybe when you're a little older."

In truth, Radha was not so certain that such an eventuality would ever come to pass. She knew that *memsahib* loved to dress well and prized her wardrobe—especially her dazzling collection of expensive *saris*—almost beyond reckoning. The silken treasures hung inside a large, antique armoire in Ashmita's bedroom, behind two ornately carved teakwood doors with wrought-iron handles, each forged into the shape of an angry cobra poised to strike. To Maya, they seemed like a pair of serpent sentinels out of a fairy tale, shielding the precious trove of fabrics from prying eyes and covetous hands.

Though leery of the snakes' venomous bite, Maya sometimes trespassed into the forbidden territory over which they stood guard. She would sneak into her mother's bedroom without permission, pull the armoire doors open, and stare in wonder and delight at the panoply of bright, colourful silks arrayed inside. She loved to feel their soft, satiny texture, so cold to the touch, yet so warm when she held them against her cheek.

Once she was caught in the act.

"May-aa—how dare you!" her mother hissed as she entered the bedroom, with Radha trailing at her heels.

"I just wanted to touch the *saris*, Mama. They're so soft and shiny. I was very careful, I promise."

"Show me your hands," Ashmita demanded.

The sight of the remains of Maya's lunch—red lentils spiced with yellow turmeric—crusted under the child's tiny fingernails stoked her mother's displeasure into outraged anger. She lifted her hand to strike. Maya braced for the blow. It never came.

Rushing to the rescue, the *malishwali* gently interposed herself between Maya and her mother, "*Ayree, ayree, memsahib,* she is just a child." Checked in her rage, yet far from placated, Ashmita closed and locked the armoire doors and then stalked out of the room without uttering another word, the keys on the key ring jangling furiously against her hip.

~

Only once, to the best of Maya's recollection, had her mother ever left the house without those keys at her side. She had been suddenly called away to attend an unscheduled meeting of the trustees of Marshall School, and in her haste to change into street clothes—a formal *sari*—she had inadvertently left them hooked to the discarded petticoat. The washerwoman found them while sorting the laundry and immediately brought the key ring to Radha, who in turn brought it to Maya's father in the courtyard, where he sat enjoying one of his rare afternoon's off from the family business by reading to his daughter from a storybook. As soon as she saw the keys, Maya lost all interest in the story.

"Papa, can you tell me what Mama's keys are for?"

"I'll do my best, little princess," Prem replied, giving Radha a conspiratorial wink. He held up the key with the carved elephant head in the bow. "There are so many of them, it's hard to remember which is which. But this is an easy one. It opens the elephant stockade in the back yard, of course. We own a whole herd of them, and they're quite tame. Do you mean to tell me that Mama never showed them to you? I'll have to have a word with her about that. Next, this long, skinny key, if I'm not mistaken, unlocks the door to the room where we keep all the cobras. We never like to open that door, because then the cobras might escape. But just in case they do"—Prem held up another key—"this is the key to the room where our snake charmer lives. He would play his magical flute to lure the cobras right back to where they belong before they can bite us." Prem made biting motions with hands, playfully nipping Maya on the nose and belly.

"Oh, Papa!" Maya cried, and Radha could not help but smile at the child's pleasure in the game. "And what is that gold key for?"

"This one?" Prem made a great show of examining a shiny brass key, the smallest on the ring, as if he were a jeweller appraising an exceedingly rare gem. "Why, this is the most precious key of all, even though it's small. It is the key to your heart. The man who holds it has the power to unlock all your secrets, and he will love you forever."

"Then you must love me, because you're the one who is holding it."

"I suppose that is so. And any other man," he growled with mock ferocity, "would have to fight me for it!"

"What about that one?" Maya asked, pointing to another key.

"Ah, that one. I'm not sure. Radha, help me out. Do you have any idea what this key is for?"

"Yes, sir. It is the key to *memsahib*'s bedroom."

"Of course, her bedroom. How could I have forgotten such a thing?" Prem smiled at Maya. "That's where Mama gets her nice massages." Now suddenly serious, he turned to Radha. "You have some free time now, don't you? I've always wondered what all the fuss is about. Perhaps you could give me one of those nice massages. Naturally, I would pay you."

"I don't know, *sahib*..."

"Oh, come now, Radha. A job's a job, and what's the harm? I'll tell you what—I will pay double the rate *memsahib* pays."

After a few more minutes of gentle and not so gentle coaxing, Radha finally agreed to *sahib*'s wishes, and Maya was sent away to sit with her grandmother for an hour. When Ashmita returned from the meeting of trustees later that day and found out what had happened, she exploded in fury. Radha was dismissed on the spot; and the ensuing argument between Prem and his wife, conducted in a tone and language deliberately intended to savage rather than conciliate, shocked their daughter deeply. Then Papa said a word that she did not understand and, for the first and only time in Maya's memory, her mother slapped him across the face, which effectively concluded the battle, but also put an end to talk.

For the next week, Ashmita sulked in her room before relenting at last and patching things up with her *malishwali*. Radha was hired back, with no hard feelings, but relations between Maya's parents were never the same after that. Three months later, Prem's mother passed away. Relieved of her duties, the dead woman's maid Malti left the Talwars' employ to live with a sister in Bombay. With the small cottage behind the house now vacated, Radha was invited to take up residence there, rent-free, as a permanent member of the household staff, and that is where she remained for years, ever on call for the indispensable services she provided, until Ashmita herself fell ill and died.

~

I miss you, Papa.

The chugging train speeding along the tracks toward Dehradun had opened the floodgates of memory. *Cheaper than hypnotherapy, and far more effective*, Maya observed ruefully to herself. As if in a waking dream, she stared through the window, still covered with that damned dark-tinted film, and watched the passing scenery flash by, so foreign now and yet so familiar. Eighteen years—was it really that long ago that Papa had teasingly told her about the elephants riding aboard this very train? Yes, how she missed her father now. Conjuring yarn after yarn from thin air, like a master magician yanking countless rabbits out of a single hat, he had kept her gleefully entertained throughout childhood with his whimsical fabrications made up at a moment's notice. Depending upon the nature of the jape, little Maya would applaud in delight, gasp in disbelief, or feign horror; but always, in the end, she laughed, emitting great peals of innocent, easy laughter. And he laughed right along with her.

Oh, Papa—you and your silly elephants!

Lost in a mist of pleasant recollections, Maya absentmindedly traced the edges of the gold pendant hanging from her necklace—a medallion depicting the head of Lord Ganesh, with his single tusk inlaid in ivory. It was an extravagant gift from her father, given on her tenth birthday and deeply cherished because it was the last she had ever received from him. This final leg of the journey home by rail resurrected one bitterly sad memory as well. She recalled all too vividly the night Papa had been killed on his way home from work, at a small railway crossing on the outskirts of town, when the guard fell asleep on the job and failed to lower the gate for an oncoming freight train. The car he was riding in disintegrated upon impact and, mercifully for both him and his driver, death was instantaneous; but Maya had mourned her father ever since, with a grief made all the heavier because she never saw her mother shed a single tear for the terrible loss of that good man. It had happened just a few years after the family's one and only vacation, when the three of them travelled together by train to Mumbai. That had been a joyous time for her. Back then people still called it Bombay. So much else had changed. Now that she was older and had been away for a while, she could see those changes throughout India with unclouded eyes. For one thing, despite the building boom in the ever burgeoning cities, the country as a whole looked a little grittier and more decrepit than before, including this air-conditioned train car, which seemed nowhere near as pristine or well maintained as she remembered it in her idealised childish perception. Why, even the once perfectly applied plastic film on the windows could be seen in places peeling away, strip by ragged strip, allowing little daggers of dim sunlight from outside to stab into the cheerless interior. One thing, however, had decidedly not changed—the way Maya felt about her mother, now also deceased.

"Madam, eat a little at least. It is free you know." A pantry boy in a faded blue uniform offered Maya a meal tray for the second time. Beseeching her to accept the extra amenities available to first-class ticket holders, he was surprised by this passenger's refusal to take advantage of them. Everybody else did. Pleasing her palate, however, was the last thing on Maya's mind. Immediately after the phone call from Radha in Dehradun, she had hastily packed a knapsack and duffel bag with whatever she might need while away and hopped the first flight she could catch out of Heathrow to New Delhi. She had not stopped moving since then. She should have been famished by now, yet all she felt was exhaustion, brought on as much by travel as by the torment of her thoughts.

"I can exchange the *dal* for extra chicken curry if you like," the pantry boy said, lowering his voice to a whisper, lest the other passengers overhear and start clamouring for the same special treatment. Maya smiled, acknowledging his concern, but declined again the greasy repast.

"Just a bottle of water, please," she said, and pressed two 10-rupee notes into his hand.

"It is a new bottle, madam," the pantry boy assured her, pleasantly taken aback. He was not used to receiving such a large gratuity for providing only meagre service. "The seal is not broken. You can check." He handed the bottle over and turned his attention to the next passenger.

In contrast, the man across the aisle accepted the proffered meal from the pantry boy with boundless alacrity, then eagerly peeled back the foil from the disposable trays arrayed before him and inspected the feast with an expression of radiant anticipation, as if he had never before seen such delicacies. Preparing to dig in with the plastic utensil provided—shaped not quite like a fork and most definitely not a spoon—he closed his eyes and inhaled deeply the steam rising off the food, savouring its mix of spicy aromas. He must have sensed the curious gaze of his neighbour upon him, for suddenly he opened his eyes and swivelled around to face Maya. "You should try some," he advised amiably. "The fare in first class is really not bad at all." Then he attacked the *thali* with unbridled gusto, scooping the food into his mouth as fast as humanly possible, beaming delightedly with each mouthful before finally scraping at the corners of the trays until every last particle had been consumed.

A lefty, just like Papa. And he loved chicken curry and rice too.

Maya could not help but notice how enormous the man was. Only his hands, nearly feminine in their daintiness, were properly proportioned. Everything else about him appeared almost grotesquely oversized, from the length of his legs and the girth of his belly right up to the immense block of a head sitting atop the broadest shoulders she had ever seen. Dressed smartly in dark tan slacks with matching blazer, he carried his weight with a dancer's ease, though it all appeared ready at any moment to burst right through the seams of his clothing. The comically large nose and protruding ears completed the picture of a great, jovial soul that had outgrown its own body.

Poor guy must be starving—if I'd only known, I would have let him have mine.

Maya took a sip of water and shifted several times in her seat, desperate to relieve the tension that had laid siege to her hips and arms. All the muscles and joints of her body screamed for mercy. Crammed for nine straight hours into her allotted cranny on a crowded non-stop flight, she had arrived in New Delhi from London at 4:30 in the morning, then stood on protesting feet in an endless line to pass through customs. As each precious second ticked by, she became increasingly concerned about the possibility—and soon the likelihood—of missing her train. "No problem, *memsahib*. Gyan will get you there on time. I know a shortcut." True to his word, the affable *taxiwala* who had picked her up outside the terminal covered the 17-km route to the railway station in record time, and Maya managed to claim her seat on the train to Dehradun with mere minutes to spare. She only wished the executive-class coach with cushioned chairs had not been sold out. *Just a few more hours of this torture.* Positioning herself this way and that, she finally pushed the small of her back firmly into the hard seatback, leaned forward, and began massaging the knots that had formed hours ago in her neck and shoulders. The relief was fleeting at best.

Only Radha's hands can untangle this mess.

"Please, Maya, you must fly home immediately. It's about your mother. She has passed away." The call from India had come early in the morning, just as she was about to leave her apartment for the clothing design house on Sloane Street where she worked. The news had hit her like a punch to the heart, not so much because of the loss she should have felt, but its suddenness. How typical of Ashmita, how perfectly in character. Maya had not heard her mother's voice in over a year and did not even know she had been sick. *Why did no one tell me?* Ever since she had moved to London, there had been scant hellos from home, and now this—not even a proper goodbye. Maya knew that she ought not to have been surprised at all. What else could one expect from a cold and utterly uncaring woman who never showed more than a cursory interest in raising her own child?

After Papa died and the new widow took over the task of running the family business, the child had seen even less of her mother. Through her teenage years and up until she finished school, Maya had grown increasingly independent. By the time she left Dehradun and settled in London, she had begun to make a life of her own, beholden to no one else and free to think and do as she chose. Not lost on her at this moment was the painful irony that just two days ago she had been sitting in an exquisitely comfortable grand tier seat in Covent Garden with her latest boyfriend, Luke Bristow, watching the premier of a new production of *Lakmé*. The most recent in a long procession of hopeful romances that never went anywhere, he had pulled some strings to acquire tickets to the sold-out performance, mistakenly believing that a musical drama about colonial India might somehow evoke a pleasurable sense of nostalgia within her. Watching the tragic love story unfold before her on stage, she had experienced nothing of the sort. Instead, a thought crossed her mind—*London is my home now; I may never see India again.* Yet here she was, a mere 48 hours later, racing right back toward Dehradun as if she had never left, compelled to do so by circumstances outside her control.

Toward the end of its journey, the train meanders through a zone of densely wooded wilderness. Those last lush miles along the Ganges mark the entrance to the Doon Valley. Maya at least looked forward to that. Meantime, she forced her attention back to the paperback novel in her hand—an impulsive purchase made at the airport, intended to keep her mind occupied during the long flight east—but the ineptly written saga of betrayal, heartbreak, and true love found at last offered no escape. The printed words on the page had stopped making sense hours ago. She closed the book for good and stuffed it back inside her knapsack, then leaned her head against the window and shut her eyes, struggling to ignore the beasts of memory that ranged round her, angling to attack like a pack of ravenous wolves. Luke had offered to accompany her; but she had refused. This was not just another trip home, it was a valediction, and it was something she had to do alone. *Just a few more hurdles to get past. Lay mother to rest. Close up the house. Dispose of the business. Say goodbye for good.*

Jet lag had finally caught up with Maya, and she fell into a deep sleep.

~

In her dream Maya felt herself floating, gliding gently forward in a boat pushed by gentle, rhythmic currents along a narrow woodland stream. Radha sat motionless beside her on the boat, humming the melody of an old nursery rhyme and, all the while, pressing the silken petals of a white flower into her hand. Luke stood on the shore, smiling and waving at her, until suddenly he grew frantic, gesturing wildly and pointing ahead, as if to warn her against some grave danger. The soft eddying murmur that filled her ears soon grew increasingly louder until it became as deafening as the terrible rush of wind flung forth by an immense typhoon. Beneath the boat, the turbid waters of the stream churned violently before flattening into an endless ribbon of asphalt, and night fell with impossible speed, like the flapping of a black wing. For several moments Maya had the sensation of helpless headlong motion through a dark, empty terrain illuminated only by a faint glimpse of the circling stars. Then she heard the blaring horn of a locomotive and, through the inky blackness, she saw its blinding headlights bearing down like a juggernaut upon the car in which she rode. Frightened, she turned toward Radha for help, only to be met instead by the sorrowful face of her father, who pushed her from the moving vehicle at the very moment of impact.

Maya awoke with a violent start to the shrieking sound of metal upon metal. Abruptly, the train lurched forward again with a force that sent spasms of pain through her travel-weary bones, then braked hard once more before resuming its normal speed. Maya moaned softly. Outside, the landscape was misty and vague. *Where are we?* Disoriented, she glanced around the coach in search of someone to ask. The pantry boy had moved on to another car, and the man across the aisle with the limitless appetite was nowhere to be seen. She yawned and stretched and pressed her face against the window to get a better look. Rising up in the distance, beyond the paddy fields and hutments, the lower foothills of the Doon Valley shimmered like a mirage. *Almost home.* But that was all she recognised. To Maya's dismay, the once familiar sight of rich, green foliage never came into view. In its place, a string of new townships, unappealing in their construction, had sprouted along the train route like an infestation of scraggly weeds in barren soil. A little past the human habitations, she caught sight of the Ganges. High in the sky, the afternoon sun glinted off the mirror-like sheen of the river, leaving the surrounding banks and bottomlands awash in the river's reflected radiance. Yet for all its brilliance, the scene outside appeared dim and colourless, for the dark-tinted window cast a shroud over everything in her purview. Where the film had peeled away, a few determined shafts of light, blinding in their intensity, pierced through the glass and cast a silvery glow around Maya. The light hurt her eyes. She blinked and, when she turned away, her gaze came to rest on something glistening next to her sandal. Leaning forward, she scooped the object off the floor and held it up for closer inspection.

"My wedding band! Thank God you found it." Maya turned to see her burly neighbour making his way rapidly down the aisle in her direction, using the seatbacks to propel himself forward with unexpected agility. The man continued talking as he ambled closer. "I have a bad habit of twirling it between my fingers when I'm bored. That last big bump knocked the thing right out of my hand, and away it rolled. I've been searching high and low for it ever since." As soon as he reached her row, she handed the ring over, and he slipped it back on his finger. "You just rescued me from my wife's wrath. Thank you so much! Do you mind?" Without waiting for any word or sign of assent, he slid into the vacant seat beside Maya.

"You're quite welcome," she said with cool politeness, only grudgingly surrendering her solitude, and almost wishing she had never spotted the elusive treasure at all. The gregarious man extended his hand in greeting.

"My name is Amit Lal."

"Uh, nice to meet you. I am—"

"Maya Talwar!" he said, grabbing her hand and shaking it with singular fervour. "As soon as I saw your face, I knew it was you."

"I'm sorry. Have we met before?"

"Indeed we have, quite a while ago. In Marshall School. You and I were classmates."

Maya rapidly sifted through her archive of impressions from that distant time, but without success. Try as she might, she simply could not place either the man's name or his face. "This is so embarrassing. I can't seem to—"

"There's nothing to be embarrassed about. Completely understandable. I've changed quite a bit since those days."

"How have you changed?" she asked, hoping for a small clue to unlock the mystery of their former acquaintance.

"For one thing, I've grown, shall we say, somewhat larger." He patted his ample midriff with unabashed satisfaction. "But let's see if I can jog your memory. It was our first day in class 5A, and the teacher—Mrs. Verma, that sweet old lady with the thick mop of white hair, remember her?—had just assigned us our seats. But the girl who was supposed to sit next to me refused to take her spot."

"She did? Why?" In spite of her reluctance to be drawn into reminiscence about the long-dead past, Maya found herself growing increasingly curious about this Amit Lal.

"Because of who my father was. The girl started chanting something at me—not in a nice way, either—and then the other kids joined in."

Something sparked in Maya's mind, a dim echo of childish cruelty. "Mali?"

"That's it. Except what they said sounded more like 'Maa-LI! Maa-LI!'"

"Now I remember. You were the son of the school's groundskeeper, weren't you? And they made fun of you." It was all coming back to her. Maya vaguely recalled a small, shy, skinny boy with perpetually dirty fingernails whom none of the other students ever paid attention to, except to mock.

"Bingo! Mind you, I was quite proud of my father. I helped him around the campus sometimes, and I saw how hard he worked to make the place bloom. But the way they said that word *mali*, over and over, made me feel humiliated, as if there is something shameful about working with plants and soil. Isn't that ridiculous? Then you pushed through the circle of kids and plopped yourself right down in the girl's assigned seat next to mine, as if you owned it. That shut them right up, and they never bothered me after that. You were like the queen in that school. Everybody always followed your lead."

"A queen? Hardly. I was just another student, nothing special. Though I never could tolerate seeing anyone bullied. It's all coming back now. Weren't you in Red House?"

"I was, and you were in Blue, our mortal rival. From what I hear, they call yours Ashoka House now and mine is Pratap. Back then we never used such glorious titles. I wonder what the principal, Mr. Marshall, would have had to say about that. Remember those savage cricket matches he used to set up between the houses?"

"Don't remind me," Maya chuckled. "Every time your team played ours, we were reduced to ashes. No wonder I never much liked playing cricket."

"Me neither. Fielding was the worst part, just standing around for long stretches of time, waiting to get my hands on the ball. Playing *pittu garam* during recess was a lot more fun, don't you think?"

"It sure was. If I'm not mistaken, you were a deadeye shot and never failed to topple my tower. So much for gratitude," she said with a grin, and nudged him in the side with her elbow.

"And you were ruthless, as I recall, and never failed to give me a good thump with that tennis ball. But I had an excuse. My uniform was always two sizes big for me. How could you miss?"

"My God, those adorable uniforms—"

"—with the school motto sewn onto the patch—"

"—right under the picture of the torch. What was it again? *Light...*"

"*Darkness to Light.*"

"Yes, that was it!"

Transported back to a more innocent time, the two former classmates dissolved into paroxysms of childlike giggles. Regaining her composure, Maya said, "It all seems such a long time ago. What do you do now, Amit?"

"Funny you should ask," he said. "I guess you could say the school motto inspired my choice of career. I work with blind children at the NIVH on Rajpur Road. Believe it or not, I'm a Braille teacher." He gave a good-natured laugh and held up his hands. "Thank God my fingers aren't as big as the rest of me!"

"How wonderful for you—and for them," Maya said. "I'll bet you are a very good teacher. The apple doesn't fall far from the tree. I remember your father too. He truly did make that school of ours bloom. How is he, by the way?"

"Retired. But do you think that stubborn old goat would ever consider taking a rest? He lives with me and my wife now. He's turned our home into a veritable Garden of Eden. And what about you—where do you make your home these days?"

"In London for the last few years. I'm a fashion designer." She smiled wryly. "That usually impresses people, but it sounds so trifling compared to what you do."

"Not at all. Whatever brings beauty into the world, or helps others see it, is a worthy profession in my book. Are you home on holiday? Living so far away, your mother must miss you terribly."

"She died, quite suddenly," she said in a way that surprised even herself, blurting the words out without softness or sentiment, as if she were announcing the weather. "It happened yesterday, in fact. I just flew in for the funeral."

Amit looked stricken. "Your mother—dead? My God, I had no idea. Please accept my deepest sympathies. She was such a kind woman."

"What? You knew my mother?"

"Why, of course. I would not be working at the NIVH now, were it not for her. I'll never know what she saw in me or why she did it, but it was your mother who interceded with the school to accept me as a student, even though I was just a groundskeeper's son. As I understand it, she put up quite a fight for my sake. You know how it is for people like us—we're welcome to labour with our hands but never our brains. She even convinced the principal to waive all the tuition fees, which my father could not have afforded in a 100 years. It's no exaggeration to say that dear Mrs. Talwar changed my life. What a wonderful person she was. But you no doubt already knew that. Say, are you feeling all right? You look like you've seen a ghost."

The rest of Amit's words faded into incoherence. Maya was stunned. She had never heard this story before and was hard pressed to believe it. "It's just that it's been such a long day and...Pardon me, I need to use the loo."

Amit rose from his seat to let her slide past, and she fled down the aisle on trembling legs toward the back of the coach. "I'm sorry, Maya," he called after her. "I hope I didn't upset you."

Once inside the W.C., she closed and latched the door, then filled the shallow, crescent-shaped basin with cold water and splashed it on her neck and face. The water felt good on her clammy skin. She took some deep breaths and dried herself off with a paper towel. Inspecting herself in the mirror, she could see the colour starting to come back to her cheeks. *A kind woman? A wonderful person?* Ashmita may have been many things, but 'kind' was not one of them. Were they even talking about the same person? Maya wondered what could have provoked her mother into such an uncharacteristic act of magnanimity. Surely, there was more to the story than even Amit knew.

She could feel the train beginning to slow. *We must be close to Dehradun.* Soon it would be entering the railway station. Maya took another deep breath and exited the lavatory. Many of the passengers had already stood up to retrieve their carry-ons from the overhead racks. The aisle was strewn with an assortment of bags, satchels, and small pieces of luggage, forcing her to squeeze past every obstacle to return to her seat. "Sorry. Excuse me. Excuse me! I need to get through." Noticing her difficulty, Amit Lal leaped up and began clearing the obstructions from her path, shoving them to the side with his foot until she was able to reach their row without hindrance. "Thanks, Amit. That was gallant of you." She snatched her knapsack from the seat and slid it across her back. "I guess the other one will have to wait until the coach clears out."

"Oh, please allow me." He reached over Maya's head and grabbed her duffel bag from the rack as the train shuddered to a stop. "I'll carry it out for you. Just follow me."

"No need," she said, but it was too late. Amit had already started down the aisle, the bulky bag slung over his shoulder as if it weighed nothing. She had no choice but to let him lead the way.

Through the tinted window, the train platform seemed to Maya much bigger and a lot more crowded than she remembered it. Amid the roiling mass of humanity, porters in red shirts and white *dhotis* swarmed around the train, hoping to be hired by the debarking passengers. Suddenly, against all odds, she spotted the familiar face of a woman in the middle of the crowd, her eyes searching urgently for Maya. She hoped Radha would look up and notice her, but then remembered that the black film made it impossible for anyone to see inside the car.

Stepping onto the platform, she eased the duffel bag off Amit's shoulder. "I can't tell you how much I enjoyed this chance encounter," he said. "I only wish it could have been under happier circumstances. Once again, I am so sorry for your loss."

"Maya, over here!" The *malishwali* had seen her getting off the train, and Maya waved excitedly in her direction. She turned to thank Amit for his help, but he had already been swallowed up by the throng and was nowhere to be seen. Dragging the duffel bag behind her, she began to jostle her way through the crowd to get to Radha.

Loss? Her former classmate could not possibly comprehend that what she felt at this moment was not sorrow, but only joy at the prospect of embracing once more the person she no longer thought of as a family servant but rather as the dearest of friends.

How can you lose something you never really had?

~

Oblivious to the maelstrom of passengers coming and going, the two women stood on the station platform and clung to each other like survivors of a shipwreck. Then Radha—her hair tied in a loose bun, her face practically unblemished by the passage of time—held Maya at arm's length for inspection. "Too thin!" she exclaimed, shouting to be heard above the hubbub of activity around them. "Just like your mother." The words were barely out of her mouth before the tears began to flow. "I miss *memsahib* already," she blurted out. The words caught in her throat, and she buried her face in her hands. "Forgive me. Seeing you again makes everything bearable."

Maya knew that her mother's death would be hard on Radha. What would she do now? Where would she go? For as long as Maya could remember, the *malishwali* had been the linchpin of the household, the one reliable oasis of peace amid the tumult of her parents' troubled marriage. After her father's death, it was Radha who had stepped into the emotional breach and lavished upon the heartbroken child all the comfort and affection that her mother would not or could not supply. At the same time, toward Ashmita she had remained as faithful, loving, and loyal a retainer as anyone could wish for. Maya's only question was—Why? Why did she stay? She could never understand what Radha saw in her cold-hearted witch of a mother that might elicit such unswerving devotion.

Once the crowd thinned out, Radha said, "It's been a long journey, and you have a hard day ahead of you. Let's get you home. I'll fix you something to eat, and then you can rest a little."

For the length of the long car ride from the train station, Maya held the *malishwali's* hand, the way she used to do as a child. It was just as soft and strong as she remembered it to be. "I almost didn't come," she admitted. "I have nothing to come home to, except you. As for the rest of it—the land, the house, the business, everything—they don't mean much to me anymore."

"Your mother knew that," Radha said. "She already took care of those things for you. The business was sold three months ago, and the property is under contract. All you have to do is sign the paper if you wish. It's all in your name. You have a nice inheritance coming. And that reminds me"—she reached down into her petticoat and drew out the silver foliated key ring, with eight keys attached, which she pressed firmly into Maya's hand—"she wanted you to have this. Now the house and everything in it are yours."

Maya stared grimly at the family heirloom gleaming inertly in her hand. "What on earth am I supposed to do with this? I still have no idea what most of these keys are for."

"I'll let you in on a little secret. I don't think your mother did either."

~

Set on two acres of land and surrounded by countless mango and litchi trees, the old bungalow appeared insulated from change, like an insect caught in amber. The neighbours on either side had sold their enormous homesteads years ago for a pretty penny to property developers, who wasted no time in razing the architectural treasures and replacing them with lacklustre apartment blocks, proud monuments to India's headlong economic progress. Maya was a little shocked at the change. Even if she were inclined to do otherwise, perhaps the time really had come to relinquish the ancestral home. It mattered very little to her now. Selling the place would at least add to the inheritance and ensure her material comfort. God knows, she had found little enough comfort here when she lived in it.

As she wandered from room to room, Maya surprised herself by experiencing so little in the way of regret. What she felt in its stead was mere curiosity. In the drawing room, she paused to reflect on what she beheld. Apart from peeling paint here and there on the walls, her childhood home remained largely unchanged. For some reason the prized Nataraj had been removed from its customary spot over the mantel. Otherwise, the white and brown garrisons on the marble chessboard still stood poised for battle. Not a single piece of china displayed in the breakfront cabinet had been displaced. Even the arrangement of silk flowers in the vase by the loveseat was exactly the same, though the once vivid hues of the petals had now faded to a dull brown. Gazing at the wooden rafters of the high ceiling, she envisioned a little girl who used to lie on the divan and stare up at the two-bladed ceiling fan, entranced by its whirling motion and the sound of its wordless lullaby. Everything around her summoned up memories which, though familiar, seemed unsettlingly strange, as if it all belonged not to a lifetime ago but to someone else's life entirely. She saw herself less as a returnee than an interloper.

And now all this is mine, Maya thought, calculating the physical extent of her inheritance not in monetary terms but in man-hours, for ahead of her still lay the arduous task of dismantling the countless appointments of the home and disposing of them piece by piece—curtains and kitchenware, bureaus and chiffoniers, brass floor lamps in need of polishing and fragile chandeliers, oversized sofas and sagging shelves stuffed with books, electric appliances and four-poster beds surrounded by wispy mosquito netting. The inventory was staggering. What in the world would she do with all this stuff? *I just want somebody to take everything.* Everything, that is, except the *saris*.

Maya stood before the armoire in her mother's bedroom.

"Go ahead, open it," Radha prompted her. "They're all yours."

Only now, here in this room, did the old familiar sensations—of boldness in the face of risk and fear of impending punishment—return with full force. Her heart raced as she grasped the cobra-shaped handles and felt their scaly texture etched into the cold metal. Maya's disquiet vanished the moment she pulled the doors open. Suddenly she became a little girl again, awed and delighted by what she saw.

Here, her mother had accumulated over a lifetime more than eighty of the most beautiful *saris* that money could buy, and in every colour imaginable. Maya reached out to touch them. Inside, carefully hung and tidily arranged, were hand-woven *chanderis*, fine Mysore silks, luxurious *kanjivarams* and *banarasis* with gilded borders, vibrant *patolas* and splendid *dhakai jamdanis*, gossamer chiffons and shimmering georgettes. Maya ran her fingers across the garments as if they were ivory keys on a Steinway piano, feeling rather than hearing the swish of the soft fabric under her hands.

An octave was missing!

"Radha, what happened to the others? There used to be more."

"Of course you would notice!" Radha bent down to retrieve a bundle from the lower shelf. "*Memsahib* had some of the *saris* made into quilts and pillow covers—for you." She placed the package on the bed and unknotted the string around the muslin wrapping that held it together. Out fell a cascade of pillow covers in scores of magnificent shades—saffron and navy, turquoise and mahogany, ruby and emerald, and colours without names at all. "The matching quilts are in the other closet."

"They're gorgeous!" Maya stood dumbfounded by the extravagance of the gift. One of the covers, peacock-blue with gold filigree, lay near at hand, and she picked it up to examine the needlework more closely. "But I don't get it. Mother adored her precious *saris*. She cared for them more than anything else. I wasn't even allowed to touch them. I can't believe she would let them be cut up like this."

"Oh, she knew you adored them too. But *memsahib* also knew you were never going to wear them—always pants, pants, pants. 'What good are these *saris* hidden away in some closet for all time?' she told me. Your mother wanted you to be able to see them and touch them every day, so you would remember how much she loved you."

"What are you talking about, Radha? You know better than anyone that Mama never loved me. She barely had time for me." From the recesses of her mind a stray memory wafted to the surface—the wisp of a conversation overheard in secret.

"I was never cut out to be a wife, much less a mother." Ashmita and her *malishwali* had been sorting through old clothes laid out on this very bed. Unbeknownst to them, little Maya was hiding under it, lying perfectly still and holding her breath for fear of getting caught. "Radha, I wish you could have been with us in Bombay. Everything seems so modern and exciting. Not like Dehradun. There, a woman can live free. She can have a career for herself if she wants, or even go a little crazy. But here," she sighed, "here I am stuck, and in this life I must play the role assigned to me."

"Oh *memsahib*, think of your fine home and your beautiful daughter," Radha had counselled. "You must be grateful for what you have. It is Lord Shiva's will."

"That may be. But those are not the things I would have wished for myself." Once the pair had left the room, Maya scampered from her hiding place in tears and sought the solace of her father's arms.

She never told anyone about what she had heard. The burden of that unshared secret weighed on her through the years until it had become at last unbearable. To escape it completely, what recourse had she but to flee not just her home but her homeland itself and put the whole of India behind her?

"Maya, you're wrong," Radha said. "Your mother loved you deeply. It was always hard for her to say the words, but she showed it in other ways. How can I explain? She was—well, she was different."

"She was selfish, that's what she was."

"Hush now, child. You should never speak ill of the dead, especially your own mother. But it's getting late. We can talk about it later. People will start arriving soon to pay their respects, and you need to be ready. Why don't you wash up and change, and I'll bring you dinner."

"I'm not hungry."

"Fine, I'll bring you some milk."

"I'm too old for milk. I don't want—"

"Nonsense. Milk is good for the bones and will help you put on some weight. I see all these young girls in town, skinny girls like you, who look like they are wasting away from some disease. Dieting, always dieting. Then they struggle after childbirth."

She escorted Maya to her room and scurried off to the kitchen.

~

Maya could not help but chuckle; childbirth was the least of her worries. So far, all her attempts at romance had fizzled out, and the prospect of marriage seemed distant, if not impossible. The budding relationship with Luke, with only a couple of dates behind them to speak of, was still too new for any hopeful prognostication.

Still clutching the peacock-blue pillow cover, she lay across the old bed of her youth, too short for her legs now, and listened to the sound of mourners arriving outside the house. She ran her hands over the patchwork quilt and remembered the cold nights when Radha—never Ashmita—would place a hot water bottle between the covers to warm her icy toes. Pressing the pillow cover to her face, she recognised the scent of her mother's perfume, however faint, still clinging to the fabric. Her mother had been right about one thing—all those beautiful *saris* would just go to waste in their present form. Better to transmute them into something useful.

Though Ashmita had always attired herself in traditional Indian garb, Maya remembered her as the very antithesis of a traditional Indian woman. She moved with strength instead of grace, as if she were wearing a man's trousers underneath the petticoat. Her demeanour was the manifestation of a free spirit testing its limits and, when it reached them, gnawing at the tether.

In the beginning, Maya's father attempted to rein her in with gentleness. When that failed, he resorted to bribery, lavishing her with gifts and dressing her in the most exquisite *saris* from every part of India, urging her to be 'more like the other wives.' But when Ashmita refused to devote herself, body and mind, to the patriarchal demands of marital life, Prem retreated into the dark purlieus of indifference and never came back.

Maya remembered all too well how the couple slept in separate bedrooms at opposite ends of the *haveli* for most of their years together. Was that to be her fate as well—a cold, lonely bed? In her mind's eye she saw her older self lying alone, shivering between the sheets without a loving husband's warm body beside her. *Perhaps mother and I are both cut from the same cloth after all.* If that were the case, then it was just as well, for she could not tolerate the thought of treating her own child the way she had been treated.

Radha entered the room with a steaming cup of milk. "I strained off the *malai* from the top and added a spoonful of cocoa powder—just the way you like it. Now sit up and drink this." She continued talking while Maya sipped the hot liquid. "Guests have arrived already. You need to go out and meet them very soon. I bathed your mother's body just this morning. Before she died, she told me to dress her in that magnificent indigo *sari*. You know the one I am talking about. It was her favourite. She still looks so elegant in it."

"Mama always liked to make a grand entrance," Maya said. "She might as well make a grand exit too."

"Oh Maya, you must not hold on to hate."

"I don't hate her, Radha. I just don't want to be like her."

"And that is how I know she loved you. She never wanted you to be like her either. She recognised a little of herself in you, but she wanted you to be free. If she treated you harshly sometimes, it was because she feared you might come to admire her too much. A long time ago she told me, 'I don't wish my daughter to make the same mistakes I did.' Her only intention was to help you find your own path."

"She picked a hell of a way to go about it."

"But it worked, didn't it? Her last words before she died were about you. She said, 'Maya has made me proud. She is living the life that I might have had if things were different.' It broke her heart that she could not show her love for you in some other way."

"She could have done it!"

"That's what I was there for," Radha said.

With that, the pent-up grief of the past 24 hours burst through the wall that Maya had erected around her heart, and heavy, burning tears welled forth from her eyes. "You were always kinder to me than Mama ever could be," she sobbed. "I just wanted to hear the words from her lips for once. I just wanted to hear her say, 'I love you.' Was that too much to ask?"

"She did say it. She said it to me, and now I am saying it to you." Radha took the half-emptied cup away and set it on the nightstand. Then placing an arm around Maya's shoulders, she used the free end of her own spotless white *sari* to dab away the tears from her face. "That gift in your mother's bedroom was her way of saying goodbye. Now it's your turn to say goodbye. It will make her soul happy to know that you came for her in the end."

The *malishwali* gripped Maya by the hand and led her out of the room and down the long hallway. Pushing open the double doors to the courtyard, she said, "Go to her. I'll join you later on, after everyone has left." As the last of the Talwars, it was Maya's solemn family duty to mingle with the mourners in attendance and accept their condolences. Radha had no place there. She was, after all, but a servant.

~

That poor child—so much pain. But no matter. Radha believed she had managed to put things right again.

She returned to *memsahib*'s room and began folding and stacking the ornate pillow covers spread out across the bed into a neat pile, pausing to admire each one as she did so. They reminded her of her mistress in so many ways. When she had finished, she tied them up in the muslin wrapper and placed the bundle back on the shelf. She knew that Maya had liked the gift. She remembered which *saris* the child used to linger over the longest, so it was easy to select the ones that Maya would find most appealing. Ashmita had been incoherent, drifting in and out of sleep, when Radha smuggled them out of the house and brought them to the tailor in the bazaar to be refashioned. She tried not to think about how it would have infuriated *memsahib* were she to learn that her treasures had been torn up in such a way. But she never found out, or was too sick to care.

As her condition worsened, Radha was tempted to inform Maya, but *memsahib* remained adamantly opposed to the idea. "There is no need. Call her when it is over." Then she had grabbed Radha's hand and pulled her close. "You have to promise me that you will go to Mumbai and live for me," she said, her voice barely audible. "Just be free. I have made arrangements on your behalf. You will never have to worry about money for the rest of your life."

Radha had no desire to go anywhere. She had all the freedom she required; anything extra would go unused.

"Please let me call Maya," she implored once more near the end. "Don't you wish to see your own daughter one more time? It has been so many years."

"No, Radha, I don't. I have nothing to say to her. She was never meant to be my child," she whispered, drifting back to sleep. Capitulating at last to the wishes of her mistress, Radha waited for the appointed hour.

~

Who are all these people?

Every room of the bungalow emptied into the wide-open expanse of the courtyard, in full bloom at this time of year with a riot of roses and jasmine. It had been Papa's sole refuge from the pressures of work and the turbulence of his marriage, the one peaceful place in the house where he could find solitude and something akin to happiness. Now it resembled Dehradun's railway station, a vortex of moving bodies and sombre faces, most of which Maya did not recognise. All that it lacked was the din of voices, for everyone around her spoke in hushed, respectful tones. She had expected no more than a small handful of distant blood relatives to show up, perhaps some of her mother's friends—if she had any—but not this multitude.

Commanding the space around the exact centre of the courtyard, Ashmita's imposing presence was hard to miss. Maya made her way through the crush of mourners, pausing here and there in her passage to greet the few she knew and to thank them for coming, until she arrived at the simple bamboo bier upon which her mother lay in repose, just inches from the ground, under a white cotton canopy erected to shield the lifeless flesh from the mild spring sun. By the side of the bier the prized Nataraj statue held vigil over the body, and an oil lamp flickered near her pallid face. The features, serene in death and still beautiful in their unconventional way, had not changed much. Radha was right—she looked elegant in the indigo *sari*, indeed quite regal, like a queen holding court while she napped. Staged around the body and even partially covering it, a profusion of flowers in elaborate arrangements enlivened the doleful occasion. Glancing through the accompanying cards, Maya could only determine that they had been sent by sympathisers from near and far. Many of the names were unfamiliar to her, but at least one stood out in high relief—it had come from Malti, grandmother's maid, residing now in distant Mumbai. All contained the customary expressions of sorrow; yet reading them, Maya sensed behind their words a common sentiment that could only be described as profound gratitude.

At the head of the bier a grown man wept openly. Maya recognised him at once as the son of one of the former neighbours.

"Hello, Pradeep."

"Maya, is that you? Why, you're all grown up now."

"What a coincidence, so are you. I'm glad you could come."

"After what your mother did for us, how could I not?" Seeing the perplexed look in her eyes, he continued. "Ah, you never heard that story? Then let me be the one to tell you." Drying his cheeks with a handkerchief, Pradeep hastily composed himself. "It happened years ago," he began, "but I'll never forget it. While you Talwars always seemed to prosper, even in hard times, my father's business began to fail. He turned jealous, and then he did something very foolish. Out of spite he tried to put a scare into your household—some silly prank involving cursed seeds and black magic, that kind of nonsense. When your mother found out who had done it, she could have made a lot of trouble for my father. Instead, she loaned him some money, which got him out of his scrape. The business flourished again, thanks to her. I run the show now. Father is abroad on holiday, or he would have come himself, but he sent me in his place. He was quite emphatic that I relay this message—our family will always be indebted to yours."

"Thank you for telling me that, Pradeep. I had no idea—"

"Maya, look who's come. Speak of the devil." Hearing again the now familiar voice of Amit Lal, she swivelled around to greet her old schoolmate and fellow passenger on the train. He had traded in his dark tan suit for a traditional white *kurta-pajama*. Supported on Amit's massive arm, an elderly gentleman holding a cane stood beside him. "You remember Mr. Marshall, our principal," he said. The frail Englishman stepped forward, removed his hat, and made a genteel bow.

"Yes, of course. Mr. Marshall, how sweet of you to come. I'm honoured."

"And it was my honour to know your mother. Mrs. Talwar was a remarkable lady and an invaluable asset to our academic community. And one tough cookie, I might add. She will be missed by many, including myself." He began enumerating the many generous contributions of time and money that Ashmita had made to the school, until he noticed that a line had begun to form behind him. He politely excused himself and stepped aside.

A shy, diminutive woman approached, and Maya said, "I'm sorry if I'm not able to recall your name. There are so many people here whom I don't even know."

"Oh, you wouldn't remember me, Miss Talwar," the woman said, "but I had to come pay my respects anyway. My name is Deepti. On the night your father was killed by that train, my husband Roshan died too. He was your father's driver. A woman alone with three mouths to feed does not have an easy time. Your mother, a widow herself, could have blamed my husband for the accident, and she had no obligation to help us. Yet she took pity and gave us money and food through that terrible time. We would not have survived otherwise. I light a candle to Lord Shiva in her name every night to give thanks."

And so it continued, with an endless stream of mourners filing past the bier from the late afternoon and into the evening, all professing their admiration for Maya's mother. As dusk fell, someone thought to light the torchère lamps positioned along the edge of the tiled patio. The hour grew late, and one by one the visitors left, promising to return for the service the next day. The house fell perfectly silent, save for the occasional guttering of the oil lamp. Seated beside the bier, Maya observed her mother's face, animated by the play of light and shadow across the placid features, and wondered if she really knew the woman at all.

It was past midnight when Radha finally entered the quiet courtyard. She lengthened the wick in the oil lamp and inched it closer to her mistress. The thought of *memsahib*'s beautiful body on a funeral pyre, a body that Radha had touched so many times, pierced her heart with sadness. Stepping back, she placed her hands on Maya's shoulders, feeling the tautness in them. "I'll go with you to spread her ashes on the Ganges. But that's for another day. It's late now, my child. You should sleep."

"I'm not tired."

"Then I will stay up with you."

Maya reached behind to clutch the *malishwali*'s hand. "Mama showed kindness to everyone else. Why wouldn't she show it to me?"

Whether by pure instinct or out of long habit, Radha started rubbing Maya's shoulders and back. She did it as much to comfort her as to unknot the muscles. "Your mother knew she had made a terrible mistake. Toward the end, over and over she told me she was sorry."

"Sorry for what?"

"She wished she could have been a better wife and mother, but it was too late. You must let it go, Maya, or you will never find peace."

"There is so much I wish I could tell her. She never gave me the chance."

"Tell her now. She is here, with you. She will listen. We will both listen."

Maya closed her eyes and began speaking. Hesitantly at first, then with increasing fervour, she let the words spill out into the night. She spoke out loud of the joys and sorrows of her childhood, of her hopes and fears, of everything she had seen in her travels or only dreamed, of her disappointments and triumphs, of her life in London and the friends she had made, of her work and the freedom it gave her, of her growing fondness for Luke, of her memories, of her deep anger and, finally, of her forgiveness. Listening, yet lost in her own melancholy thoughts, Radha let the sounds wash over her, like wave upon wave advancing upon a desolate shore, their cadence silencing, at least for a few moments, her infinite sadness.

Banished by the flickering lights to the dim edges of the courtyard, the ghosts of the past rose and subsided, impotent and futile shadows clamouring under the wide firmament of stars, until dawn broke and consumed them; and all, unto the last, were burnt away to cinders.

~

"Please take this. Give it to Maya when you see her. Everything is hers now. And tell her I'm sorry." Solemnly, Ashmita handed the key ring to her *malishwali*.

"You can tell her yourself."

"Too late. You must do it. I was never meant to be a wife or a mother. I'm sorry I ever brought a daughter into this world."

Tears welled up in Radha's eyes as she clutched the key ring to her breast. "Yes, *memsahib*, I will make sure she gets it. And I will let Maya know that your last thoughts were about her."

"Oh please, Radha, stop calling me *memsahib*."

Radha smiled coyly and said, "You will always be my beloved mistress."

With her last remaining strength, Ashmita grasped Radha's hand in hers. She held it to her lips and kissed it, over and over, until with her final breath she whispered, "I will see you in another life, Radha, my darling, and we will be lovers again."

Kebabwala

No good opera plot can be sensible, for people do not
sing when they are feeling sensible.

—*W.H. Auden*

Shyam pushed hard on the rusted pedals of his bicycle,
traversing a kinetic maze of pedestrians, hawkers, beggars,
and vehicles of all types and sizes. In the distance, the
evening sun inched down toward the Arabian Sea, willingly
submitting to its cold, dark embrace. Street lamps along
the embankment began flickering to life, casting a soft,
yellowish glow upon every surface that they illuminated. It
was Shyam's favourite time of day. The gathering darkness,
the subtle drop in temperature, and the salty-sweet whiffs of
ocean breeze created the illusion of cleanliness in a place
where there was little to be found. How he wished the sun
would take with it all the ugly remnants of the day.

As he pedalled, Shyam took caution to avoid the hurdles
of garbage and occasional clumps of excrement—animal
and human—edging the sidewalk. Lashed securely to the

handlebars were two large canvas bags loaded with freshly marinated lamb. Ferrying the precious cargo to his kebab stand, he was determined to keep it safe from contamination.

The street vendor held a coveted spot on a South Mumbai pavement near the Gateway of India. The imperious old edifice, with its massive arch and austere decorations, looked askance upon the gleaming, majestic Taj Mahal Palace Hotel across the way. Slightly scruffy now but still proud, the colonial monument seemed almost envious of the other's extravagant upkeep. Yet together the two seaside landmarks drew countless visitors all year round, sustaining a marvellous assemblage of roadside entrepreneurs like the *kebabwala*.

Shyam rolled up next to a large pushcart propped on irreparably ruptured tyres. The ramshackle food stand belonged to his friend Babu, the *bhelwala*. Shyam paid a monthly rent for nocturnal use of the cart, which would be all but worthless were it not for its auspicious location, made more or less permanent by the heavy, red bricks that held the wheels in place.

On schedule, Babu had relinquished his lucrative post just prior to Shyam's arrival. As usual, however, he had failed to clean up to the *kebabwala*'s satisfaction. "Aah, that dirty fellow will never learn," Shyam grumbled as he pulled a spotless dishcloth off his shoulder and began meticulously brushing away all the remaining flecks of *bhel* from the work surface. A savoury mix of spiced rice flakes doused in a slew of tangy chutneys, *bhel* is a popular snack during the day. After dark, however, people crave something more filling.

To lure men walking past his *bhel* cart, Babu would describe the act of consuming his crunchy, sweet-and-spicy concoctions as partaking in hurried, illicit sex. *Then I suppose eating my moist, succulent seekh kebabs is akin to making love to one's mate,* Shyam mused, though he would never articulate such an intimate thought. Besides, he had no need to hawk his goods vocally, for few in the vicinity could resist the seductive aroma of lamb sizzling on his portable grill. Roasted to a turn on thick metal skewers and served piping hot, the *kebabwala*'s flavourful fare was popular among homeward-bound office workers yearning for meaty comfort, international tourists seeking the exotic Indian street food experience, and nightclub revellers with ravenous appetites.

Shyam took immense satisfaction in choosing the best quality meat for his *kebabs*. He never used leftovers. His grandfather, who served as a butler and cook for a British family during the Raj, had schooled him in the merits of hygiene. Like him, Shyam washed his hands on the hour and kept his domain scrupulously free of bugs and rodents. The constant presence of fair-skinned tourists clamouring for the toothsome treats, dripping with fat as they came off the grill, assured his wealthier clientele that their countryman's merchandise was indeed safe to consume. He even supplied paper napkins of peerless quality, a small convenience well appreciated by patrons who wished to consume his mouth-watering cuisine with decorum. All in all, Shyam did well for himself.

I am just as good as any chef at the Taj Hotel, he would boast to himself. All that he lacked were the checkered pants, double-breasted jacket and fancy toque hat.

Dishing out kebabs was more than just a job to him; it was his calling. Shyam may have lived off the profits, but he thrived on praise. When a customer from England or America complimented his culinary skill, he would respond with 'Easy as pie' or 'Thanks a million,' or 'Horses for courses,' followed by a gentle bow. Then, cheeks reddening, he would turn away, as if attending to the next batch of kebabs roasting on the fire; but inside, he was bubbling over with pride.

For Shyam, conversing in English was the mark of a superior man. As a young boy, he had coveted the education available to kids of affluent families. He longed for the opportunity to master a tongue not his own. As much out of protest as desire, the kebabwala had taught himself the language in bits and pieces, listening carefully to the foreign tourists who frequented his stand. In this way he had culled entire lexicons of words and phrases overheard in conversation and committed them to memory. Now, from behind the dais of the pushcart, he declaimed them nightly in a relentless stream, like an elaborate fusion of flavours concocted from his motley spice rack. His non-stop banter, liberally sprinkled with Anglo idioms and expressions, was almost as delectable as his kebabs.

~

Though self-reliant by nature, Shyam did not work alone. In a city where everything—from fruit to foreign currency—could be summoned to one's doorstep at will, Shyam was compelled to offer home delivery service to keep up with the other street vendors. Babu's son, Raju, an industrious lad of 15 who could slice recklessly through traffic on a bicycle at high speed without fracturing or disfiguring in the least a single kebab, was the express delivery boy. He did, however, make an alarming dent in the profits by helping himself to Shyam's wares whenever he got hungry—which occurred quite often. Also on the payroll was Radha, his friend and business partner, who served as both sous chef and cashier while Shyam kindled the coals.

During the day, Radha worked as a nanny in Malabar Hill, an upscale neighbourhood a few miles north. The evenings brought her to his side, her presence both comforting and exciting. In her company, Shyam dispensed with his English phrases in favour of home-grown verse, carolling melodies from old Hindi films instead. Rocking his head from side to side, he sang 'Mere Sapno Ki Rani,' evoking the euphoria of young love. And on nights when the moon appeared in full splendour, he serenaded her with 'Chaudhvin Ka Chand Ho,' playfully comparing Radha's beauty to that of the luminous orb in the onyx sky.

During the day's final clean up, Shyam made the minutes pass more quickly by whistling 'Yeh Duniya Agar Mil Bhi Jaye' from his favourite film, *Pyaasa*. The words of the song—a lamentation on the cruelty and injustice in the world—sounded more like poetry to him. It's lilting melody never failed to lift his spirits. Raju, himself an ardent fan of cinema, teased his employer about those outmoded tunes and urged him to try singing the newer Bollywood hits instead. Shyam stubbornly refused. He had no appetite for music that, in his estimation, lacked true lyrical flavour.

Radha too poked fun at his warbling, but with kindness. "Do you have any idea how off-key you sing?" she giggled, jabbing her finger into his soft belly. "Why don't you play the radio here instead? Your customers will thank you." It was a suggestion made in jest, for both of them knew that a radio was no match for Mumbai. Perhaps the only thing Shyam missed about Dehradun—the peaceful little city where they had lived as neighbours until a few years ago—was listening to the radio while grilling. Here, on this hectic, noisy street, with its deafening traffic and babble of voices, no one would be able to distinguish melody from mayhem.

Shyam had never imagined life beyond the borders of his northern hometown. It was Radha who orchestrated their move to this burgeoning coastal metropolis. Abandoned by a worthless husband in Dehradun, she used to pay Shyam to guard her door by night; and for years, and in all seasons, he had slept on her front porch, as a loyal *angrakshak* pledged to her protection. After the wealthy woman whom Radha had served as masseuse and caretaker passed away, she learned to her astonishment that she had been written into the *memsahib*'s will. The more-than-respectable inheritance that she received was sufficient to finance their move to Mumbai, with a substantial nest egg left over. Shyam never inquired into the particulars of the unusually lucrative bequest, or Radha's desire for an urban adventure, but he always felt a deep gratitude toward the dead woman for her act of benevolence.

The decision to pull up stakes could not have come at a more fortuitous time. From the very beginning, the location of his kebab stand had been ideal—right outside *Doon Mithais*, a popular sweet shop in a big, busy bazaar in Dehradun. To the envy of the other vendors and shopkeepers surrounding him, Shyam cooked up a sumptuous profit. "There is indeed money in meat," he proclaimed. But when the sweet shop sealed its doors and installed air-conditioning, foot traffic to Shyam's stand soon dwindled to almost nothing. His regular patrons, men who stopped by after work for a luscious appetiser, chose to purchase sweetmeats from the fancy *mithai* shop instead.

The looming failure of his once-thriving kebab stand struck fear in Shyam's heart, for it threatened his relationship with the woman who was, after all, the nearest thing to a wife he would ever know. The opportunity to play house with Radha, even if only on the front porch, quenched his desire to be close to her. He knew that she cared for him, albeit without passion—a bitter reality that lost something of its edge when Shyam considered his handicap. The bus accident that orphaned him in his youth had also permanently rendered his manhood incapable of arousal. Practically speaking, what woman would ever want such a man? Now, without a reliable means of support, he had even less to offer her.

It had not always been thus.

After that terrible accident, 16-year-old Shyam and his twin sister Shanti were left in the care of their grandfather. The loss of both parents, along with his mortifying disability, had steered the boy away from wasteful juvenile diversions such as gambling and smoking *ganja*. Instead, he channelled his energy toward more sensible business pursuits and so took over his grandfather's *chai* stall, relieving the frail old man of the burden of putting food on the table for them every night.

In the bazaar, the *chai* stall attracted a small but steady stream of customers throughout the day. They would congregate around a wooden bench, discussing the state of their compact little world between satisfied gulps of tea. As he served them, Shyam became privy to their conversations, which involved animated analysis of both public and private matters. He tsk-tsked upon hearing about the *paanwala*'s scandalous love affair with his sister-in-law. He shook his head sadly at the news of the violent rape and murder of the *policewala*'s daughter. But his ears perked up when he heard that there was money to be made in the meat business.

"People are getting richer these days," one of the men said. "Now they all want to eat meat like the *maharajas*."

Meat! Shyam remembered how his mother used to put money aside in an empty pickle jar to purchase that luxury food for the family once a month. On those special evenings, she would let him help her prepare the meal, tossing a potpourri of ground spices into a bowl of minced lamb while he kneaded it, squeezing the savoury mixture in his fists until it oozed between his fingers. Then together they would wrap and shape the lamb around thick metal skewers and cook the kebabs over smouldering coals, watching and smelling the feast sizzle to pleasing perfection.

That single off-the-cuff remark about meat and *maharajas* planted the seed of an idea in young Shyam's head. Three days and countless trial kebabs later, he had tweaked his mother's old recipe, already quite good, into something more than delicious. The secret lay in the blend of spices, which he arrived at by trial and error. The next day, he repainted the 'Shyam Chaiwala' sign on his cart to read

'Shyam Kebabwala,' added another bench and a folding table, and went on to earn wholesome profits.

Following his grandfather's death, Shyam became by default the ranking male of the family; and thus the onus of Shanti's marriage fell on his adolescent shoulders. As tradition demanded, he approached other families within their caste, luring eligible suitors with the prospect of a sizeable dowry. He settled on a good-natured tailor from the neighbouring town, and even took the unconventional step of consulting Shanti for her approval before finalising the nuptials. He ascribed his sister's wordless acceptance to deference, and was therefore dumbfounded when, out of the blue, she eloped with a *harijan* boy and disappeared from his life.

Bad enough that she married without his permission; but to marry an untouchable went beyond the pale. A few years later she wrote to him, begging for forgiveness. Shanti invited him to visit her and her husband in New Delhi, where she worked as a *safaiwali* and earned a modest living by cleaning people's homes. Shyam's pride could not consent to a reconciliation, even though Shanti was all the family he had, and he often reminisced about the bond they once shared. Unable to overlook the stain upon the family reputation that her actions had inflicted, like yellow splashes of curry on a white *kurta*, he was forced to lower his head in the community. The shame proved unbearable, and he never responded to her letter. Now that he was getting older, he had come to regret his aggrieved intransigence. He missed his sister and realised, at long last, that paying too much heed to other people's opinions was a recipe for heartbreak.

He was done with Dehradun, or it was done with him. The time had come to move on.

~

Shyam and Radha arrived unceremoniously in Mumbai, a pair of provincials from the hills. The city of 18 million took them in, albeit unwillingly. "Maharashtra is for Maharashtrians," they were told grudgingly, "not for outsiders like you."

Unschooled in the etiquette of scarce resource allocation, Radha once suffered a blow to her head for inadvertently jumping the queue at a community water tap. Among the offended assemblage, those most prone to outrage called her *villager*. "Follow the rules or you'll get run over," a *paan*-chewing woman warned disdainfully, hawking a crimson stream of betel juice into Radha's empty bucket.

Shyam too learned some harsh lessons. He would never forget one incident in particular. He discovered the exact cost of an imported luxury sedan when he accidentally bumped up against the car with his rusty bicycle, leaving behind a small, fine scratch. Screaming obscenities, the driver leapt out and proceeded to beat him savagely in the presence of a gathering crowd—curious but mute witnesses to the dispensing of pitiless street justice. "*Madarchod!* Do you know how much this car costs, *sala?*" the angry young man shouted. "Huh? Do you?" It was not a rhetorical question. The ordeal ended when the man finally spat out the figure, in rupees and its equivalent in dollars—in either case a mammoth amount of money—branding it forever in Shyam's memory and wresting from him an abject apology.

"So sorry, *sahib*, it will never happen again. Small man made big mistake."

Satisfied but still spouting expletives, the driver hopped back into his car and roared from sight on squealing tyres. Shyam considered himself fortunate to have escaped what would have been an enormous debt for a minor repair. "The bruises will heal," he assured Radha as she helped him peel off his torn, bloodstained shirt.

In time, the couple learned to cloak their small-town sensibilities beneath a street-smart hide—trusting nobody, feigning subservience where necessary, and sharing little, except between themselves. They became shape-shifting denizens of the metropolis, pledging allegiance to neither place nor people, but solely to their own mutual survival. And so they learned to make money the only way they knew how in this unforgiving city, and thereby held onto their souls.

They also learned that mere space—the nothingness of air and blessed solitude—was scarce, and thus the most valuable commodity in an overcrowded city. Like the millions around them, they erected severe, makeshift barricades, both physical and psychological, to guard their fragile lives and meagre possessions. Only late at night, lying chastely side-by-side on a small bed bathed in the neon glow of the electric hoardings outside their window, did they venture beyond their defensive walls; and only then did the inhospitality of urban living fade temporarily from consciousness as they escaped into an expanse of dreams. Yet, like a tethered dog running madly toward freedom, at any moment the couple would be yanked abruptly back to reality by one of the myriad discordant alarums of the street—the blare of horns, the crunch of metal, the ululation of sirens, a howl of rage, or a human scream.

~

Shyam carefully slid the heavy canvas bags off the handlebars and placed them on the worktable. They were filled to the brim with containers of ground lamb, seasoned with smoked spices and ready to roast. Before unloading the meat, he filled four pint-sized plastic bags with water and hung them high on the posts of the cart. In this way he sought to repulse whole legions of ravenous flies, spooked away by their own distorted reflections in the improvised mirrors.

As he prepped and cooked, evening slipped into night, altering the landscape like a dramatic backdrop change in a theatrical production. The vegetable and fruit vendors vanished, while mothers hurried home with their tired children. Simultaneously, yawning prostitutes emerged from their hideaways like sun-shy vampires rising from musty crypts, and pot-bellied cops swarmed in for their happy-hour handouts.

Shyam served the first batch of kebabs to two policemen assigned to the Gateway area for the month. They smiled grimly, acknowledging the 'dessert'—envelopes stuffed with cash—tucked under their paper plates. Befriending the lawless sentinels of the law with *baksheesh*, Shyam had learned, was crucial to any successful street enterprise in Mumbai.

Radha arrived just as the cops were wiping the grease from their thick moustaches with soiled handkerchiefs, which they hastily stuffed back into their pockets as soon as they caught sight of her. With wolfish grins they greeted the woman, still attractive in middle age. Accustomed to unsolicited male attention, Radha masterfully swatted them away. She complimented their ruddy complexions and protruding bellies, crediting their wives' culinary prowess for keeping such worthy physiques in shape. The cops slunk away, leaving the couple to prepare for the Saturday night rush.

"Raju isn't here yet?" Radha asked, wrapping the free end of her *sari* around her waist before tucking it into the petticoat.

"No, his mother came by to say that he has a high fever. If it's malaria, he'll be sick as a dog for a few days."

Though they missed the extra set of hands, Radha and Shyam were free to discuss private matters without Raju eavesdropping.

"Maya is going back to London next week. I don't know when I will see her again," Radha said, making a perfunctory attempt to count the change in the moneybox. "By Durga's will, I was never blessed with children of my own," she added, sorting the coins in her palm and dropping them one by one into the designated slots. "But there are days when I feel as close to her as if she were my own daughter." She looked up at Shyam, teary-eyed.

For more than two decades Radha had served Maya's mother, Ashmita Talwar, in Dehradun. Over the years, the mistress–servant relationship had blossomed into a precious bond. Watching the child grow into a young woman, she felt the social shackles loosening, until finally they fell away for good. Now Maya was family to her.

"And you know the feeling is mutual, Radha. She loves you just as much. I've seen it myself. Be happy with that." All his life Shyam had known his exact place in society. It lay only a few inches off the bottom, just above the untouchables. To see Maya—a wealthy girl from the upper class—show genuine affection for Radha was not only remarkable to him, but unique in his experience.

"She keeps asking me to visit her at the Taj, that fancy hotel for the *paisa walas*. I tell her, 'How can I go in there?' She knows that is no place for people like me. 'I don't care,' she says. *Ayree*, that girl has so much of her mother in her." Radha rambled on, her voice breaking with emotion at the memory of her dear *memsahib*, now long departed.

Shyam proffered no opinion on the matter. He recognised that the moment called for mute attention. When women do the talking, men do the nodding, his married friends had advised.

"She too is stubborn like her mother," Radha went on. "She doesn't care about boundaries. But one of us has to do the right thing. I mustn't give in to her naive demands. Correct?"

Fortunately for Shyam, their conversation ran aground at that point. With Raju away, Shyam and Radha found themselves suddenly swamped with customers.

"*Oye, kebabwala*, hurry up and take my order. You're getting slow in your old age. *Sala*."

Without even looking in the man's direction, Shyam immediately recognised the owner of that voice—Rohan Saluja. The American-educated brat riding up in his big car had the wardrobe of a prince and the mouth of a whore, and he took pride in peppering even the most casual conversation with gratuitous insults and gross profanities. The sole heir to one of the country's largest telecom companies, he would never have to worry about earning his bread or, for that matter, his kebab.

"C'mon, c'mon, pack it up. I don't have all night. I'm taking my girlfriend to Juhu tonight. Do you know what the traffic is like out that way? Huh? *Sala*." Rohan honked impatiently. "And throw in some extra napkins, okay? Don't be stingy, you little fucker."

Shyam approached the car and politely handed the parcel over to Rohan. Rupees flew out of his hands like cards from a blackjack dealer. A few fell to the ground, and Shyam stooped to pick them up.

"Oh, and I need you to deliver 10 plates of kebabs to my house on Monday night. I've invited some friends over and they'll want something to eat, the pigs. Come by at nine o'clock sharp, okay? Is that too much to remember? Better write it down, *sala*."

With Raju out of commission, Shyam was tempted to refuse. He would never forget the savage beating that Rohan had given him a few years ago—for scratching the twenty-something's Mercedes. Then again, he could use the money, since he wanted to buy something nice for Radha to cheer her up after Maya's departure.

"Yes, yes, I will remember, Rohan *sahib*, no problem," Shyam answered, his head bobbing from side-to-side in affirmation. "Monday, 10 plates, nine sharp. It won't slip my mind."

Speeding away in his SUV, the latest addition to his father's fleet, Rohan suddenly swerved sharply to avoid running down the stray dog that resided at the end of the street, its filthy coat mottled with mange.

"*Kutta, sala!* I am going to kill you one day," he howled, cursing at the mongrel before powering up his window.

~

Chowpatty Beach was surprisingly crowded for a Monday afternoon.

"The kids are on summer vacation," Radha explained, sipping coconut water with Maya. "Your mother would have liked living in Mumbai," she added, angling her straw to reach every drop of the ambrosial juice in the bottom of the shell. "Plenty of drama in this city. She would never have complained about being bored, the way she did in Dehradun." Radha smiled, as if she could hear her mistress grumbling in the distance.

"And what about you, Radha—do you like living here?"

"It was hard at first," Radha admitted. "The city is a little rough, and it could get lonely if you don't know anyone. But I'm lucky to have Shyam. He is a decent man, and his kebab stand brings in enough for the both of us. The money your mother left me is a big help too."

"Then why do you still work? You could just take it easy now and enjoy life."

"The day I stop using my hands is the day I will die. Whether it is massaging a baby or rolling out kebabs, I must remain useful, Maya. That is my purpose. We all have a purpose. We must serve the best we can."

"All right, enough with the philosophy! Just promise me you won't overdo it. I've already lost one mother. I don't want to lose another."

"Don't worry about me, Maya. I'm okay. Shyam takes good care of me."

"It seems like you take care of each other. I'm glad."

"So tell me, how are things in London?"

"I've already told you, everything is fine," Maya said, smiling.

"Yes, yes, you have told me—whatever 'fine' means. I want to know more. Tell me about your job. Does it keep you very busy?"

Maya proceeded to describe her workday routine in detail. "When I was hired straight out of design school," she said, "they started me on the bottom rung and paid so little that I had to deliver pizzas at night just to make ends meet. Once the boss saw what I could do, though, it's been one promotion after another. But never mind the money. I've made my own way and I'm working at what I love. That's what really matters."

"How wonderful! Your mother would be so proud of what you have done with your life." As was inevitable, the conversation eventually veered off in a quite different direction. "And what about that special fellow of yours?" she asked, turning her eyes toward the expansive ocean in an attempt to appear casual.

"You mean my boyfriend?" Maya said with a coy smile. "Things could not be better. Luke is the most attentive man I have ever known—not to mention an incorrigible romantic. In the beginning I thought it must be an act he put on just to impress me. But we've been together over a year now, and he still likes to surprise me with thoughtful little gifts. And whenever we kiss, I feel like my knees might buckle under me. I've met his family, and they are the nicest people. To be honest, things have gotten very serious between us."

Radha's eyes widened, and she cupped her hands over her mouth. "Oh Maya, I am so happy for you!"

"That makes two of us. I never thought it possible, but the idea of getting so close to someone no longer scares me." An attractive woman with a bewitching smile, Maya had never lacked for suitors in her younger years, but a deep wound in her heart had kept them at bay. More than anything else, Radha always hoped that one day Maya would taste the delicious splendour of love—the kind of love that she herself had once experienced, the memory of which still sweetened all her days and nights. Now that it had happened to Maya, she could not have been more grateful. She offered up a silent prayer of thanks to Lord Shiva and Maa Shakti.

"Then I must meet your Luke," Radha demanded. "He sounds very nice."

"And Luke insists on meeting you, since I never seem to be able to shut up about the wonderful *malishwali* who helped raise me."

"So it's settled. When will you be back?"

"In just a few months, actually. We have a show opening in Mumbai, and it will even include some of my own designs. I'll bring Luke along."

Radha clapped her hands in delight. "I will count the days."

"Here's something funny I didn't realise before," Maya said. "When we first started dating, I learned that Luke had an inexplicable passion for grand opera, and I thought to myself, 'This will never work out.' All those people in crazy costumes running around stage shrieking at the top of their lungs about heartbreak and revenge—I just couldn't stand it. But now that he's taken me to a few shows, I find it's starting to grow on me. I guess love does change you after all."

With that, they both choked on their coconut water and broke into a fit of laughter. Turning suddenly serious, Radha reached out and stroked Maya's cheek with her hand. "I will miss you, my darling Maya," she said.

"Oh please, don't get all sentimental on me." Maya tossed their empty coconut shells on top of an overflowing garbage bin and turned sideways on the bench. "Make yourself useful and massage my shoulders the way you used to when I was little." As always, the tension in her muscles eased instantly under the *malishwali*'s expert fingers. She was thankful to be facing away from Radha, which made it easier for her to conceal her tears.

~

Shyam was surprised when Maya showed up unexpectedly at his kebab stall.

"My flight doesn't leave until 2:00 A.M., which means I have a few hours to kill. So I decided to swing by and say goodbye to Radha."

"I thought you already said your goodbyes over coconut water," he said with a teasing tone. "Still, it would give her great joy to see you one more time before you leave. Be warned, though. She might cry like a baby."

Maya liked Shyam. It warmed her heart to see Radha with a kind man who treated her with affection and respect. More than that, it was obvious that he loved her as more than just a friend.

"Where is she?" Maya asked.

"Out making a delivery on Colaba Causeway. I hope she returns soon—I need her to make one more stop. It's very important." Shyam pointed to the large bag in his hand.

"I have time. Let me deliver it for you. Is the customer close by?"

"No, no, Maya*ji*," he said respectfully. "This is not a job for you."

"Why, because I am a *memsahib*?" Shyam did not answer. Of course that was the reason why, but he dared not say so to her face. Maya eased the package out of his hands and glanced at the street address scribbled on the side. "Look, it's not far away at all."

"I don't think this is a good idea," he said. "Radha would never allow it."

"So we don't need to tell her, do we?" she said with a smirk and wave. "Trust me, Shyam, I've done this before. If I can deliver pizzas in London, then I can deliver kebabs in Mumbai."

~

Maya double-checked the address before entering the six-storey building situated in a decidedly upscale part of the neighbourhood. The security guard in the lobby gave a perfunctory salute with a listless hand and directed her to the elevator for the penthouse suite. Since the package weighed more than a few kilos, and the walk from the kebab stand had been a bit longer than expected, Maya was grateful to be spared lugging it up six flights of stairs.

A young man with thick, dark eyebrows and bleached-blond hair answered the door. He was dressed in a black satin shirt pulled over tight leather pants, and he reeked of expensive cologne.

"I have a delivery for Rohan Saluja," Maya announced in a cheery voice. "From the *kebabwala*."

The man surveyed Maya's svelte frame with open admiration and called out to Rohan without turning around.

"Ya, what is it?" Rohan yelled back. Out of habit he almost added something obscene; but upon entering the foyer, he was stopped in his tracks by the sight of the striking woman standing at the entranceway. For once he found the good grace to hold his tongue.

"She says it's from the *kebabwala*."

"Oh, right. Good, you got here early." He accepted the package from Maya's hands and invited her in while he retrieved some cash from a snakeskin wallet. The heavy door shut behind her and locked itself with an audible click. A mild sense of unease overtook her. For a brief moment she almost felt as if she were trapped inside the apartment.

On first impression, she did not much like this Rohan Saluja. She knew the type—rich, young, shallow, and irresponsible. Modern India was full of such men and women now, overeducated yet ignorant, the frivolous children of privilege who purchased their status in society without earning it and who felt entitled to take whatever they did not already own. Glancing around the room, however, she had to admit that it was rather tastefully furnished. She even recognized some of the artwork on the wall. Here was an original Souza; on the opposite wall, another by MF Husain. Perhaps this callow boy who possessed them had some class after all, she thought.

"I haven't seen you before," Rohan said, handing the money over. "So what's your name, beautiful?"

"I'm only helping Shyam for the night," she explained. Without warning, Rohan thrust his face just inches from Maya's. "He's a family friend," she stammered, smelling the sickening odour of beer on his breath.

Rohan laughed, loudly and grossly, showing a mouthful of large, white teeth, so close that she could almost count them. "Is that so? Did the old dog send you as part of the package? I owe him a big tip for that."

He laughed again, and this time he grabbed Maya by the waist and crushed her body against his. She grunted and tried to push him away, which merely provoked a more earnest struggle. Noticing the swelling bulge behind the zipper of his friend's pants, Rohan shouted, "You want a taste of this too? Wait your turn, *sala*." With that invitation, the other man stepped forward to help, and together they each grabbed an arm and pinned Maya against the wall. "Mmm, nice perfume." When Rohan crouched over to sniff her breasts, she lunged for his ear, biting down on the soft flesh until she could taste blood. He screamed in pain and staggered backward, cradling the side of his head. With her free hand, she gave the other man a forceful shove to the chest, and he released her immediately, lifting his arms in surrender lest he suffer something worse. Maya turned and headed toward the door.

"Bloody hell, where do you think you're going?" Enraged, Rohan leaped forward and slapped her hard across the mouth, which sent her tumbling onto the smooth marble floor. He slouched toward her prostrate body, a menacing scowl plastered across his face.

"Stop, please," she begged. With her back against the wall, Maya slid up slowly to a standing position. "I'm sorry. Don't hurt me. I promise to be good. Hey, let's make it fun." She exaggerated her British accent, knowing that someone like Rohan Saluja could not resist the allure of anything foreign. "Your Indian girls have nothing on me—I know some Anglo tricks that would put the *Kama Sutra* to shame," she boasted, undoing the top button of her silk blouse with trembling fingers. "You both can undress me—but *gently*," she continued, suggestively licking her lips.

Somewhat placated, her attackers exchanged glances and warily approached their prey. Maya then surprised them both, one with a vicious kick to the groin and, for the other, a sharp elbow jab to the chin. With both men stunned and momentarily immobilised, she flung open the door and flew out into the hallway, pursued by howls of pain and a furious stream of epithets.

"*Sali kutti! Sali randi! Haramzadi!*"

Past the elevator and down the stairs she ran and, upon exiting the building, raced through the dark streets and dank alleyways of night-time Mumbai, not stopping until she arrived, out of breath, back at the *kebabwala*'s stand.

As soon as Shyam saw the dishevelled state of her clothing and the reddening welt on her cheek, he gasped in dismay. He did not even have to ask what had happened.

"That Saluja boy," he hissed. "*Chutiya kahin ka!* Are you hurt? Let me get a taxi, I'll take you to the hospital."

"It's okay, Shyam. I ran away. Don't worry, it's over." She smiled wanly and let a fistful of crumpled rupees fall on the worktable. "At least we got paid."

"It's no laughing matter, Maya. We have to go to the police. That bastard can't be allowed to get away with this." A customer approached the stand, but Shyam roughly ordered him away.

"What good will it do to go to the police?" Maya said. "The boy is rich. You know how it is. Let's not cause a big *tamasha* over this." She tried to fight back tears, but they came anyway. "Where's Radha? Why isn't she back yet?"

"Monday nights are always slow. She must be chatting with the *phoolwalis* somewhere. I'll go and find her."

"No, don't do that. I have to catch my flight. Don't even tell Radha I came by. Don't tell her anything."

~

Shyam packed up early. When Radha finally arrived back at the stand, he instructed her to walk home with her friends, the *phoolwalis*.

"What's the matter?" she asked. "You look troubled. I'm sorry I took so long."

"No, it's nothing you did. I just have to take care of something tonight. Don't ask me what. I'll see you later."

Radha wondered what had gotten into him. Bidding farewell to Maya earlier in the day had drained her, and she was in no mood to put up a fuss. She simply shrugged and headed home.

Shyam found the two cops sitting beside the *seenghwala*'s stand, eating peanuts near the Gateway. The murky ocean behind them looked deceptively pristine in the moonlight. He approached them with folded hands.

"*Oye, kebabwala*. You sold all your kebabs already? It's only 10 o'clock!" The cops chuckled humourlessly.

"Oh no, sir. Please, sir. I need to talk to you for a minute, sir," he begged, making as much of a pretence of humility as he could muster. "One single minute of your precious time is all I ask."

Without divulging too many details, Shyam told them that he wanted to file a report against the Saluja boy. The cops stopped chuckling. Instead, they laughed out loud, their bellies jiggling like bagfuls of coins. They told him to forget about it, for his own good. Unless Shyam had witnessed the boy murdering the prime minister in broad daylight, there was no way to pin anything on him.

"Look, *kebabwala*, we like you. You don't make trouble. So trust us when we say this, nobody will touch the Saluja boy. Whatever it is you think he has done, let it go." The cops patted him on the cheek and resumed tossing peanuts into their gaping mouths.

Seething under a calm façade, Shyam was tempted to push them over the embankment and serve them to the ocean sharks. But these fools were only the custodians of crime, not its perpetrators. Without further remonstration, he turned and walked away.

Like the flames from the hot embers smouldering in his grill, a fierce fury consumed him. He wanted to burn down the world.

Cutting through a dimly lit alley to get back to his stand, Shyam lost his footing on something slippery and fell face forward, landing in an oily puddle. The mongrel dog that Rohan had sworn to kill lay mangled before him. The wretched beast looked as though it had been run over and, judging by the odour wafting from the carcass, it had been dead for a while. A maggot emerged from its gaping, twisted maw and crawled away, burrowing into the wet, matted fur along the lip. Springing to his feet in revulsion, Shyam shook the greasy filth from his hands and fled down the alleyway.

A half hour later, he returned to the spot with a canvas bag and scooped up the bloody remains of the dead animal.

~

The following evening, Shyam entered Rohan Saluja's building through the service entrance located in the rear, where it was always dark. Climbing slowly up the six flights of stairs, he sang 'Yeh Duniya Agar Mil Bhi Jaye' from *Pyaasa* in a lilting, quiet voice, almost a whisper. He had reached the middle of the last verse by the time he stepped onto the sixth-floor landing, and then his singing trailed away into silence. He rang the gilded doorbell to the penthouse and waited. Dressed in a starched white *kurta* and clutching a bottle of beer, Rohan greeted the *kebabwala* at the door with a phony smile and a pat on the back.

"What are you doing here? I didn't order anything."

"Sorry for my mistake, sir. I sent the wrong girl to you last night. She's new and got scared. I hope you will forgive me," Shyam implored with folded hands. He could not help but notice with secret pleasure the gauze dressing on Rohan's ear and the swollen bruise beneath his jaw. He resisted the urge to wrap his hands around the boy's neck and throttle the life out of him, to pummel his face with clenched fists until the blood gushed out and crimson spatters spoiled that nice white *kurta* for good. But no, he must be patient.

"*Ayree, sala*, don't worry about it. Just take my advice and fire that crazy bitch. She's bad for business." He took a swig of beer. "So what is it you want?"

"Look, I've made some fresh kebabs for you, sir, with the very best cut of meat, to repay your kindness and understanding. I used a very special recipe, just for you. I hope you like them. Please, sir, try one."

"Sure, why not? I'm famished anyway." Rohan reached into the bag and plucked out a plump kebab, still steaming from the grill. Shyam watched him devour the meat with gusto, washing it down with the ice-cold *Corona*. "Mmm, it tastes different today."

"The secret is in the spices, *sahib*."

"Not bad. I like it." Rohan hungrily reached for another.

"*Kutta* eat *kutta*, *sala*," Shyam murmured to himself with deep satisfaction. "Dog eat dog."

Safaiwali

But let there be spaces in your togetherness,
And let the winds of the heavens dance between you.
                                                    –*Khalil Gibran*

The bulb was out on the third-floor landing, leaving the space illuminated only by a small, dust-covered skylight overhead. Shanti had just come inside and still felt almost blinded by the blazing New Delhi sun. Standing in the semi-darkness and slightly out of breath from her climb up the stairs, she groped around her commodious faux leather handbag, swirling its contents with impatient fingers. From the bowels of the bag she extracted a chintz coin purse and tugged at the cheap zipper until it reluctantly split open to reveal a gleaming brass key. Grasping it firmly, and with not a little pride, she inserted the key into the lock, turned it, slowly pushed the door open, and ceremoniously crossed the threshold into Mandira's apartment. Had any of Shanti's fellow domestic workers been watching, they would have applauded in awe, for low-born cleaning ladies like her are seldom granted such easy access into upper-class homes.

She knew that Mandira madam would still be fast asleep, even though the sun stood near its meridian. The one-bedroom terrace apartment rose just above the abundant shade of the *gulmohar* trees that surrounded the building, so only the thick gingham curtains across the two large windows kept the dazzling sunlight from disturbing Mandira's youthful slumber.

Shanti flitted past the supine figure, her tatty flip-flops slapping against dirty, calloused heels with every step. The soft moan of pleasure that escaped madam*ji*'s lips betrayed to Shanti the mildly erotic nature of her dreams. Dropping her bag with a soft thud, she made a beeline for the bathroom, where a towering pile of laundry—everything from blouses to bed sheets—awaited her. Without further ado she set to work, making a token effort to muffle the noise that always accompanies such toil. She was sure that the vague, unavoidable commotion would soon begin to seep into Mandira's dreams, crowding out whatever nebulous visions that might be keeping her in thrall to sleep.

Shanti's job description had increased in scope since her employment with Mandira madam began. It now encompassed much more than mere cleaning duties. Besides dusting the furniture, sweeping and mopping the floors, washing laundry, and keeping the kitchen spotless, she now prepared small meals and performed a growing list of onerous but necessary tasks. The latest, and now her least favourite, required that she stand in endless queues to pay the household utility bills.

Unbeknownst to her employer, Shanti also served as sentinel and spy on behalf of someone keenly interested in what transpired inside these four walls.

Mandira's widowed mother lived in Jaipur, a few hundred kilometres west of the capital. Contrary to custom, she had granted her grown-up daughter the freedom to live independently and pursue a career of her choosing. Never having been the beneficiary of such emancipation herself, she derived vicarious satisfaction from knowing that Mandira would soar without the tethers of tradition to hold her down. But such knowledge came at a cost, which could be reckoned in ever-deepening worry lines, chronic headaches, and frequent bouts of insomnia.

On a recent visit to New Delhi, she had become especially troubled to find Mandira uncharacteristically depressed. Her voice sounded dull and distant, and her expression appeared vacant. A great, dark cloud had swept in to cast her daughter's spirits down. "What ever happened to my happy-go-lucky child?" she asked, her face furrowed with a distress so deep that she feared it could easily precipitate some physical malady in herself or, worse yet, trigger another migraine. "Something is wrong. I can see it in your eyes."

"I'm fine, Mama," Mandira assured her. "Please stop bugging me." She meant no disrespect. While dismissing her mother's unease with breezy nonchalance, she spoke with a subtle edge in her voice that maternal intuition could not fail to detect.

"You are not fine. Your father sounded just the way you do now whenever he was trying to keep something from me," her mother pressed on. "You don't smile anymore, you barely eat, and you always seem to be lost in a fog. And you never visit your aunt anymore, even though she lives in the same city, practically at your doorstep. She's worried about you. Why shouldn't I worry too?"

"Because you don't need to. I'm just a little tired, that's all. Flying five days a week is exhausting." Mandira reflexively threw on the bright, plastic, and thoroughly imperturbable smile that she had perfected over many years when welcoming throngs of airline passengers as they boarded the plane. "Being a flight attendant is a tough job, just as you warned," she added, keeping her voice light and playful. She did not want to give her mother any more grounds for disquiet. "Everything is okay with me."

Despite these assurances, the woman knew that behind her daughter's unconvincing smile lurked a profound and mystifying unhappiness. When all attempts at persuasion, gentle and otherwise, failed to get to the root of it, Mandira's mother stopped digging in one spot and instead widened the perimeter of her search. Knowing that household servants—omnipresent yet seemingly invisible—are privy to some of the most intimate secrets of their employers' lives, she decided to recruit the cleaning lady to her cause. As soon as the opportunity presented itself, she pulled Shanti aside and instructed the *safaiwali* to meet her at the teashop down the block that same evening.

~

"I know you work for my daughter and not me, but that is about to change," she announced by way of preamble, wrapping her bony fingers around the teacup and bringing it to her lips. As she took her first sip, she fixed a piercing gaze directly on Shanti's large, round face. "From now on, consider yourself to be on my payroll as well. You will serve as my eyes and ears in Mandira's home." Though loyal by nature, Shanti understood that refusal to accept such a job from this determined woman was not an option available to her. And what was the harm, after all, if it benefited Mandira madam? Besides, she could always do with a little extra cash. The *safaiwali* maintained a respectful silence to signal her acquiescence.

"So, Shanti, tell me everything you know about my daughter. How does she spend her time? Who are her friends? Do not hold anything back."

Ever the obliging servant, Shanti held dear the notion of keeping one's employer satisfied, and for that there is no time like the present. She bit happily into the crispy crust of the *samosa* that had been served along with their tea and began to divulge the facts that Mandira's mother so desperately craved, garnishing the truth with a smattering of unsolicited opinion and sage advice.

"Don't worry, *bibiji*, you go back to Jaipur in peace. Mandira madam is a good girl, not like other young girls these days, drinking beer and smoking cigarettes and going around with boys. She comes straight home after work." Then wiping the crumbs off her lips and lowering her voice slightly, she confided, "Only that one man—he must be around 30-35, I think—he comes to meet her a few times a week. Always dressed in a suit and tie. I think he comes to visit her from office during lunch break. But he never shows up when I am working there, only when I am on my way out. I think they like to be alone with each other."

"What man?" Mandira's mother grimaced as she uttered the word *man*.

"His name is Pratap. I once overheard him say that he lives in Panchsheel Park. That is a very nice area. If you wish, I can go with my neighbour—he is a taxi driver—and we can follow Pratap home, just to be sure." Shanti spoke fast, as though mildly excited (and not a little surprised) by her own demonstration of initiative in advocating surveillance as a prudent precaution.

"No need to do that," Mandira's mother answered, deep in thought. "At least, not yet." While she had not yet succeeded in ferreting out the whole truth, what little had been revealed was already cause enough for concern.

"As you wish." Shanti had no desire to raise more alarms, but some things must be said. Dropping her voice to a whisper designed to thwart the curiosity of even the most determined eavesdropper, she added, "Maybe you should talk to Mandira madam about marriage before something happens. You know...." Her voice trailed off suggestively. The *safaiwali* wiped the plate clean with her forefinger and deposited all the crumbs on the tip of her tongue before gulping down the last of her tea.

"Thank you, Shanti, you have been a big help. This is for you to keep."

Tossing her head from side to side, the *safaiwali* humbly accepted the scribbled phone number and 50-rupee note offered in payment for her time and service—the first of many to come in her new career as family informant. With the money tucked safely in her bra, Shanti promised to keep an eye out and to call *bibiji* immediately should Mandira madam land in trouble of any kind.

~

On weekdays, Shanti worked at three different homes in Kailash Colony, beginning with the Iyers' at 9:00 A.M. The household consisted of a young couple along with the man's elderly parents. Relatively recent transplants from Madras, they held on to a set of habits that she frequently found baffling. As a northerner, she had not yet completely reconciled herself to the family's idiosyncrasies, which she viewed as quintessential to the character of south Indians. Challenging the grey-haired Mrs. Iyer in a battle of wills had by now become an almost daily ritual.

"What does it matter if I sweep the kitchen without bathing? I prefer to go home and clean myself at the end of the day," Shanti declared firmly, standing with arms akimbo, her thick lips clasped in defiance.

"Do not question the ways of the Lord," the five-foot one-inch Mrs. Iyer growled in a resolute voice. Once again, as she did every morning, she ordered the *safaiwali* to bathe in the servant's bathroom before entering the kitchen.

Located behind the house, that particular bathroom— barely larger than a broom closet—was not fitted with a geyser, which made showering on winter mornings brutal. The icy water made Shanti's teeth chatter, and her squeals of agony when it first touched her skin were loud enough to scare the pigeons off the tin roof. If the Iyers could afford the services of a *safaiwali*, she often asked herself, could they not also afford an inexpensive water heater? *Those stingy buggers!*

Of course, she could pretend to bathe by making loud, sloshing noises behind the door, but she feared the crazy old lady might see right through that ruse and fire her. She was half-convinced that the vermilion *bindi* on the woman's forehead really was an all-seeing third eye, capable of looking through solid walls. Why take the chance? In the end, her best recourse was to show obedience and avoid the wrath of her employer.

Shanti showered quickly, lathering the best she could with the pitiful shard of lemony soap provided for her use, then dried herself off, got dressed, and re-entered the house. Smelling fresh and clean (and, she opined, a little like a piece of fresh fruit), she tied the long ends of the *dupatta* around her sizeable waist as she ambled her way toward the kitchen.

"*Namaste*," Shanti said, smiling politely at Mrs. Iyer, who stood waiting impatiently by the door.

"*Namaste, namaste*," Mrs. Iyer responded, "You spent five minutes extra in the bathroom today. Get to work—do the dishes first." Shanti was certain that the old woman had sniffed her as she lumbered past, like a police dog on the hunt for contraband.

The heavy aroma of coconut, mustard seeds, and *hing* emanating from the sink overpowered the lingering scent of lemon on the *safaiwali's* dark skin. The exacting Mrs. Iyer (who intensely disapproved of melamine because it might poison the food, and porcelain because it could chip so easily) scrutinised her every movement as she began washing the tottering stack of steel *thalis*, as if it were possible to ruin such plates simply by scrubbing them with a dishcloth. Shanti next tackled the soiled cutlery. Once she started on the glassware, however, the vigilant old woman, routinely distrustful of the help, could not help but interject with stern instructions.

"Be careful with those," she ordered. "Remember, if you break anything–"

"–you will deduct the cost from my salary. How can I forget, Iyer madam? You remind me every time I touch them." *Pagal aurat!* In the five years that she had worked for the family, she had never broken a thing. *And yet this lunatic still watches me like a hawk*, she thought. It made no sense.

With the dishes cleaned at last to Mrs. Iyer's satisfaction, Shanti swept and mopped the floors of the entire house, which she did every day, for dust is ubiquitous in Indian homes. Even with the windows shut tight, it finds a way inside, blowing in through invisible interstices and accumulating at an alarming rate in every nook and cranny.

Quite often, Mrs. Iyer would give her overtaxed servant the wearisome chore of preparing fresh *ghee*, and sometimes the *safaiwali* was ordered to grate mounds of coconut for the family's meals. Although Shanti relished the occasional dollop of coconut chutney with *upma*–the semolina cereal that the Iyers ate for breakfast most mornings–she could not imagine incorporating coconut flakes in virtually all her food, the way the south Indians did. Finally, before leaving for the day, Shanti was required to warm a pot of milk to set curd, for Mrs. Iyer considered the very idea of buying yogurt from the bazaar tantamount to culinary sacrilege.

"We are not like those lazy Punjabis," she proclaimed arrogantly, waving her crooked finger in the air. "We always make our own curd and *ghee*."

"Yes, Iyer madam, you are very wise to do that," Shanti lied. In actuality, she saw no point in it. *Ghee* was *ghee*, no matter where you got it from.

Around noon, she would head over to Mandira's apartment. Everybody in the colony—from Mrs. Iyer to the roadside *chaiwala*—solicited Shanti for juicy information about the high-flying lifestyle of the emancipated air hostess. How many lipsticks does she own? Have you seen her drink alcohol? Does she have any boyfriends? But the *safaiwali* refrained from disclosing even the smallest personal detail, at least in part because she felt a protective allegiance toward her young employer, who treated her well. Mandira's mother might be entitled to the truth, but the neighbourhood gossips were just looking for dirt, and so she ignored them.

Besides trusting Shanti with a key to her home, Mandira had the good grace not to chivvy the *safaiwali* with constant instructions, nor did she threaten to fire her one or more times a day just to keep her in line. "Clean properly or we'll find somebody else for the job," the other home-owners warned. That never happened here. Best of all, Mandira never placed any limitations on what Shanti was allowed to eat and drink on the job.

"Do you like soft drinks, Shanti?" Mandira had asked one afternoon while sipping a cold soda.

"I don't remember the taste, madam*ji*. It has been a while since I had one," she said, reaching for dust balls under the bed with her *phool jharu*. The long broom, with its dense, bushy head made of bamboo grass, was her preferred tool for the job.

"There are plenty cans in the fridge. You are welcome to have one if you get thirsty." Such generosity was unprecedented in Shanti's experience. Her other employers would have vehemently accused Mandira of 'spoiling the *kaamwalis*.' For that very reason, this *kaamwali* required no special scrutiny when madamji was absent from the apartment on one of her afternoon flights. If anything, such lack of supervision prompted Shanti to work even more diligently. On every visit, without fail, the *safaiwali* subjected the entire apartment to an exquisite cleaning from top to bottom. She scrubbed each individual bathroom tile to a glossy sheen. She removed the cobwebs from every corner. She organised and reorganised the contents of the refrigerator and kitchen cabinets until they looked not just tidy but orderly. She carefully collected the mislaid pieces of jewellery she always found scattered about the apartment—tossed cavalierly on counters and tabletops, secreted in piles of laundry, or dropped behind furniture—and put it all away in one spot. And when every task had been performed to her own stringent standards, only then did she take the liberty to indulge her modest appetite and imagination.

First she would try on some of Mandira madam's jewellery, from which there was much to choose; and then, with a soft drink can in one hand, she would slip into a pair of madamji's elegant high-heeled shoes. Marvelling at the fact that two women with vastly different girths could have the same shoe size, she would do a little coquettish twirl and admire the stylish 'Shanti madam' in the mirror. Other times she would help herself to some of the apartment's ample bounty, never taking anything valuable, but just everyday items that her employer would not miss—a half-used roll of aluminium foil, a box of cornflakes, a bar of scented soap. She did not think of it as stealing. Rather, she bestowed these small tokens of luxury upon herself as rewards for such remarkable industry on her part, an act of largesse that madam*ji* herself would surely have performed ungrudgingly, were she present.

Finally, at 2:00 P.M., Shanti would leave the apartment and saunter along the tree-lined street, past the *chaiwala*, to what she called the 'big Punjabi bungalow,' where two brothers resided together with their respective families, which consisted of a wife and two children each. Both brothers shared the burden of caring for their uncle, a cantankerous octogenarian and former brigadier in the Indian Army. Shanti pictured him as Mrs. Iyer in pants, except taller.

To service their large and demanding *ménage*, they employed four drivers, three live-in nannies, two cooks, one washerwoman for clothes, one cleaning lady strictly for the kitchen, and the *safaiwali* herself, who swept and mopped the floors. Territorial battles raged constantly between mistresses and maids, cooks and drivers, siblings and cousins, pet dogs and stray cats, and the senile uncle, who was at war with everybody. To survive the frequent bursts of ack-ack fire that erupted in the household at the slightest provocation, Shanti had learned early to fly far below their radar. The family members valued her policy of strict neutrality, and for that reason they often called upon her to negotiate temporary truces between belligerent parties. Thus, as a non-combatant allied with none, she created the illusion of favouring all.

~

"Wake up, madam*ji*!" The sound of Shanti's high-pitched squawk intruded upon the mellifluous quietude of Mandira's dream, putting to rout all the amorous visions roosting in her head, like a flock of birds scattered by the sudden shriek of a hungry raptor in their midst. "Don't you have a flight this afternoon?"

"*Uff*, Shanti, not so loud. It's like waking up next to a Boeing 747." Mandira laced her fingers together and stretched her arms overhead. As always, her large watch with the phosphorescent dial had remained fastened to her narrow wrist throughout the night. In fact, it came off only when Mandira bathed or hand-washed her dainty undergarments (thus saving them from Shanti's merciless wringing). This timepiece served as the indispensable compass and telltale that helped her navigate busy workweeks filled with ever-changing flight plans.

"Damn, look at the time! I have to leave in an hour. Could you brew me some *chai*, Shanti? And please go light on the sugar. You always make it too sweet."

Twenty minutes later, Mandira slipped into a freshly ironed Jet Airways uniform that complimented her slim figure. Appraising herself in the narrow, full-length mirror, she deftly harnessed her thick brown hair into a chic French knot and then twirled a few strands on either side to frame her delicate features. As though annoyed by the seductively fragile reflection gazing back at her, she brusquely tamed the rogue strands with two bobby pins. She purposely disregarded her supervisor's precise instructions—to look sexy for evening flights by wearing red lipstick and plenty of blush—and declared herself ready with a touch of kohl around her almond-shaped eyes and just a hint of colour on her full lips. Her intention was not to revel in rebellion for its own sake; rather, principle now dictated that she look alluring for one man and one man only.

Mandira left for the airport buoyed by the prospect of seeing Pratap later that night. She thought back on the day when she had met him almost two years ago at a friend's party, where he surprised everyone present by publicly declaring his resolve to marry a woman of his mother's choosing and not his own. At a time when revolt against the time-honoured institution of arranged marriages had become the norm among many of her peers, holding such a contrarian stance struck her as curiously out-of-step if not downright archaic. How could one surrender free will in a matter so important as romance? She was at once appalled and intrigued. Yet, the other young men at the party slapped the handsome reactionary on the back, congratulating him on his brilliant strategy to circumvent the marital commitment issue.

But that was then, when mutual attraction had yet to couple the pair and before flirtation had blossomed into passion. Now Mandira could not imagine Pratap consenting to marry another. He would have to fight for her, of course. His mother surely viewed air hostesses as little above glorified waitresses—and certainly not daughter-in-law material for families of stature. It was a testament to her love for Pratap that she felt so much confidence in his courage to oppose his mother's wishes and take a stand for their everlasting bond of love.

~

The wind picked up as Mandira boarded the aircraft with the rest of the crew. Cleaning personnel bustled up and down the aisle, scrubbing curry stains off the tray tables, untangling seatbelts, and extracting trash from bulging seat pockets. While her colleagues hurried to fix their wind-blown manes, Mandira helped the cleaning crew restock the seat pockets with in-flight reading material.

The first leg of the 6:00 P.M. New Delhi–Mumbai–New Delhi flight was Mandira's favourite route. The sun would begin to set just as they reached cruising altitude, smearing the pale blue sky with bursts of coral, celebrating the day's glory before the night staked its claim. Sometimes, in the middle of meal service, Mandira would try to draw her passengers' attention toward the portholes to admire the molten light brimming over the horizon. Sadly, the motley contents of her food cart always proved more enticing to them.

That evening's beverage and meal service went like clockwork. Working in tandem with Anu, her colleague and trusted friend, Mandira managed to push all thoughts of Pratap to the back of her mind and focus on the task at hand. Once they were back in the galley after collecting food trays, however, she spoke of nothing but the man she hoped to marry. After a while, Anu had had enough of it.

"Mandira, however much you think he loves you, Pratap may not want to spend the rest of his life with you. You do realise that, right?" Without warning, a rill of tears began to wash away the kohl around Mandira's eyes. Drawing a paper napkin from the pile on the counter, she dabbed at her cheeks, leaving black blotches on the airline's yellow flying sun logo imprinted on the paper.

"But we are *so* much in love. How could he not want to be with me? Mark my words. He will ask me to marry him, Anu, if his mother lets him."

In truth, she was not completely convinced that Pratap's mother even knew of her existence. She had never been brought to his home, never introduced to his family, and there was something strangely suspicious in the way he asserted, "Of course, I have told them about you, sweets."

"He will explain to her—kindly, of course—that just because I am a stewardess, it doesn't mean I don't have good values," Mandira pressed on, holding back the remaining tears, but barely masking the distaste she felt for people who judged others based on their profession. "And then he will ask me to marry him."

"Personally, I think a 32-year-old man shouldn't have to seek mummy's approval to marry the woman of his choice," Anu said. "But that's beside the point. Why must you cement a relationship with marriage? What's the rush? You're so young, Mandira. Can't you simply live in the moment? It's no use getting all wound up worrying about what comes next."

"That 'live in the moment' stuff is all bullshit, Anu. Everybody makes plans for the future. Or they should. All I want is to be with Pratap. We have so much to experience together in life."

"What have you experienced so far, pray tell? He rarely takes you out because he is afraid someone will see the two of you together. You should be going to the movies, eating out, dancing—like normal couples. All you do is stay at home or go for drives in his fancy car. I'll bet it even has tinted windows. That's not dating. It's skulking!"

"It doesn't matter. I never liked the clubbing scene anyway."

"Since when? You used to go out all the time! Now I know why he dislikes it when you hang out with me. It's because he thinks I might knock some sense into you. And I hope he's right. Because when you're not working, you just sit cooped up in your apartment, waiting for him to show up at your door. From where I sit, it looks like he's after only one thing."

A few passengers turned around, some drawn by the personal nature of their conversation, others annoyed by the disturbance.

"He doesn't want anyone to see us together because he's afraid his mother might think I am fast, like the other girls," Mandira whispered.

"Oh my God, do you actually believe that? The truth is," Anu continued, nudging Mandira toward the aircraft door, "he just doesn't want anyone else to know that he's attached."

Mandira pulled open a jump seat and slumped down, cradling her chin between two cold palms as she mulled over Anu's words. Although they did not seem convincing, they had certainly knocked the wind out of her sails.

"Okay, forget all that," Anu said, sliding into the seat next to her friend. "Just tell me at least three things you want to experience with him as his wife, things that you think you will enjoy for the rest of your life."

The question took Mandira by surprise. Having invested herself entirely in the relationship, she no longer thought in terms of what would please her and her alone. The wide-open roads of adventure that she used to travel in her imagination had now become barricaded by love. Bungee-jumping in New Zealand, snorkelling in the Maldives, shopping in New York—she dusted off the old desires filed away in the archives of her memory, as if she were staring at yellowing postcards sent to her long ago by someone she could barely recall.

Not once had she talked about such adventures with Pratap. Without a doubt, this passion had completely consumed her. But had it also compromised her zest for living? If love is supposed to be so uplifting, Mandira wondered to herself, why did it sometimes make her so unhappy? Soaring somewhere over the deserts of Rajasthan, she stared through the tiny porthole at the sunless sky and made one last attempt to persuade her friend that Pratap was worth all the agony.

"I feel his love when we are together. You can't fake emotion like that. And I'm not talking just about the physical, Anu. There is magic in the air when he is around." Though the words were loosely borrowed from an article in a lifestyle magazine that she had read during take-off, the sentiments they expressed were genuine. "I don't think I can live without him."

Anu rolled her eyes in exasperation. "Sure you can! Contrary to what you believe, you won't wither away. You are an attractive, salaried, 24-year-old woman living by yourself in the big city—that's something most Indian girls never get the chance to do. Look, Mandira, I know the two of you have been together for a while. If he stays, wonderful. But if not, you will be just fine. The whole world is spread out before you, my dear."

Mandira stood up and straightened the stiff fabric of her uniform skirt. "Thanks for the pep talk, Anu. Things will work out in the end, you'll see. I just have to be patient." She glanced at her watch. "We'll be nearing the approach soon. I'd better go make the rounds of the cabin."

The passenger with the gelled-back hair in 24E snapped his fingers to get Mandira's attention for the third time that evening. Now he wanted some water. Given his manner of dress—pinstripe navy suit, button-down white shirt, and flashy paisley tie—she could tell that he was no novice flyer. After three years of interacting with passengers as varied as cloud shapes, she was able to determine their level of experience almost at a glance. The less-travelled passengers were usually nervous, overly polite, and unsure of just how much was available to them, while the seasoned travellers demanded everything with authority, and then stirred up a storm if their wishes were not met at mach speed.

Mandira brought 24E his cup of water, served up with a fabulous smile. "Here you are, sir," she said. "And should you require the attention of a flight attendant again, there's no need to snap your fingers—simply use the call button. It is located on the overhead panel directly above you. This is how you operate it." With a slow, deliberate motion,

Mandira held up her middle finger and drove it into the panel until the large button glowed blood-red.

Anu watched the scene from the galley, aghast. "What the hell is the matter with you? Do you want to get fired?"

"People like that have to be taught a lesson," Mandira fumed. "We are not their *kaamwalis*. How dare they snap their fingers at us!"

"*Ayree*, forget about that idiot. Let's eat something before we land. The biryani looks yummy." Anu took two meals out of the oven.

"I can't eat that. I'm only allowed fruit today. My *safaiwali* told me I should fast on Mondays as an offering to Shivji."

"Oh. And the great Lord Shiva will reward your self-denial with a good husband, right? I've heard that one before," Anu said, scooping up a spoonful of biryani. The captain turned on the fasten-seatbelt sign. They would be landing shortly. "Mandira, you really need to relax. Why don't we do something together after this flight? Just you and I. Girls' night out!"

"Maybe next week, Anu, but thanks anyway. Pratap is coming over tonight. He's been away on a business trip to Bangalore—some big, important case he's been working on—and I haven't seen him in three whole days."

~

Shanti found Mandira asleep in the apartment, still dressed in her uniform. An empty strip of sleeping pills lay beside her head on the pillow. She wondered if it might be time for parental intervention. Concerned, she placed a cup of masala *chai* by the bedside and sat down on the floor, waiting for the aroma to revive madam*ji*. As soon as Mandira's eyes fluttered open, Shanti began to fuss over her.

"Why are you not eating the food I make for you these days? The *dal* and potatoes are still in the fridge. You look so thin, and so sad. What is the matter?"

Mandira wanted to tell the *safaiwali* to go away and let her sleep some more. Instead, the truth spilled forth like a confession to a priest.

"Last night, Pratap told me that his mother is looking for a girl for him to marry."

To Shanti's surprise, the news upset her, as though she were the one being passed over. "But madam*ji*, didn't he tell his mummy about you?"

"He says he did, but his mother doesn't want him to marry an air hostess."

"That's what he told you, huh? Then why does he come here if he has no balls?"

"Because he loves me," Mandira replied defiantly.

"Mandira madam, don't waste your love on that *chokra*. You are a very good girl, very pretty. Your mummy can find many nice boys for you."

"No, Shanti, you don't understand. I cannot live without him."

"*Ayree*, I understand everything. Look at that boy, doing everything his mummy says. And you? Your mother, poor widow, sends you, her only child, to a big city just to make you happy. How sad it will make her to see you waste your life over some *chokra*."

"I don't want to talk about it anymore, Shanti. Go boil some water—the last batch for drinking is almost finished.

And be sure to let it boil for a few minutes, okay? That's the only way to kill all the germs."

Spewing expletives all the way to kitchen, Shanti filled a large pot of water and heaved it onto the stove. *How foolish we women are*, she thought. *We sacrifice everything we care about in the name of love. Even I.*

It had been a long while since the *safaiwali* had thought of the boy she eloped with at the age of 19. Dressed in tight pants, like some kind of film hero, Mohan came to her window on a still June night. His powerful arms glistened in the moonlight; and Shanti, still young and foolish, mistook his muscle for mettle. Fearing no future, she fled her beloved brother's home—that kind, generous brother who had cared for her since the untimely death of their parents—equipped only with a sack of clothes and enough love to last a lifetime.

Just two months into their self-conducted marriage in a run-down temple, the man she loved more than anything in the world was gone, lured away from the marriage bed by laziness or wicked friends or a different woman or who knows what. She was devastated. Whatever his reason for abandoning her, Shanti had never wanted to see the *chutiya* again.

Now she imagined flying to Mumbai on a Jet Airways plane to visit her brother at his famous kebab stand near the Gateway of India so that she could beg for his forgiveness. *Oh Shyam, dear Shyam, what a mistake I made*, she would say. She would tell her brother what that *chut* Mohan had done to her, and together they would curse his name. *May wild tigers tear the bastard to pieces and devour his guts!*

And then she would tell Shyam about her new husband, Anand, whom she had met a few years ago and who was a much better man.

Shanti sighed and watched the pot rumble, spouting vast plumes of steam into air until the water was safe for consumption.

~

Anand often spent many days at a stretch away from home. Working as a truck driver, he traversed hundreds of miles every week over the potholed highways that spanned the country. Upon his return from each back-breaking trip, Shanti gladly played the part of the dutiful wife. She massaged his aching spine with *ayurvedic* oil, and then soaked his feet in warm salted water to ease the discomfort. At dinner, she reduced her portion size in order to give him a bigger helping. Granted, once in a while cheap country liquor loosed Anand's fist, but their partnership thrived under the duress of frugality, and that was surely worth the occasional bruise or black eye. Most of the time, though, he appreciated her well enough, and even applauded some of the little thoughtful things she did—lining the utensil racks with shiny aluminium foil, serving him cornflakes for breakfast instead of a greasy *aloo paratha*, or surprising him with a bagful of plump Goan cashew nuts from Mandira's house. Such treasured treats, thanks to Shanti's employer, were extravagances that otherwise lay far beyond the truck driver's reach, though certainly not beyond his range of vision. For Anand entertained lofty dreams of living large, and he was nothing if not tenacious in his pursuit of clever shortcuts to achieve those dreams.

"Guess who I met today. Go ahead, guess?" Anand asked Shanti urgently; but like an importunate child, he did not wait for an answer. "Dinesh! He just came back from Dubai. He is making a lot of money there." In one large gulp, Anand drained the bottle of *tharra*—the sugary home-brewed alcohol that he purchased on his trips—and continued. "He said he can get me a job there."

Without waiting for a response, Anand grabbed his wife as she walked past, pulled her down to his lap, and buried his head between her heavy breasts. She tolerated his attentions, not to mention the belching, without complaint, wondering what it would feel like to have a baby at her bosom instead. They had been together so long that by now Anand could practically read her mind.

"I know you want a child, Shanti. I know, I know. Believe me, I also want one. But I have to make some more money first. This Dubai job is exactly what we need."

"I have heard about your get-rich-quick schemes many times before," Shanti countered, squirming to free herself from his arms, "but we'll never have enough money until you stop your *matka* gambling."

Anand tightened his grasp around Shanti's waist, a crazed look spreading over his eyes like hot tar across concrete. "You don't get to tell me what I can and cannot do," he hissed, and grabbed a fistful of her hair. Jerking her head back, he clasped her thick chin in a vicious grip, his fingers digging into the side of her face. And then he kissed her hard on the lips, pushing open her reluctant mouth with a stiff, demanding tongue. Shanti struggled under the onslaught, but not for long. She was born a strong woman, and years of manual work had made her stronger still. She pulled away from her husband and stood up, clenching her hand into a fist and wagging her thumb at him.

"You're drunk. You can tell me about your silly schemes once you've sobered up."

Anand met his wife's reproving look with sheepish eyes. The sudden anger that had inundated him mere seconds ago receded just as quickly. "Shanti, if I go with Dinesh, I can earn what we need," he said, as though the brutal kiss had been but the preamble to an earnest promise. "And then I will give you a child."

Wiping his sweet, sticky saliva off her lips with the back of her hand, Shanti began mulling over Anand's proposition, as if she had bitten into something new and exotic and was trying to decide whether or not it tasted good. The yearning for a child had been growing stronger with each period, and now it was a force in itself, perhaps stronger than any misgivings she might have harboured.

"Has he asked you for money to make all this happen?" Shanti said. It was a statement of fact rather than a question.

Anand paused, considering his next move on the chessboard of matrimony. "It is not that much, *jaanu*," he answered. "Just the plane ticket, plus Rs. 5,000 for the *dalal* in Dubai. And then I have to give Dinesh Rs. 4,000 for the referral. You know it is only fair." Anand spoke forcefully, like a politician before a restive mob, making the case for enduring temporary pain if it will yield a greater good in the long run.

They spent the rest of the evening mapping out the details of their future—a year of living apart, the exact amount of money they could expect to save after expenses, and the child (surely a boy!) at the end of it all. Just one small obstacle stood in their way.

"Dinesh needs someone now. He is not going to wait around for me. I need to pay him immediately," Anand said. "We have our savings, but I am still Rs. 3,000 short," Anand added, a forlorn look on his scraggy, unshaven face. "We will have to borrow the money from someone."

Shanti knew that the only person who would even consider lending such a large sum was Mandira, but she also knew that she could lose her job if the girl's mother ever found out. Over the past few months, the woman had visited her daughter often, and she had compensated Shanti generously each time for the information she provided about Mandira's daily activities and emotional state. A request for a loan would stink of greed.

"Or maybe you can pinch some jewellery," Dinesh suggested encouragingly. "You're always stealing anyway."

Never before had Shanti been called a thief to her face.

~

The windows of the apartment were dark, as expected, since Mandira was away on a scheduled layover in Goa that night. *Was it possible? To have a child of her own at last—or perhaps even two, if God was good!* Impelled by the distant yet perceptible prospect of motherhood, Shanti tiptoed up the stairwell to the third floor landing and quickly slipped the key into the lock. She wanted to get the job over with as quickly as possible. The gold earrings she planned on taking looked expensive, but she had never seen her employer wear them. *Mandira madam won't even miss them*, she assured herself.

After she flipped on the light switch, it took her a few seconds to comprehend in its entirety the horrific scene that unfolded before her eyes. Most alarming was the blood—not a frightful amount at first, just a few streaks on the kitchen floor, but then a widening trail of it leading to the bed, and two crimson blotches saturating the green bedspread, with Mandira splayed face down and fully clothed on top. Both her wrists appeared to have been deeply slashed. Three empty strips of sleeping pills lay on the floor, right next to a soft drink can. A large cockroach, perched on the rim of the can, explored the sticky, syrupy surface with its whip-like antennae.

Shanti was not sure what to do next. If she stole the earrings now, she would never forgive herself and, if she did such a thing, it was highly unlikely that God would bless her with a son. She pressed two fingers against the side of Mandira's neck, but felt nothing beyond the drumming of her own heart. Then she heard a faint cough and a muffled groan from the prostrate figure on the bed. Madam*ji* was still breathing!

At first Shanti considered calling for an ambulance, but then thought better of it. Emergency services in the city were too unreliable, she reasoned. *By the time the first aid people get here—if they get here—she will already be dead.*

Instead, Shanti called her husband from the phone near Mandira's bed and ordered him to come immediately in a taxi. Afraid that the driver might refuse to ferry a bleeding passenger, Shanti instructed Anand to call upon their neighbour Gyan, who owned a taxi of his own. A kind man whose wife had died the year before, the *taxiwala* was always quick to offer assistance to anybody who asked for it.

When Anand arrived and assessed the situation, he counselled against taking Mandira to the hospital. Anyway, he was sure she was already dead, so what good would that do? "Forget it, Shanti, let's get out of here," he pleaded in a nervous voice. "The police will blame it all on us. You have no business being here at night. Let's just take what we need and go."

"You want me to steal from this poor girl, and then leave her to die?" Shanti did not wait for her husband's response. Instead, she stepped out onto the balcony and called down to Gyan.

Mrs. Iyer, who happened to be out for an evening stroll with her husband, watched in horror as the *safaiwali* and the taxi driver emerged from the shadows of the *gulmohar* trees, lugging the limp body of her neighbour, the air hostess girl that everyone was always wondering about. Anand took up the rear, grumbling something indistinct about Dubai and babies. Shanti looked up at Mrs. Iyer and pointed her chin toward the door of the vehicle parked in front of the apartment building. Too shocked to ask questions, the old lady reached for the handle, and whispered a prayer as they slid Mandira into the back seat, slammed the door, and sped away into the night.

~

It had been four days since her last flight. Four days since she had learned of Pratap's engagement to some Oxford-educated hussy from Kolkata. Four days since she had tried to kill herself.

Tired of lying in a four-poster bed at her aunt's palatial house, where her mother had brought her from the hospital, Mandira sat up and let her feet dangle a few inches off the floor. In place of a watch, she wore white bandages around her slender wrists. She had no idea what time it was, nor did she care. Staring at her unpolished toes without really looking at them, she marvelled at how the simple need for love had very nearly killed her. *Oh Pratap, what a fool I've been*, she thought to herself. She had given up too easily. *I should have taken a stand and fought for you, my love.*

She was startled by the sudden appearance of a pair of anxious eyes staring at her through the doorway.

"I see you're up. You must be feeling better," Mandira's mother said in a casual tone that veiled a grim sadness. She had arrived in New Delhi the same night that Shanti had called from the hospital with news of her daughter's unsuccessful suicide attempt by knife and pill. Hesitantly she stepped inside and drew back the curtains, inviting the mellow afternoon sun into the spacious room. "Can I get you anything, my dear?"

"Please don't fuss, mother. I'm fine. Really."

"Then come join us in the living room for some *chai*."

"Why? So I can listen to you and *masi* discuss my disastrous love life over tea and biscuits? That sounds like a lot of fun."

Mandira's mother resisted the urge to slap her petulant child. But all contact with Pratap had been forbidden, and the last thing she wanted to do was drive her daughter back into his arms. "Why the attitude, Mandira? We are only trying to help."

"Look, Mama, I'm sorry. I appreciate all that you and *masi* have done for me. But I am okay. I made a stupid mistake, that's all."

"When you stub your toe, that is a mistake. Slicing your wrists open—well, that is something else." It was time to lay out some boundaries. "Look me in the eye, and promise me that you will never see that man again."

Mandira turned away, not knowing how to respond truthfully to her mother's impossible request.

"In that case, you are to return home with me," she continued, and watched with satisfaction the look of alarm spreading across her daughter's face. "If that is not acceptable, then you have only one other choice. You can keep working in New Delhi, but you will live here with your aunt. She has very graciously offered to take you in. You will have a roof over your head and someone to keep you company. In the meantime, I will begin a search for a suitable boy for you to marry. Now get dressed and make yourself presentable. I'll let you know when dinner is ready." With that, she turned on her heel and left the room.

The evening meal was a quiet, awkward affair. No one knew what to say, or to whom. After it was over, Mandira retreated back to her bed and turned off the light. Later on, when the house fell silent and she was certain that her mother and aunt were fast asleep, she threw back the covers and crept out of her room and down the hall into the expansive living room. In the darkness, she carefully navigated her way around the couches and end tables all the way to the phone perched on a tall brass stand in the far corner. Without her watch, she had no idea what time it was, but that did not concern her. She knew that Pratap would be overjoyed to hear from her after all these days. She dialled his number, her fingers trembling with excitement, and slid down against the wall as she waited for him to answer. *Pick up. Please pick up.*

"Hello?" The sleepy male voice at the other end of the line sounded aggrieved. "Who the hell is this, calling in the middle of the night?"

"Pratap! It's me, Mandira." Crying softly into the mouthpiece and stumbling over her words, she explained why she had not called him since their last meeting, which had been so unpleasant for the both of them.

For his part, Pratap said, he had been worried sick. How relieved he was to hear from her again! This was all his mother's fault, and he was sorry that he had agreed, in a moment of weakness, to marry someone she had chosen, a stranger whom he did not know and obviously did not love.

"You're the one I want to be with," he swore, lowering his voice to barely a whisper. If Mandira could get away from her aunt's house, he promised to meet her somewhere, and then he would put everything right.

When she finally hung up, she heaved a great sigh of relief.

~

In return for saving her daughter's life, Mandira's mother had agreed to loan Shanti Rs. 3,000 with no interest—exactly the amount Anand needed to go to work in Dubai. The deal had been struck at the hospital, when the woman was utterly distraught and profusely grateful.

What happened after that was not so fortuitous, though it was entirely predictable. Instead of flying off to Dubai, Anand gambled away the entire sum, and then came home reeling drunk. An argument ensued, and Shanti's refusal to listen to his excuses infuriated him. In his intoxicated state, he raised his fist to teach her some respect. Before the blow could land, however, she slapped him hard in the face. She did not know who was more surprised—Anand or herself. Without another word, he slunk off to bed to nurse both a split lip and the hangover forming in his brain.

~

Dressed in a pink and yellow *salwar kameez*, Shanti came to visit Mandira and her mother with a small bouquet of roses that matched her sprightly attire. She accepted the invitation for tea and sat on the floor a few feet away.

"*Ayree*, Shanti, come sit on a chair," Mandira's mother said, patting the seat beside her.

"No, *bibiji*, my place is right here at your feet," she said, nodding her head.

"You are like family now, Shanti. I can't thank you enough."

"Do not thank me. Thank Shivji that I forgot my purse and returned to madam's apartment to fetch it. And just in time. God is great."

"Yes, he is. I am certain God will bless you with a child soon." Mandira's mother patted her shoulder affectionately.

Unbidden tears welled up in Shanti's eyes. The prospect of having a child with Anand seemed more distant than ever. In fact, she was no longer sure that she wanted to stay married to such an unreliable man.

"*Ayree*, Shanti, don't cry. Sometimes these things take time, that's all. Now wipe away those tears." The kindly woman gave Shanti a napkin from the tea tray.

"*Bibiji*, why don't I take Mandira madam to the Shiva temple?" Shanti suggested, changing the subject. "Today is Monday. It is the best day for Shiv *puja*."

"I don't know, Shanti. She still looks a little weak to me. I don't want my daughter travelling in those rickety scooter rickshaws, especially in this heat and with the *loo* still blowing." The dry afternoon wind, typical for that time of the year, had been blustering of late with exceptional ferocity, as though perturbed by the knowledge that its time was almost over and the monsoons were about to begin.

"Don't worry, *bibiji*, my neighbour brought me here in his air-conditioned taxi. We will take Mandira madam to the temple and bring her right back. She will be very comfortable."

~

A hot wind blew dust in their faces as Mandira and Shanti made their way to Gyan's taxi. The *safaiwali* used her long *dupatta* to shield them from the onslaught, but dirt got in their eyes anyway.

"*Jaldi, jaldi!*" Gyan held the door open, urging them to hurry inside. Cocooned in the stillness of the taxi, the two women travelled in silence, each one caught in an emotional whirlwind conjured up by the men in their lives. Shanti now knew that Anand would never change, and she felt a twinge of despair at the thought of spending the rest of her life with a man who could not match her strength or loyalty.

As for Mandira, she still pined for Pratap, someone with whom she truly believed she could spread her wings and fly. But what had she to show for all her deep yearnings and romantic flights of fancy except these two bandaged wrists that reminded her of handcuffs, she wondered. An image of Pratap's face floated before her eyes. How she loved his rakish smile and deep-set raven eyes! The voice of reason was banished, yet again. Instead, she weighed the pros and cons of the various stratagems that she had devised to slip out of her aunt's house and meet her lover in secret.

Mandira had already begun to settle on a viable plan of escape when Gyan, perhaps made uncomfortable by all the silence and sombre expressions in his back seat, began pointing out some of the notable sights of the city along the way. "Back there we passed the ruins of an ancient fort. And over here is Mayfair Gardens. Inside that park is an old mosque, very beautiful. Have you seen it, Shanti?"

"No, I haven't...," Shanti answered distractedly and then, after a quiet moment passed, she added, "But I would love to see it someday."

"Tell Anand to take you."

"Anand? Humph. He is always busy playing *matka* and getting drunk on his days off from work."

"I would be happy to accompany you, if you like," the *taxiwala* offered kindly.

Dust from the *loo* still irritated Mandira's eyes, but she stopped rubbing them as soon as she heard Gyan mention Mayfair Gardens. Looking up and recognising familiar landmarks of the neighbourhood, she felt a small thrill of excitement. "Where are we going?" she interjected, rubbing her eyes again. "This isn't the way to the temple, Shanti."

"First I have to pick up my bag from the new house I work at," the *safaiwali* explained. "Why don't you come inside with me and wash out your eyes?" she suggested helpfully, as Gyan pulled up to the curb.

Exiting the taxi, Mandira followed Shanti up the steps to the front door and waited while the *safaiwali* insistently rang the doorbell.

"Don't you have a key to the house?" asked Mandira.

"Not everyone is as trusting as you, madam*ji*."

Finally, a tall, skinny young woman dressed in a gaudy printed bathrobe answered the door. "Yes, can I help you?" she demanded impatiently, tying the ends of the belt around her slim waist. Without a word, Shanti pushed past the woman into the foyer, dragging Mandira behind her and down the hallway. "Hey, where the hell do you think you're going? Pratap!"

They found him sprawled on a white leather couch in the living room, wearing only his paisley boxers and a look of pure astonishment on his face. "Mandira, what...what are you doing here?" Pratap stammered.

"You know each other?" the woman in the bathrobe said, equally astonished.

Mandira ignored her and looked directly at Pratap, who was struggling to put on his pants. "I thought you said your fiancée lived in Kolkata. Who is *she*?"

"Who am I? I'm his girlfriend. Who the hell are you?" the girl barked at Mandira.

"She is just a friend," Pratap sputtered, caught like a bug between the accusing stares of two women. "I can explain!" He started to say something while he buttoned his shirt, but by then the *safaiwali* had already ushered her employer from the room.

"What fiancée was she talking about?" Mandira heard the woman in the bathrobe screaming as she and Shanti walked out the front door.

"Come, come, madamji. Let's get out of here." Before another gust of hot wind could blow more dust in their faces, they hurried toward the waiting taxi and slid into the back seat.

"I am sorry to hurt you, Mandira madam," Shanti said, "but you really needed to see that with your own eyes." She wrapped a protective arm around the dazed woman's shoulders as they drove away in silence.

"How...how did you know he was cheating on me?" Mandira asked finally.

"Trust me, I know the type. They're easy to fall for, all smooth and slick, like some kind of film hero. I had my suspicions, so I asked Gyan to help me find out where he lives and follow him around, just to see what he's been up to while you were recovering. It didn't take us long to figure out he had another girl on the side."

Gyan turned around to inform them that they were not far from the temple.

"No. Never mind the temple today. Let's just go home," Mandira said. And then she added—"My home".

When they pulled up to the curb, Mandira took some rupees out of her wallet to pay the *taxiwala*, but he refused, saying that he would never accept money from anybody who was a friend of Shanti. "Should I wait for you here?" he called after the *safaiwali* as she followed Mandira up the stairs. "I see some clouds. It looks like it may rain tonight!"

"That would be nice. These poor *gulmohar* trees could use a good washdown." She stopped to smile over her shoulder at Gyan and said, "Don't wait. I may be a while."

With the key entrusted to her, Shanti unlocked the door to the apartment and pushed it wide open. Entering her home for the first time in many days, Mandira strode directly to the window and pushed the curtains apart. In the golden light of the evening sun that burst through the monsoon clouds lowering on the horizon, they saw that a fine film of dust had settled on the floor, almost concealing the trail of crusted blood.

"It's time to clean up, Shanti. Will you help me?"

Kismetwali

Non temer; ché 'l nostro passo
non ci può tòrre alcun: da tal n'è dato.
            –Dante Alighieri

Sometimes she could see the future without even trying, an unwitting spectator to imminent mishap or miracle. Too often it was the former she saw, not the latter. So on a wet, ray-less morning such as this, she felt thankful for the evanescent vision of impending sunshine.

Such was the nature of the ever-turning wheel of the seasons. Standing by the window, sipping her tea and listening to the pouring rain—relentless, implacable, and seemingly everlasting—Mannat Jogi chuckled. Even amid this deafening cascade of water, it did not take any great power of clairvoyance to foresee that the monsoon season would eventually come to an end. It always did. She could almost mark her calendar down to the day. And though it was still early in the morning—one hour and 23 minutes before sunrise, to be exact—she could also predict with certainty that at least one of her clients, daunted by the particular ferocity of today's downpour, would cancel their appointment.

All her patrons swore that the well-regarded 'Mannat auntie'–a moniker that had been conferred upon the clairvoyant–possessed a remarkable gift. Unlike her father, an amateur astrologer in his own right who laboriously charted personal horoscopes based on the time and place of one's birth, Mannat did not divine the future by calculating the precise configuration of celestial objects. Rather, she had learned to navigate forward through time by relying strictly on her ears.

Everyone who came to her had a tale to tell, and no two were ever alike. Simply by taking a person's hands in her own, asking a few encouraging questions, and opening her heart to the inevitable flow of revealing words, she was able to forge what appeared to be a mystical connection with individual fate that no paper chart could ever achieve, and one that allowed her to glimpse deeply into that person's past—and future. Her gift, if gift it was, consisted of the ability to listen better than most and to see her subjects in all their frail, hopeful wholeness. As a consequence, her appointment book was always full, and people from all walks of life came to her seeking insight into what was to be and the fulfilment of urgent wishes.

"Can you help me get a good job with a multinational company?"

"Will I marry a wealthy man from a good family?"

"For my daughter-in-law to give birth to a son, what must I do?"

"Mannat *auntie*, please make my husband remain faithful to me."

How many times had she heard such yearnings and thousands like them? *I want! I want!* And what was this wanting, after all, except a sidelong glance toward one future out of infinite possibilities? Compulsive worry, thwarted ambition, thankless duty, overwrought vanity, love gone awry—there was no end to the long tapestry of troubles that wily humanity wove for itself. People came to her for help. Yet, she had no more power to grant personal wishes than a teapot.

Her clients seemed like children lost in the monsoon, Mannat thought, blinded by the rain and wandering aimlessly through waterlogged streets. It was her job to guide them to safety and open their eyes. This she did by making the right inquiries, learning their deepest desires, and then steering them toward the expectation of outcomes that were reasonable, practical, and even magical in their own way.

But there was always a caveat. "Remember," she would tell each client awaiting her propitious forecast, "every wish comes at a price. If you gain something, you must also be prepared to lose something."

Oh yes, her gift—if gift it was—surely was one that all possessed to some degree. Mannat could not make the future happen. Invariably, her clients chose their own futures.

She drained her teacup and headed toward the bathroom, wiping the perspiration from her forehead with the back of her sleeve. Born and raised in Kashmir, high in the glorious hills of north India, the clairvoyant always felt hot in Mumbai. To make matters worse, water shortages were common in this coastal city, even during the four months of monsoon rains. She stepped into the shower and bathed quickly, enjoying to the utmost the brief, rationed luxury of cleanliness. *Water, water everywhere—and barely a drop to bathe in.* Mannat could not help but find amusement in the irony of it.

Beads of perspiration reappeared on her forehead even before she had finished drying herself. Undismayed—for nothing dismayed this woman—she dressed as quickly as she had bathed, and with equal efficiency. At five feet nine inches, Mannat towered over many of her fellow citizens, which rather pleased her. Attired this morning in an embroidered red tunic smartly sized for someone with trim and youthful contours, she cut a statuesque figure, the envy of many other women her age and vaguely intimidating to weaker men. Returning to the kitchen (where her maid Kanta, as if reading her mind, had prepared a fresh pot of tea), she poured herself another cup and took up her post once again by the window.

Like a genie summoned from a lamp, steam rose from the cup and enveloped her face. *Why is it,* she wondered, *that Indians like me find such comfort in a cup of hot chai, even on sultry September days such as this? Don't we do enough sweltering?* She sipped slowly while her mind wandered at its leisure through a treasure trove of memories, riffling through recollections of the precious, bygone years she had spent with her husband Amar in Mumbai. Only when the cup had been drained to the last drop did Mannat permit the present to intrude on her thoughts once more. She felt at peace. Delighting in the life-giving, world-cleansing music of the monsoon, she reluctantly turned away from the window, ready to begin her day.

The rain was coming down hard.

~

The rain was coming down hard. It drummed through the streets of Mumbai like the angry beat of an invading battalion, it assailed the sidewalks, it bombarded the rooftops, and it ricocheted noisily off the windowpanes, waking the woman from a restless sleep. Although every portal was shut tight, she felt as if the monsoon were about to besiege the house.

Karuna Malhotra cursed under her breath. Her right hand lay heavy and numb under the pillow. Once again she had fallen asleep in a cramped position, cutting off the circulation to her arm. She sat up and eased herself out of the narrow, uncomfortable bed, fumbling for her spectacles on the nightstand with clumsy, tingling fingers. Karuna was long accustomed to sleeping on a king-size mattress, but her old bedroom had been converted into an extravagantly decorated nursery for her beloved grandchild, Avinash. Relegated now to the guest room, the limited dimensions of which could hold only a much smaller bed—barely a cot, in fact—she had discovered in short order, and much to her dismay, that she herself would also have to shrink in stature if she ever hoped to inhabit with any kind of tranquillity the confines of her newly rearranged world. By no means did she begrudge relinquishing her former accommodation to the precious infant; but the transition to such attenuated living quarters had proven more arduous than one would have expected.

Rubbing the last remnants of sleep from her eyes, she remembered that today was her birthday. *Another year older. Would anyone else remember?* No matter. Right now she was in no mood to celebrate. The clock on the nightstand read 5:04 A.M. She yawned and stretched. Sameer needed to leave the house by 7:30 to get to work on time, so it was still a little too early for him to wake up. The newspaper would not arrive for at least another hour, and her hair appointment had been scheduled for much later in the morning. Though tempted to fix herself some tea, she feared that even the slightest commotion would disturb the family. Sleep had become a precious commodity around here; and who was she to misappropriate it?

Karuna also remembered that she had booked a session in the afternoon with that astrologer woman everyone was talking about. She dreaded venturing outside in such inclement weather, but she had to do *something* about her situation. Nepean Sea Road might just be a sodden mess today, but many of the other streets in the city and suburbs would look like rivers. *Perhaps the rain will let up later on.* At this predawn hour, the only illumination in the room came from the street lamps. She stood by the window and glanced outside, but the view from her vantage point was obscured by raindrops sliding down the surface of the glass like the tears of an inconsolable child. Her mother had once told her that raindrops were more precious than diamonds. Pressing her face to the pane, she could see flowing through the avenue below a black, raging torrent of water, burdened with dirt and refuse dislodged from every nook and cranny of the city and carried away by the deluge. *Diamonds mixed with dross,* she reflected sadly. Karuna detested the monsoons in Mumbai. They lacked the organic splendour of the kind of rain she recalled from childhood in her hometown of Nainital. She still held the deed to the ancestral bungalow where she grew up and wished that she could hear again the sweet pitter-patter of drops falling softly onto the leaves of the *kafal* trees encircling the house, like kisses bestowed upon the hands of a lover. Instead, her ears were assaulted by the vicious tumult outside her window, loud as a stampeding herd of elephants.

Nainital. Perched high in the mountains, the town of her memory seemed as different from Mumbai as a foreign country. Even its monsoon season was different. The mild afternoons, the mists rising off the hillsides and filling the valleys, the aroma of rain mixing with the rich, black soil, the magnificent sunsets—how beautiful she remembered it to be! Yet sometimes it could be perilous too. Silently to herself she recited a few lines from a poem about the place that she had committed to memory as a schoolgirl—

> When suddenly, they who had calmly felt
> So safe one little span of time before,
> Discovered in dismay the swollen floods
> Meant danger—that the safety of their homes
> Was menaced, walls were tottering, waters rose,
> Sapping foundations, threatening precious life.

Sharp as ever! She could not resist the triumphant boast. *At least you still have that.*

Karuna began laying out her clothes for the day, choosing from the small chest of drawers a pale blue *salwar kameez.* While the outfit was both sensible and stylish, and of course perfectly proper for her status as a widow, something about it stuck in her craw. She had long ago grown weary of wearing sombre colours all the time. *I need to cheer myself up*, she decided. In an act of rebellion, she added to the ensemble a bright red *dupatta* with flowery *phulkari* embroidery. Then, satisfied with her wardrobe selection, she knelt down on the tiled marble floor and pulled a yoga mat out from under the bed. Though the purple slab of foam looked quite worn out—it had been a steadfast companion for years—she was reluctant to replace it. This little rectangle remained the one place where she could reliably jettison her discontent every morning.

She removed her spectacles and unrolled the mat directly underneath the speeding ceiling fan, for what little it was worth. Though she felt asphyxiated by the thick, humid air in the room, she forced herself through her daily routines, as quietly as she could, contorting her slender frame in an elaborate sequence of *asanas*. Then, with the help of a resistance band, she worked on improving the strength and steadiness of her favourite yoga poses, until the lean muscles of her arms and legs began to ache.

The rigorous morning workout always culminated in a meditative *savasana*. Closing her eyes and lying perfectly still in a corpse-like pose, she struggled to shut out the sound of the rain and focus entirely on the breath entering and exiting her body. Even at her age, she was fit enough to recover quickly from her exertions. As the rise and fall of her chest slowed, she began to drift into a pleasant, half-waking state. She felt as if she were floating outside her own body, connected to the earth only through the insubstantial tether of her quiet, rhythmic breathing. A sense of peace enveloped her entire being.

Then the shrill cry of a baby forced Karuna back into her body and into her constricted surroundings, back into the world of humid air and the pounding rain.

~

The pounding rain came to a sudden, temporary halt at a propitious moment, bringing brief respite to the pedestrians unlucky enough to find themselves outside and at the mercy of the remorseless elements. Seizing her chance, the young, well-dressed woman paid the *taxiwala*—with a little extra to wait *right here* for her return—and leaped from the vehicle onto the rain-glazed sidewalk. Before her stood a dilapidated three-storey building boxed in by gleaming high-rises that seemingly had sprouted up overnight. *Was this the right place?* She glanced at the address scribbled on the back of an envelope. Yes, this was it. An inner voice chided her—*What else did you expect?* For a fortune teller's place of business, it certainly looked the part.

As she approached the entranceway, a man with an open umbrella held in front of him darted past. He had not seen her, nor had she seen him, and the force of their collision knocked her to the pavement. He bent to help her back up, only to be met by the woman's basilisk stare, which instantly caused him to think better of inflicting gallantry upon this forbidding stranger. Muttering profuse apologies, he scurried away, more intent anyway on arriving at his destination before the next cloudburst. The woman had not been injured by the fall, but her freshly pressed wrap-around *ikat* skirt was now wet and soiled. *This is not a good omen.*

Once inside the building lobby, she was welcomed by the sight of peeling wall paint and the odour of mildew and stale cooking. Fighting the urge to beat a hasty retreat back to the relative safety of the waiting taxi, she climbed three long flights of creaky stairs, navigated the length of a gloomy corridor, and at last came to a halt in front of the fortune teller's door. For the hundredth time that morning she thought of her precious infant son. She had been out of the house barely an hour, and she missed him already, longing to gather him up in her arms and shower him with kisses. Though she had left him in Radha's care, she felt rather anxious. She only hoped that the nanny would be up to the task. *It's not too late to turn back.* But she had come this far. What did she have to lose?

The shrill sound of the doorbell silenced the importunate voices of reason and fear.

Almost immediately the door swung open, revealing the spacious foyer of a clean, well-appointed apartment. The grey-haired woman who greeted her had a hooked nose and gaunt frame and carried a broom.

"Madame...Jogi?"

The woman threw back her head and cackled loudly. "Of course not!" she answered in a thin, raspy voice. "I am Kanta, her maid." Consulting a list of names in an appointment book lying open on a table by the door, she motioned for her visitor to step inside. "And you must be Rhea Malhotra. Lucky for you there was a cancellation just before you called; otherwise nobody gets in to see Mannat *auntie* so fast. She is very busy, you know." Broom in hand, she led Rhea down the hall to an empty waiting area.

"You said she was busy," Rhea protested. "There's no one here!" If the maid's words were to be believed, one would expect the room to be crowded with supplicants waiting their turn to receive timely portents. As a former advertising executive, Rhea had been well trained in the art of making the mundane appear modish, even exclusive. She could smell gimmickry a mile away. *It's all a ruse to attract customers*, she concluded, beginning to grow furious with herself for having allowed an acquaintance to talk her into something she knew to be entirely contrary to common sense. Surely this so-called psychic was a sham after all. *How could I be so gullible?*

The maid let out a throaty laugh. "How suspicious you are! Many people who come here don't want anyone to know about it, so *auntie* keeps a wide gap between appointments," she explained. "She is not like some of those other money-grubbing astrologers who pack in their clients like sardines. She takes her time with each one. And after every consultation, she does *dhyan* on the balcony, cleansing all the negative energy through meditation."

Rhea smiled inwardly at the maid's attempt to parrot the arcane jargon that her mistress no doubt employed while plying her trade. The explanation had the ring of truth, however, and Rhea resolved to give this Mannat *auntie* a fair shot. She was not normally superstitious, but who knows? *There might be something to all this mumbo-jumbo after all.* At the very least, when all was said and done, she would have an amusing tale to share with her friends. *What few friends*

I am left with. Regrettably, the demands of motherhood had wreaked havoc on her social life.

"Now wait here and think about your problem and the wish you want to make," Kanta instructed, clearly enjoying her provisional authority over this *memsahib* from the nicer part of the city. "I'll be back soon."

After a few minutes the maid reappeared, dragging the broom behind her. "Auntie is ready to see you now," she announced, crooking her bony finger, and ushered her guest down a narrow hallway and through a beaded curtain. "This is the consultation room. Please have a seat." Rhea turned to thank the woman but only caught a glimpse of the broom as it vanished from view.

Settling into a generously proportioned rattan chair, Rhea took in her surroundings with a growing sense of relief. This was not at all what she had expected. The room had been modestly but tastefully furnished, and a faint, pleasing odour of jasmine and vanilla hung in the air. No devotional *bhajans* or vapid New Age music played in the background, no cheesy idols or smouldering joss sticks cluttered up the tidy space, no tarot cards were splayed out across the table in front of her, and no garishly coloured prints of Hindu Gods stared fixedly at her from every corner. Instead, the walls were lined with framed charcoal sketches of landmarks from around the world—the Eiffel Tower, Machu Picchu, the Parthenon, and some places she did not recognise. Propped on an easel in one corner of the room was a half-completed oil-on-canvas painting, done in the style of Monet and depicting what appeared to be a panoramic view of fog-cloaked hills. Oversize illustrated travel books on Egypt and Ecuador lay open on top of an antique steamer trunk. Though the sky outside remained overcast, two Battenburg lace panels draped in front of a tall French window let in enough light to infuse the room with a subdued but cheery ambience. Rhea noted with appreciation that the lace cloth covering the small, round table in front of her matched the pattern of the curtains. A vase with freshly cut roses stood nearby on a mantelshelf amid a collection of ornate and exquisitely fragile teacups, antiques by the look of them, and no two alike.

So preoccupied was she by the delightful décor and quiet serenity of the room that the peremptory greeting of someone unseen gave her a bit of a start, breaking the reverie into which she had fallen.

"Don't get up," said the clairvoyant as she passed through the beaded entranceway and marched across the room toward the window. She parted the curtains and glanced outside. "I see it has stopped raining—at least for a little while. We won't have to shout to hear ourselves above the noise." She turned to face her guest, smiling. "It is very nice to meet you, Rhea Malhotra. My name is Madame Jogi. But please call me Mannat *auntie*. I trust you have made yourself comfortable."

"Of course," said Rhea. "How could I not? You have a lovely home."

"*Shukriya*," said Mannat, seating herself on the opposite side of the table. "How kind of you to say so."

They took a moment to size each other up. The first thing that struck Rhea about this reputed fortune teller was that she bore no resemblance whatsoever to the short, squat, and ill-groomed astrologer whom her uncle used to consult. On the contrary, this Madame Jogi—or rather, Mannat *auntie*—was remarkably tall and, even more remarkably, smartly dressed. For her part, Mannat discerned with secret amusement the ill-concealed look of surprise on the face of this new client, who—like so many of her other clients—arrived with the presumption that a clairvoyant, however famous, must be costumed appropriately for her profession and inhabit less graceful surroundings. She had seen that look many times before. More importantly, she could not help but observe with some concern the web of worry lines etched into the younger woman's brow, not to mention her anxious energy and the dark circles under her eyes.

"Down to business, then," Mannat began without preamble. "Tell me a little about yourself. Then we'll address the circumstances that have brought you to me."

A year and a half ago, Rhea would have introduced herself through her record of academic excellence and professional triumphs, starting with an advanced business degree from IIM-Bangalore, followed by a steady rise through the ranks of an internationally renowned advertising agency with a major office in Mumbai. But that was then. She began her story instead at its new epicentre—her six-month-old son.

"Becoming pregnant so soon after I got married was never on the agenda. I wanted to establish myself in my job before starting a family. My husband Sameer and I were in no rush to have children, and we were deliriously happy together. But last year, everything changed. When I saw those blue lines appear on the test strip, my first reaction was surprise. We had been so careful! Then came dismay.

I was doing so well at work, which I found rewarding in every way. Taking time off now would put the brakes on my career. But after all those unsettling thoughts and emotions passed, I was suddenly overcome by a great sense of purpose. I began to think of motherhood not as an inconvenience, but rather as the ultimate promotion. So I quit my job and threw myself wholeheartedly into the most important project of my life—our beautiful little child, Avinash." Rhea paused to catch her breath. "May I?" Without waiting for a reply, she reached for the jug on the table and poured herself some water. Mannat took note of the slight tremble in her client's hands as she held the glass and took a few tentative sips. Clearing her throat, Rhea proceeded to describe her life as if it were a sales seminar, presented in a sequential series of vignetted slides.

"I read every book on pregnancy and parenting that I could lay my hands on. I watched what I put in my body, religiously attended the birthing classes, and never missed an appointment with my obstetrician—who happens to be one of the best in the city, from what people tell me. Sameer and I chose the nicest room in the house for the nursery, and I decorated it myself. And needless to say, we ignored all that superstitious claptrap about not buying anything for the baby before it is born. Way ahead of time, I stockpiled everything—tubes of nappy cream, formula cans—all the good-quality, imported things that cost a bomb."

"You like being prepared, don't you?" Mannat interjected.

"Indeed, I do!"

"And yet...."

"And yet nothing prepared me for the actual day-to-day reality of being a mother. I don't just strive to be good at it. I want to be excellent. But I have to admit, this is the hardest thing I have ever undertaken."

Mannat smiled sympathetically. "Then you have begun to learn what every other experienced parent already knows. Do you have any help with the baby?"

"That goes without saying," Rhea answered smugly. "I interviewed several nannies before hiring a mature country woman from Dehradun—not too young and not too old—who came with stellar references." Rhea paused for air, and continued with her story. "Avinash has been a bit colicky ever since he was born, so I spend most of my time with him. It can be exhausting. But the nanny comes by at noon and washes the baby clothes by hand, folds laundry, cooks sometimes, and pitches in with the housekeeping, so I can concentrate on being a mother. It is a very efficient support system, don't you think?" The deepening furrows on the young woman's face gave her the contours of an age that should have been decades away. "You can't imagine how tired I would feel without Radha to assist. It is quite hard on me as it is."

"Child-rearing is certainly not for the faint-hearted," Mannat wryly observed. "Or so I'm told. However, I'm not sure anyone can solve that problem for you. It just comes with the territory."

"That is not the problem I came to you for," Rhea declared. "It's my mother-in-law, Karuna. I'm sure she hates me! She hardly ever leaves the house. But would she ever think to offer a helping hand with the baby? Not on your life. She doesn't say anything directly. Yet, I can sense that she is always standing behind me with an invisible clipboard, grading me, waiting for me to fail. Even when she is in her room, doing her stupid yoga tricks, I can feel her beady little eyes boring through the walls, finding fault with everything I do. And to make matters worse, she manipulates my husband."

Karuna. The very name had become anathema to Rhea. When Sameer first introduced his parents to her at the Willingdon Club, she initially liked them both. They came across as being very modern and altogether progressive in their outlook; and, from all appearances, the amiable couple took an immediate shine to Rhea as well, especially the indefatigably cheerful Mr. Malhotra, who professed admiration for her steely strength, business acumen, and independent spirit. "You will be very good for my son," he had told her.

No one could miss the signs of deep, genuine affection that passed among all three members of this close-knit family, the Malhotras. Thus, when she accepted Sameer's proposal, which came in the form of a clear, one-carat diamond set in platinum, Rhea knew ahead of time that his mother and father would be part of the package. "I want us to be one big, happy tribe, my dear," he had proclaimed, the ever-dutiful Indian son who still lived in the home where he grew up and would care for his ageing parents in the only way he knew how—by staying close to them.

"So right after the honeymoon, Sameer insisted we move in with them. Their home in Malabar Hill is rather large, and we were newly-weds just starting out. From a financial standpoint, it made perfect sense. How could I say no?"

"That is the way it is," Mannat agreed. "In India, you don't just marry the man, you marry the clan."

"And, to tell you the truth, at first I didn't mind this arrangement at all. Up to a point, there is something to be said for such traditions, however archaic. I should mention that I lost both my parents when I was quite young. As luck would have it, the uncle who generously took me in—my closest living relative—was a very enterprising man. You could say I inherited my nose for business from him. But he was also a crusty old bachelor who did not know the first thing about raising a child. So I thought that having Sameer's mom and dad around might fill a void in my heart. Besides, it wasn't as if we got in each other's way. Lord knows, the house is no rat trap. They never interfered in our lives or tried to tell Sameer and me what to do. The two of them travelled abroad frequently, giving us the run of the place. We hardly ever saw them, in fact. Eventually, they planned to leave the house to us when they retired and then settle down in Nainital."

"But something happened?" Mannat glanced at the clock on the wall. Her next client would be arriving soon, and she had to hurry this along.

"Something awful!" A rogue tear rolled down Rhea's cheek. Impatient with her own emotions, she roughly wiped it away. "Last year, they flew to Australia for an extended visit with family. One week into their trip, Sameer's father keeled over in a karaoke bar in Sydney. A massive heart attack, they said. He never came home."

"*Ayree.*" The situation was becoming clearer now to Mannat. "But Mrs. Malhotra—Karuna—she *did* come home."

"That's right! And she's been with us ever since. Granted, it is her house. But I had grown so used to being alone with my husband all the time; it seemed almost like an imposition. Believe me, I am not unsympathetic. A widow's grief can't be much different from the grief of an orphan. You never get over it, of course; but you have to move on. A month later, I learned that I was going to have a baby, and Karuna would be a grandmother. I thought maybe the news would cheer her up and give her something to look forward to. Instead, it only seemed to make her sadder. And Sameer was not much better. The two of them moped around the house constantly, reminiscing about the past and feeling sorry for themselves. It was all I could bear to watch them together. And me, with my tummy getting bigger and rounder with each passing day—"

"You felt alone and abandoned," Mannat interrupted.

"Utterly alone," Rhea echoed. "Yet there was much preparation left. Someone had to take charge. Who else if not me?"

"And once the baby was born?"

"Sameer perked up somewhat after that. Actually, he dotes on our son, and he loves to pick out the family resemblances in Avinash's face. I know he can be as wonderful a father as his own father was to him. But it's been over a year now since his dad died, and he still clings to his grieving mother as soon as he gets home from work. 'Don't be a crutch,' I told him. It's one thing to be supportive; but he doesn't need to spend hours holding her hand every evening. I even suggested that perhaps his mother would be happier if she moved to Nainital. What a look he gave me!" She began to sob. "For that he accused me of being 'insensitive'."

"I think I get the picture." Mannat patted Rhea's hand and held out a box of tissues. "Now the time has come for you to tell me exactly what it is you want."

"I want her gone!" Rhea almost shouted the words. "My mother-in-law has such a stranglehold over her son that it is ruining our marriage, ruining my life—ruining everything."

Mannat stood up and walked to the French windows, giving her client a few seconds to compose herself. The sky outside was darkening ominously, and in the distance she could hear faint rumblings of thunder. Soon the rain would start up again.

"Can you do that?" Rhea asked. "I know it sounds heartless, but can you do whatever it is you do to make Karuna Malhotra go away?"

"Rhea, I learned a long time ago that the universe gives us everything we require in this life. We need not even ask." Returning to the table, Mannat sat down and stared deeply into this troubled client's eyes, as if to underscore the seriousness of what she was about to say. "But when we do ask the universe for something, and it answers our call, it always exacts a price. The price may be cheap, or it may be dear, yet it must be paid. Do you understand?"

"Yes, of course. And I am willing to pay it—anything to get rid of that woman!"

"Just so you are clear. Now, I am going to hold your hands and recite a prayer. Then I will ask you to make a silent wish. The wish must be very specific, and you must never ask to bring harm to anybody. Apart from that, you may use your free will to wish for anything. Are you ready?"

"Yes." Rhea closed her eyes and concentrated. She could hear the wind rise outside, at first gently, then in gusts that blew violently against the windowpanes. She had already plumbed the depths of her own desire, and she knew what had to be done. *I want my mother-in-law to be the cause of something bad*, she thought to herself, petitioning the invisible fountainhead of fate. *Something that will shake my husband's love for her and drive her out of my home.*

Mannat felt her insides constrict as Rhea's dark intentions crystallised into a wish—benign or diabolical, it was hard to say. Sweat seeped from her client's slim, nervous fingers onto the clairvoyant's warm, dry hands. The rain began to fall in torrents, and a sudden clap of thunder pealed through the room, rattling the teacups on the mantelshelf.

Rhea's eyes shot open in alarm. She stood up abruptly, releasing her hands from the fortune teller's grip. A premonition pierced her heart, a hellish vision of her child's pain or terror. She realised with a sense of dread that she had never been separated from Avinash for such a length of time. So many things could go wrong. The poor nanny would be beside herself with worry.

"I must leave right away. How much do I owe you?" Rhea inquired hastily, unzipping her wallet. "Traffic will be a nightmare with all this rain," she added in frustration, addressing no one in particular. She had to get back home, back to her son, back to Radha.

~

To Radha, the morning spent alone with Avinash had seemed like a small slice of paradise. With *memsahib* and her mother-in-law both away from the house at the same time—an unprecedented occurrence!—the nanny had the boy all to herself, and she took full advantage of the opportunity.

For her first order of business, she freed the little *raja* from the cluttered confines of his crib, rescuing him from the tyranny of approved toys specially hand-picked by Rhea for his amusement—though they had ceased to amuse some time ago—and set him loose to crawl undisturbed around the rooms of the house and to discover for himself, by touch and tongue, a few of the wonders of his wide domain. A colourful, crocheted potholder, a hairbrush, and a bunch of shiny keys he found most fascinating, as evidenced by the stream of joyful gurgles emanating from the little boy and filling the air like a billow of luminescent bubbles. She would have liked to stroll him over to Kamala Nehru Park, but she knew that the playground would be knee-deep in water. So instead, for the next hour of his unscheduled furlough, Radha played with Avinash on the floor, sometimes helping him stand upright and, when he grew tired of that, rocking him in her arms and dandling him on her knee. Later, she sang to him a medley of age-old Hindi songs that her own mother used to sing, which entranced him; and then she made silly faces at him, which elicited delighted peals of laughter from both nanny and child. She even took the liberty of feeding him his first solid food, combining a bit of mashed rice with warmed-up baby formula and spooning the watery mixture into his eager mouth. There would be hell to pay if *memsahib* were ever to find out what she had done!

Of course, Radha had no intention of telling Rhea any such thing. Then again, she did not look upon this decidedly subversive act as the taking of a liberty, but rather as a dire necessity. In her eyes, the child was clearly long past ready to assay that culinary milestone. Though childless herself, Radha had helped raise the children of numerous other *memsahibs* over the years, and she felt more than qualified to play the role of mother to the son she never had and to make bold executive decisions affecting his well-being.

The proof of the pudding could be inferred from the fact that not once in all their time together that day did Avinash cry, as he often did for hours on end. When he showed signs of growing fussy with colic, she drew upon her considerable skills as a former masseuse, rubbing his front and back as only she knew how, which provided both immediate relief and a prophylaxis against later discomfort. And now, thoroughly exhausted by the day's activities and with his belly full, he lay fast asleep on the daybed in the nursery, ensconced safely behind an impregnable fortress of pillows. While her eyes devoured this picture of pure contentment before her, Radha's mind contemplated the case of poor *memsahib* Rhea.

True, as a first-time mother she was bound to make mistakes. But did she not appreciate the advantage of having under her roof not one but *two* experienced helpmates always at her beck and call—women who would be more than happy to impart the hard-won lessons of parenting to the young novice, should she only ask? Radha shook her head in bewilderment as she folded the last of the laundered rompers and other baby garments and put them away. Too proud or too headstrong to solicit advice from others, much less accept it, Rhea insisted on doing everything herself.

As a result, everybody was miserable, yet no one seemed capable of doing anything about it.

It was not the nanny's place to say a word about such matters, of course. Not that she worried much whether her boldness in speaking up might be mistaken for impertinence. She just knew that it would do no good.

The deluge outside showed no sign of abating. Though loud, the thrum of falling rain had a rhythm to it that had helped lull the child to sleep, despite the occasional thump of thunder. The house seemed extraordinarily peaceful in this moment. So it was with some alarm, and not a little annoyance, that she heard the front door burst open and the sound of Rhea's voice calling out frantically, "Radha, where are you? Is Avinash all right?" The nanny rushed out of the nursery to intercept Rhea and prevent any further disturbance, lest it rouse the baby from his rest.

"Please, *memsahib*, the boy is napping," Radha implored in a half-whisper. Soaked to the skin and seething with anxiety, Rhea had swept into the foyer of the house as if pursued by some fierce, unseen juggernaut. *Napping? Impossible!* Avinash never napped at this time of day. She had learned to synchronise her downtime with his, stealing bitter, bite-sized slivers of nightmarish sleep whenever she could. Now the remainder of the afternoon and evening would be completely thrown off schedule. Ignoring the nanny's admonitions, she kicked off her sandals and marched straight toward the nursery, leaving behind a trail of wet footprints on the recently swept floor. A look of dismay overspread her face as she stood before the empty crib.

"*Where is he?*" Rhea asked in a panicky voice. Radha pointed mutely toward the daybed on the other side of the room. "What? Oh, you must never leave him alone like that! Avinash only sleeps in his crib. What if he were to roll off and fall on the floor? And look at all these pillows—there are too many of them. Don't you know he could accidentally suffocate?"

Relieved yet exasperated, Rhea dropped her handbag at the foot of the bed and testily tossed most of the pillows aside. Then she knelt down for a closer inspection, verifying that all her child's limbs were intact and that he was, indeed, still breathing. It took every ounce of her self-control to rein in her petulance. What had happened was not the nanny's fault. It was her own.

"I'm sorry I lost my temper, Radha. This was too much responsibility for you, and I should never have left you with the baby for so long. Still, if you weren't sure what to do, you could have asked Karuna for assistance."

"Oh, no, *memsahib*, I could not. Madam left the house soon after you did."

"*What?* Where did she go?"

"I do not know. And she did not say when she would be back."

Karuna! Fury surged anew in Rhea's breast, and angry thoughts careened willy-nilly through her head. *She left her grandchild all alone with a servant! How could she be so reckless? If I was not home, it was her duty to stay and keep a close eye on things.* Such behaviour was unimaginable, much less forgivable. Had Karuna not heard all the horror stories about babies left unattended by their nannies?

If any further evidence was needed to establish that Sameer's mother lacked all normal human tenderness and regard for the welfare of her only grandchild, this was it. Rhea recalled the fervent wish she had made just a little over an hour ago; and at last she dared to believe that Mannat *auntie's* ability to influence the future was not just legitimate, but supremely effective.

With vexation tempered by hope, she rifled through the handbag for her cell phone. She had half a mind to call Sameer this very second and let him know what his mother had done. But no, he might be busy at work, and she did not want to disturb him and spoil his mood. She reluctantly tossed the phone onto the bed next to the baby. Better to wait until he got home and had eaten dinner. First she would fix him his favourite meal, a sumptuous lamb lasagne topped off by a delicious chocolate soufflé for dessert. Only afterward should she tell him about his mother's frightful act of negligence. Doubtless, he would be livid! In fact, he may even suggest she head for Nainital! *Where she belongs.*

Almost elated now, Rhea was impatient to begin preparing the evening's feast.

"You can leave, Radha. There is nothing more for you to do."

"I have not finished cleaning up the kitchen, *memsahib*. Or if you like, I could watch over the baby while you change into dry clothes. You see, he is sleeping soundly. Now would be a good time for you to take a nice nap too."

"I'm not tired at the moment," Rhea answered, smiling warmly. "Take the rest of the day off. Don't worry about the money. I will pay you your full amount."

Recognising that prolonging the discussion might only vex *memsahib*, the nanny exited the room without further ado. The early dismissal did not bother her one bit. Her friend, the *kebabwala*, would be busy tonight with home deliveries, and he could always use the extra set of hands at his popular roadside stand. On the way out the front door, it occurred to her that she had never seen Rhea in such a seemingly happy state, yet it left her feeling uneasy. Radha rubbed her head in perplexity. *Dark clouds one moment, clear skies the next.* Rich people were like the weather, she concluded. She would never understand them.

For Rhea's part, there was nothing perplexing whatsoever about her unexpected bout of happiness. For the first time in months, she felt a faint glimmer of jubilation ignite in her soul. The rain had stopped again. Did this portend the end of the monsoon season? She would listen to the evening's forecast to find out.

Her eyes were drawn irresistibly to the still form of her son, with his shiny black tuft of hair, round head, and perfect, unblemished skin, lustrous in the gloomy half-light of the nursery. *So beautiful!* The sight of him filled her with wonder and gratitude. Standing alone in the suddenly quiet room, watching Avinash sleep, she felt waves of tranquillity wash over her. Having grown accustomed to his incessant wailing, she had almost forgotten what silence sounded like. Truth be told, there were times the past few months when she had felt the urge to take one of these pillows and smother him with it—anything to drown out the din of endlessly importunate crying. Of course, she could never really act on such a dreadful impulse. She was a good mother. No, she was an *excellent* mother.

Rhea recalled the interminable taxi ride back home from her appointment with the fortune teller. The monsoon had unleashed a fresh deluge, forcing the driver to slow to a crawl on Pedder Road. Through the fogged window, she watched a throng of shirtless children playing along the curb. They had amassed an assortment of empty plastic water bottles, pieces of plywood, tin cans, cardboard boxes, and other detritus liberated by the storm—anything that would reasonably be expected to float—and organised the collection of trash into a regatta of sorts, launching their improvised boats into the rain-swollen rapids of the gutter, where they bobbed along on a torrent of filthy water that lifted and sped them away toward certain destruction in the roiling drains. The wake of the passing taxi capsized the less seaworthy vessels in the fleet, eliciting groans of disappointment from some of the children, victorious cheers from others, and gleeful hoots of mutual derision. Rhea was appalled. They seemed like a pack of wild animals. She wondered what kind of mother would permit her child to play outside in such weather. It was too dangerous!

The scene only served to remind her that perils abounded in every direction and that her own child, like a snail on a thorn, could slip into harm's way at any moment and without warning. For the remainder of the ride, her mind had conjured up bloodcurdling images of Avinash in distress. There was nothing vague about these images. She pictured him with his head stuck between the bars of the crib, choking, struggling for breath, shrieking till he became blue in the face, while Karuna in her room read *Light on Yoga* for the umpteenth time and Radha at the sink washed baby clothes, oblivious to the danger. *Oh God, she won't be able to hear the baby cry over the sound of the tap running.* By the time the driver turned onto Nepean Sea Road, just blocks from the house, Rhea had been about ready to jump out of her skin.

But now she was home, Avinash was safe, and all was right with the world.

Well, almost all. Lifting her shirt, Rhea stole a glance at her waistline in the wall mirror. She did not much like what she saw reflected back. What was once an appealing, feminine roundness had now been replaced by the nearly shapeless pudginess of belly fat, made uglier still by a spidery mesh of stretch marks covering the rotund expanse of her abdomen. The uncomfortable, corset-like bellyband she had worn on and off for the past six months had done little to help her slim down. For a moment, her thoughts drifted back to the woman she had been before assuming the mantle of motherhood. In those days, she could slip with ease into her size-two skinny jeans, and her greatest fear was turning into a fat Indian *gharwali*, a housewife whose only accomplishments consisted of accumulating babies and blubber. *Just look at yourself now.* She felt old before her time, frumpy and unattractive, and could hardly bear to let Sameer touch her. She knew he was only being polite when he told her that she looked as beautiful now as the day they met.

Oh, how she longed for those days when she found sanctuary in her husband's embrace, longed for those endless hours of tenderness and all their tireless passion. Above all, she missed their frantic lovemaking—in every room, on every surface, and using positions of such acrobatic virtuosity that even the *Kama Sutra* had failed to catalogue them. *But what man would want to seduce a woman with a sagging stomach like this?* In disgust, she clutched at the gelatinous flesh with both hands, lamenting the oversized skirts that her too-generous hips now compelled her to wear.

I'm tired of dressing in gunny sacks, she declared to herself. With a fresh resolve, Rhea turned away from the mirror and smoothed down her shirt. Soon this too would change. She would get into shape again and, with the intrusive presence of her mother-in-law exorcised from the house, she would begin to win back her husband's affections. Picturing this satisfying tableau in her mind's eye, she was filled with a profound sense of peace.

The sudden, insistent jingling of Rhea's cell phone lying on the daybed shattered her euphoric calm. She lunged for the device, but too late to silence it. Avinash stirred from his sleep and began whimpering. She glanced down at the screen. It was a text message from her husband—

> Today is mom's birthday, and I want to take you both
> out to a nice dinner. It will be just like old times.
> Leave the baby with Radha for the evening and meet
> us in front of Indigo at 7 P.M. Let's celebrate!
>
> Sameer

Rhea wanted to scream.

She felt the incandescent glow of impending triumph fade quickly from view, like the flame of a candle snuffed out in a pitch-black room. So this is how it was to be. She would never realise her dreams. Karuna had won after all.

Avinash was crying loudly now, demanding immediate attention. Rhea scooped him up from the daybed, a little too roughly perhaps, though with the sole intent of consoling him. She cooed softly and smothered him with kisses, but to no avail. Holding him tight against her breast, she felt at least a little thankful that Karuna was not present in the room to witness her daughter-in-law's defeat. She did not think that she could tolerate the look of pity and disapproval that would be lavished upon her by that despicable woman. Others may fault her for leaving the baby alone with the nanny, or scoff at her failure to soothe him now, but Rhea knew that she was a good mother—*an excellent mother!*—devoted to her child and attentive to a fault. She did not care what Karuna or anyone else might think of her. Their judgements were not her concern. *Let people see what they want to see.*

~

People see what they want to see. An Indian woman smoking a cigarette is viewed, at least by her own people, as being morally corrupt. Mannat Jogi did not care much about what others thought of her, but she was not inclined to ignite a revolution either. She sat down on the bench under the awning of her balcony, secluded from the prying eyes of those who would look askance at such scandalous conduct, and lit a cigarette.

"People see what they want to see." That is what her father had once told her when she asked whether anyone ever doubted the accuracy of his predictions, especially if they happened to be unfavourable. A man of modest circumstances, the *cablewala* installed and repaired cable television services in bucolic Srinagar for a living. To supplement his meagre income from that line of work, he also served a few families in the neighbourhood as their trusted *jyotishi*. "What the planets decree and the heart desires are two different things," he continued. "All I can do is show my clients their charts and explain what I think the future holds for them. How they choose to act on that knowledge is up to them. But fate is a funny thing. Sometimes their wishes do come true, no matter what the planets may say." He gave his daughter's long, black hair an affectionate caress. "After all, my sweet child, why do you think we named you *Mannat*?" He had already seen early signs of her gift for prognostication, and the hope that she might follow in his footsteps filled him with paternal pride. She grasped her father's hand and levelled her wide, earnest eyes at his.

"Papa, why don't we look at your chart?" she said. "Maybe you could become rich, and then we can buy a big television!"

Grinning at that memory of the little inquisitive girl brimming with questions, and the wise father who always seemed to have the right answers, Mannat took a long, deep, satisfying drag on her cigarette and gazed out from underneath the balcony awning. The rain—now little more than a light drizzle—provided some added cover for the clandestine pleasure. Mere rain, however, did not seem to deter her nosy neighbour in the new high-rise across the way. Almost every afternoon over the past week she had noticed the man out on *his* balcony, flagrantly aiming a pair of binoculars in her direction, and today was no exception. From this distance she could not get a clear view of his features, though she felt quite certain that he was bald. *And no doubt excessively hairy everywhere else, with yellow teeth and bad breath to boot.* However hideous he may be in other respects, he did seem unusually tall, almost as if he were walking on stilts. *How he stares at me!* She knew that calling the police would accomplish exactly nothing. It was at moments like these that she missed her husband the most. *Amar would have set him right, that ogler.*

Pushing aside the unflattering images of the brazen voyeur that her mind had conjured up, the clairvoyant puffed contentedly on her cigarette and turned her attention to the cherished collection of rose plants adorning her balcony. Amid a swirl of smoke that followed her around like a ghostly presence, she drifted from container to container, examining the leaves of her prolific floribundas for any sign of black rot, which was a constant risk in monsoon season. *So far, so good.* With her free hand, she clipped off a few stray withered flower heads, along with several unruly branches. She loved colour, and her balcony garden pleased her much. But it required work and unflagging vigilance. *Pick pick pick pick.*

The faint, anxious chirping of a bird that had lately taken roost somewhere above the awning reminded her of the preciousness and fragility of life. She took another deep drag from her cigarette, thinking about the phone conversation she had just finished with her friend in Mussoorie, whose husband had fallen gravely ill and who, most likely, would soon join Mannat in the ranks of widowhood. "Tell me what is going to happen," Kaveri had begged. Saddened by her friend's impending bereavement, the clairvoyant wished (as she sometimes did) that the future would simply arrive unannounced. What good was this ability to sense the nebulous shape of a dear friend's looming misfortune—as if through an out-of-focus telescope—if she could do nothing to avert it?

"*Jyotishis* must not use their gift for personal advantage," her father had warned. "You can help build *mahals* for others, but never live in them yourself. That is your *kismet*, your destiny."

The ineluctable truth of this statement had become painfully evident when Mannat and her husband, who longed for a child, repeatedly failed to coax life out of her inhospitable uterus. Not quite finished with her, kismet then rubbed her nose into that truth by neglecting to warn her about the sightseeing bus that would collide into Amar and erase his future entirely.

Mannat stubbed out her cigarette in one of the flowerpots. Convinced that the nicotine residue in the filter acted as a natural pesticide that would help keep aphids and other destructive insects at bay, she pushed the butt deep into the soil, then stepped back inside the apartment. The next client would be arriving soon, and she had to prepare. Her post-cigarette ritual involved chewing on a chunk of vanilla bean, followed by the application of several small drops of jasmine oil on her hands to mask the odour of tobacco. While vigorously rubbing the oil into her skin, she surveyed with a small ache of nostalgia the souvenirs lovingly displayed in a large vitrine that dominated the room—a porcelain windmill from Amsterdam, a brass sphinx from Cairo, the carved stone visage of a Mayan deity from Mexico and many more. Each had a story to tell, and she could recount them in her mind with the ease that comes from constant practice.

Once upon a time, Mannat and Amar worked hard and saved well. With no children of their own to feed, clothe and educate, they had vacationed often and far afield. Amar was a kind, easygoing man who shared her love of *chai* and tobacco, and together they roamed the world, indulging their mutual fascination with its architectural wonders. Upon their return from each trip, she would transfer the scenes of their expeditions from memory to canvas in the form of impressionistic landscapes, some of which she kept, though most she sold to the owners of small tourist hotels seeking to add artistic flair, at a reasonable price, to the walls of their humble establishments. Who knows how many thousands of visitors to Mumbai had meandered past her ethereal paintings and drawings, which hung in lobbies and hallways and other impersonal public spaces throughout the vast city, without giving them so much as a cursory glance? Had they paused to look, all would have agreed that she was quite good. Yet, however impressive her skill as an artist, it was her indisputable talent as a clairvoyant that had brought her renown. After her husband died, she lost all desire to travel, but instead threw herself wholly into that work, finding solace at last not among friends but in the company of strangers who needed her help.

She entered the consultation room to welcome her next visitor. Like a schoolteacher, Mannat sometimes chose favourites without consciously wishing to. She took an instant liking to her last client of the day, an athletically built woman with a salt-and-pepper mane like hers. The modish cut of her hair—recently done, by the look of it—left an impression all the more favourable precisely because it had not been dyed back to a more youthful colour, which would have seemed affected on this woman. The pale blue *salwar kameez* that she wore combined with a few spare pieces of jewellery and an embroidered *dupatta*, which added a splash of red to the woman's ensemble, gave her an air of understated but unmistakable elegance. Even at the end of middle age, she still looked quite beautiful. Yet that beauty could not mask the underlying sadness lurking in her eyes.

"Someone in my yoga class raved about you," the woman began, smiling amiably. "Though I have to confess, I am a bit apprehensive about meddling with fate. For that matter, it would take a lot to convince me that it's even possible. If it were as easy as reciting some mantra or keeping a fast to manipulate the future, wouldn't everyone do it? But I'm at the end of my rope with my daughter-in-law and need to do something. If you are unwilling to take on a sceptic like me as a client, I would completely understand."

The woman's candour was refreshing. Usually it was the other way around. Most of the clients who came to Mannat *auntie* professed unquestioning confidence in her abilities. They begged, sometimes literally on their knees, to see the celebrated clairvoyant and swore to do preposterous things—climb barefoot up the mountain to the Vaishno Devi shrine, tattoo their flesh with prayers from the Upanishads, pay her in real gold—whatever it took to appease, persuade, or bribe the higher forces and bend those forces to human will.

"It may shock you to hear this," Mannat said with a chuckle, "especially from me. But frankly, faith is overrated. The future comes to us, or we to it, one way or another. It doesn't matter what you believe. All I can do is help you discern what is possible and then guide you toward an outcome that you can live with."

"Good," the woman said, visibly relieved. "Then I suppose we should get on with it. Forgive me, but I've never done this before. Will it take long? I only ask because my son is meeting me for dinner later this evening and I don't want to be late."

"It can take as much or as little time as you need. Please have a seat and let's begin. We don't want to keep your son waiting! What's the occasion?" The pair continued to converse a while longer, with the clairvoyant posing a series of probing questions, and her new client answering them with singular honesty. Finally, Mannat took the woman's hands in her own, noticing immediately how cold her thin, knobby fingers felt. "Now, do you know what you want to wish for?"

"Yes, I think so. I am ready."

Mannat watched her client as she closed her eyes and bowed her head, as if in prayer. The session concluded within minutes. The woman withdrew her hands and opened and closed her fists a few times.

"The yoga should help with the circulation. Keep up with your practice."

"What? How did you—? Don't answer that. You'll make a believer of me yet. But thank you, Mannat. And don't be offended if I decline to call you *auntie*. You're younger than I am!"

"That's fine," the clairvoyant laughed.

As Karuna stood up to leave, her glance fell on the incomplete painting on the easel behind Mannat. She walked closer for a better look.

"Is this your work?" she asked.

"Yes, it is. I've been meaning to finish it, but I'm afraid I may have lost my touch."

"It's beautiful. It reminds me of my hometown Nainital."

"Well, it appears we have something in common! I'm from the north as well. I miss the sight of beautiful hills outside my window."

"I know exactly how you feel. How did you end up in Mumbai?

"Fate!"

They both laughed.

"I want to hear all about it. Go on," Karuna insisted.

"Well, my father had arranged for me to marry Amar, the son of his distant cousin in Mumbai whom I had never met. I was rather surprised at how my father had secured such a good match. After all, Amar had a real job in a big city and our family could barely make ends meet. Surely his family would demand a big dowry, I thought."

Karuna sat back down, eager to hear the life-altering events of Mannat's life.

"I saw Amar for the first time on the day of the engagement. He walked with a limp—a result of polio, I was told. I understood immediately why a man of his financial standing had settled for me. His handicap had lowered his prospects of finding a wellborn girl with a sizeable dowry in tow." Mannat eased herself into a chair and carried on, aware of how the tables had turned, for now she was the one sharing her life with a stranger, documenting her path from little to plenty. "But Amar's disability did not bother me."

"Good for you."

"Yes, it all worked out well."

"You've had a good life, by the looks of it," Karuna said, admiring the array of curios in the vitrine. "And a well-travelled one."

"Yes. Amar's job as a travel agent allowed us to sate our wanderlust," Mannat said with a wistful look in her eyes. "Unfortunately, he passed away a few years ago. I don't travel anymore."

"I am sorry to hear that," Karuna said, acutely aware of the magnitude of Mannat's loss. "Such is life."

"Oh dear! Look at the time!" Mannat exclaimed suddenly, "You'd better hurry or you'll be late for your birthday dinner!"

After the client had left, Mannat summoned her maid into the consultation room. "Please cancel all my appointments for tomorrow. Plans have changed." While Kanta made the calls, Mannat stepped out onto the balcony to enjoy her roses at the end of the day. Lighting a cigarette, she stole a glance at the building across the way. He was still there, watching her—the man with the binoculars.

~

The man with the binoculars scanned slowly left, then right, and back again. "Don't be shy," he whispered slyly to himself, then abruptly stopped in mid-motion. *There you are—beautiful!* He had found what he was looking for. *But what happened to the other one?* A flash of red caught his eye, and he zeroed in on it, turning the centre focus knob ever so slightly. *Ah-ha! Thought you could hide from me, did you?* He only wished he could hear their chatter, but alas they were too far away.

In his excitement, he barely noticed that Orff's *Carmina Burana*, his favourite piece of music, had begun playing on the CD player positioned directly behind him. He let the expensive Bushnells hang loose around his neck while he leaned down and made a brief entry in a notebook lying open on the table in front of him. '*Pycnonotus cafer*—2,' he wrote, jotting beside it the date, time, and location of the sighting. Then he poured himself a cup of steaming chai from a thermos, took a quick sip, and without wasting another moment picked up the binoculars, pressed the eyecups against the gold-rimmed Gandhi-style spectacles he wore, and resumed his observations. *Short, dark crest...brownish body with lighter feathers below...and of course the telltale daub of crimson underneath the white rump*—now that the rain had at last begun to let up and he could get a clear view, there was no doubt in his mind. The birds roosting in the eaves of the dilapidated building across the way were red-vented bulbuls. *A mating pair, no less, if I'm not mistaken.* He would have to add that to the notation, once he was sure.

He welcomed with a profound sense of relief the imminent end of the monsoons. The non-stop precipitation made his regular outdoor activities all but impossible; and he had lately begun to feel caged in by the forest of modern high-rises that surrounded his own. Their sleek, shiny surfaces and angular corners were largely inhospitable to most birdlife and provided at best only a temporary perch. Given the painfully limited view from his balcony, he considered himself fortunate that at least one of the old buildings, with its multitude of nooks and crannies, had not yet been razed and still offered a suitable home to something more interesting than a few common pigeons.

A tall man with a long face, hazel eyes, prominent chin, and receding hairline, Dr. Sanjay Deshpande had come to birding relatively late in life. Or rather, it had come to him. In fact, he was hardly aware that such a thing existed until he overheard a nurse at Hinduja Hospital boasting about what a lucrative salary her husband earned as a local guide for birdwatchers. Intrigued, he picked up a second-hand copy of the *Clements Checklist* and began spending his weekends in Borivali National Park, as did so many other like-minded enthusiasts, learning to recognise the distinctive calls, plumage, and behaviour that differentiated India's abundant avifauna. He had developed an elaborate taxonomic record of individual species; and he could speak with authority on subjects like Malabar larks, laughing doves, pied kingfishers, crimson sunbirds, and a dozen others.

Bookish and naturally reserved, with an equal penchant for scientific inquiry, medieval philosophy, and the poetry of the English Romantics, Dr. Deshpande had found in this new pastime the ideal complement to his particular sensibilities. Not lost on him was the irony that the pursuit of his hobby, which gave him immense pleasure, originated in deep personal loss. That spring he had booked a birdwatching excursion to Spain through Cox & Kings, where his sole companion was the prized pair of field glasses, purchased expressly for the trip. The long overdue vacation was also his first visit abroad. Until then, he had never envisaged travelling alone. Indeed, given his late wife's fear of flying, he had never travelled very far outside the city. When an ectopic pregnancy resulted in Sevati's untimely death—a calamity that Dr. Deshpande, reputed to be one of the finest obstetricians in Mumbai, could do nothing to prevent—he doggedly buried himself in his practice in order to escape the grief that had consumed him. Whenever concerned colleagues probed the doctor about his excessive workload and ungodly pace, he reassured them by saying, "My *dharma* is to work, so that I can give." It was only after he took up birding that he began to live fully once again.

His stomach gave a loud grumble, an audible reminder that it was almost time for his evening meal, which he would prepare (as he did every evening) with surgical precision. Once it was cooked, he would serve the food to himself at a table designed to accommodate six and consume it in his customary manner—hastily, silently, and in perfect solitude.

However insistent his hunger pangs, today he did not much relish the chore awaiting him in the kitchen. Though a creature of habit—much like his winged friends— Dr. Deshpande had long ago grown weary of solo dining. Preoccupied with his birds and brooding thoughts, he began absentmindedly mouthing the words of the cantata playing in the background, which he knew by heart—

> Fortunæ rota volvitur
> descendo minoratus
> alter in altum tollitur...

Much as he missed his sweet Sevati, he was at last learning to let her go. What he had felt most keenly during his tour of Spanish birding sites was not her absence but his own loneliness. Despite the somewhat alarming onset of alopecia, he knew he did not look his age. A healthy vegetarian diet and a regimen of brisk walks at the crack of dawn helped keep the years off and his core tight. Now that a longing for the warmth of female companionship had made its tentative return, he had no idea how to proceed. He found the prospect of dating ridiculously daunting. How did one ask a woman out these days? What would people say? Surely, the nurses would gossip and giggle behind his back.

With a wry smile at his own expense, Dr. Deshpande thought that perhaps he could learn a thing or two about courtship from the two red-vented bulbuls across the way, whom he had christened 'Boethius' and 'Rusticiana.' In the course of his observations, he had not failed to notice the handsome woman who occupied the apartment above where the birds had built their nest. Half hidden behind a veil of cigarette smoke, and standing amid the profusion of roses that took up much of the space on her balcony, she resembled some mysterious nature spirit or flower-bedecked Hindu deity. She also appeared to be unmarried, for he had never spotted a man on her balcony. Not knowing her name, he had bestowed on her the title 'Sultana of the Nightingales.' On a few occasions she had glanced in his direction, and his physical reaction had surprised him—his pulse began to race and he could feel his skin flush. The doctor wondered if someone like that would ever care to accompany him on his weekend jaunts through Borivali.

A dreadful thought suddenly occurred to him—*What if she thinks I'm spying on her?* Not a little embarrassed, he hastily slipped the binoculars into their case and began gathering up the rest of his things. *Just as well–it's time to go inside anyway.* He had a long, busy day ahead of him tomorrow, with early-morning rounds at the hospital and an afternoon crowded with patient appointments in his office. He needed to eat dinner and then go straight to bed.

~

"Go straight to bed, young man," Karuna commanded in a peremptory whisper. "Your wife is waiting for you."

Ignoring her injunction, Sameer kicked off his wet shoes and followed his mother from the front foyer into her bedroom. "Just a little while longer, mom. Besides, if Rhea is asleep, I might wake her up when I go in. And you know that never turns out well."

"Keep your voice down!" she said, softly shutting the bedroom door.

Sameer continued as if he hadn't heard her. "Did you like the restaurant? Without question they make the best chocolate soufflé in the city."

"Yes, it was divine. I ate too much, and I think maybe you drank too much–just like your father." She gave him a peck on the cheek. "Thank you for remembering my birthday."

"What kind of son forgets his mother's birthday?" Sameer said. "I only wish dad could have been there. I miss him."

"I do too. But he's gone, and life is for the living. It's a shame Rhea wasn't able to join us. She sure could do with an evening out." Karuna sat down cross-legged next to Sameer, who lay face down on the bed, his feet dangling off the edge.

"I texted her in the afternoon, telling her to come," he protested. "How was I to know she would send the nanny home early? It's not my fault!"

"It is nobody's fault, Sameer. But you have to understand that you're a parent now. You can't just make plans on the spur of the moment, like you used to. Try to be more considerate toward her."

"Believe me, Mama, I want to. But every time I offer to give her a break from Avinash or show her any affection, she just pushes me away."

"I know." She shot her son a pitying look. "Having a baby changes a woman in inexplicable ways."

Sameer thought about that for a moment. "Then tell me—did you drive dad crazy like this when I was born?"

"Why, of course I did," she answered, ruffling his hair. "You were quite a handful! But at least Rhea has some help from the nanny, which is more than I had. You should ask her whether she has thought about returning to work. It might be good for her to get out of the house. She needn't worry about leaving the child behind for a few hours. Radha is very reliable. And I'm always here."

"That's what I think. But Rhea says she's not ready, that our son needs her. Maybe in a few more months."

Karuna let out a long sigh and turned toward the nightstand, squinting through her spectacles to see the clock. She covered her mouth to conceal a yawn. "My goodness, look at the time! You should go to your room now."

"One more minute, please."

"Not one more second! It's late. If you don't listen to me, I will leave for Nainital first thing tomorrow." After a pause, they both snorted with suppressed laughter, recalling the many times that Karuna had extracted compliance from her husband with the same threat.

Sameer reluctantly sat up, and his expression suddenly grew serious. "I've lost dad; I can't lose you as well. No matter what happens, I need you to stay here with me. You can't leave. Promise me."

Karuna had told no one about her visit to Mannat Jogi earlier that day, and now she thought about the wish she had made in the fortune teller's consultation room—*Please let something happen that will free me from this tense, unhappy house, so full of painful reminders, and give me a reason to go home to Nainital.* She did not want to upset her son by revealing the secret desire that she had been harbouring in her soul for months. Yet she did not want to lie to him either. Looking him in the eye, she placed her hand on his chest, directly over his heart, and said, "Don't worry, I will always be here."

With these words, Karuna saw his lower lip begin to tremble, and she feared he might burst into tears any moment. "All right, that's enough talking for one night, my son. Off with you!" She playfully shooed him out of the room, sealing the door behind him with a firm "Good night."

Undressing for bed, Karuna thought about Sameer's predicament, and she wondered if his recent tendency toward clinginess might be part of the problem, or just a symptom. What he said was true, though. Rhea had not made it easy for anyone, least of all herself. She insisted on bearing all the burdens of child-rearing, when clearly they could be shared. The monsoons had not helped either.

Cooped up in the nursery with a colicky child all day, week after week, and barely sleeping at night—was it any wonder she had become so sullen and unapproachable?

More than once Karuna had been tempted to sit down with Rhea for a serious woman-to-woman discussion, but then always thought better of it. She remembered all too vividly the torture of living under the same roof with her own mother-in-law, a domineering woman who controlled her life with an iron grip. To this day she felt the sting of humiliation in having to beg that miser of a woman for a few rupees to buy sanitary napkins every month. The young couple, newlyweds bound to tradition, had little choice in the matter. Karuna's husband knew that failure to submit his entire salary to the matriarch of their household would result in a diatribe against his wife for being a corrupting influence, and so he had stayed silent for the sake of peace. For years, the couple endured the old lady's tyranny with stoic patience. All Karuna could do, by way of rebellion, was to make a solemn oath to herself—when the time came, she would never act in such an imperious manner toward *her* daughter-in-law. Still mindful of that long-ago resolve, she had deliberately and conscientiously given Rhea complete freedom to manage the house, her husband, and now her own child.

Perhaps, after all, I should have intervened. It was not too late, Karuna thought, trying to get comfortable on the narrow bed. *Tomorrow I will talk to her.*

She fell into a deep sleep almost as soon as her head hit the pillow.

~

The pillow somehow developed a crimp during the night, which pressed against her wrist for hours while she slept. And because of the narrowness of the bed, she had lain in an odd position, cutting off circulation to the other arm as well. Thus, when Karuna awoke at 8:01 A.M., her first conscious thought was that she could feel no sensation whatsoever in either hand. What actually awakened her, however, was an unpleasant and unexpected reveille. Rhea had burst into the bedroom, cradling a crying baby in her arms, and now stood over the bed with rage boiling in her eyes and her breath coming out in shallow hisses. Karuna sat bolt upright and began fumbling for her glasses on the nightstand to see what the matter was, but her inert fingers stubbornly refused to respond. It was as if they did not even exist.

"You think I'm crazy, do you?" Rhea accused in a disquietingly calm tone. "That I should get out of the house and leave my son? With *you*?"

Still half asleep and disoriented, Karuna got out of bed and tried to make sense of what she was hearing. "Rhea, what are you talking about?"

"Don't deny it. I heard you both through that door last night, talking about me. And now you've told Sameer that you'll be here forever. I thought as much. Since we both know you are never going to leave, why not make yourself useful? Here, take him!"

She thrust the wailing Avinash into Karuna's hands—the hands that had become useless appendages incapable of movement or response, like two slabs of frozen meat. When the baby slammed against the marble floor, the crown of his head was the first point of contact.

Karuna gasped in disbelief, shocked at how suddenly quiet the room had become.

~

Sameer gasped in disbelief. The peaceful, early morning calm in his office had been shattered in one calamitous instant. No sooner did he arrive at his desk that the frantic, nearly incomprehensible phone call came in from Rhea. Avinash had been hurt, and Karuna was driving them to Hinduja Hospital. In the background he could hear the blaring of car horns and the screeching of tyres. Still groggy and a little hung over from the night before, he tried to connect the pieces of his wife's disjointed narrative. There was no mistaking the terror in her voice. Then he heard Karuna yell, "We're here—get out, get out. Hurry!"

Sameer rushed to the hospital, driving at breakneck speed through water-slicked streets, expecting to meet them there; but when he entered the busy emergency ward, they were nowhere to be seen.

He had spent the last 30 minutes making repeated inquiries at the reception desk, and he was told the same maddening thing—"Be patient, sir. Someone will be with you shortly." In the meantime he anxiously paced the floor, dodging the chaotic procession of speeding gurneys propelled by oblivious EMTs while trying in vain to reach his wife on her cell phone. Where was Rhea? Where was his mother? Why would no one speak to him? *What the hell was going on?* He felt lost amid the roiling mass of doctors, nurses, orderlies, and the steady stream of Mumbai's sick and injured citizens entering the crowded ward in search of healing.

Nearly out of his mind with worry and exhaustion, he slumped into an empty chair. Suddenly, a face he recognised separated itself from the throng and approached him. It was their obstetrician.

"Dr. Deshpande! Can you help me? I'm looking for Rhea and Avinash. No one at the front desk seems to—"

"Ah, Mr. Malhotra, there you are. Yes, your mother brought them both here and as luck would have it, this is my day for hospital rotation. I bumped into your wife at the entrance and personally took charge of the case. She said you might be arriving soon. Apologies for the holdup. I had a few things to take care of before I could go looking for you. Where is Mrs. Malhotra, by the way?"

"I was going to ask you the same thing. Rhea's not with you?"

"No. Perhaps she—"

"Is my son all right? I need to see him."

"In a few minutes, Mr. Malhotra. He's being examined by the hospital's top paediatric surgeon, a colleague of mine who owes me a favour. Avinash is in very good hands." Towering over Sameer, the doctor wiped the sweat from his balding head with the back of his sleeve and gazed solemnly at the distraught father. "I won't lie to you. Your son took quite a blow to the head, and his condition appears to be rather serious. But I promise we are doing everything we can. Just wait right here. As soon as we know more, I will come find you."

"Will Avinash be all right?"

"I'm sorry, I must go now," Dr. Deshpande said, and began walking away. Suddenly, he stopped and swung around to face Sameer, his keen hazel eyes radiating kindness and sympathy. "Considering the circumstances, you gave your son a good name. That makes me optimistic." Then he was gone.

Sameer slumped back down into the chair, his eyes scanning the crowd for Rhea and his mother. *Where is everybody?* Alone and anxious, he began weeping uncontrollably.

~

Weeping uncontrollably, Rhea bolted from the still-moving taxi, ran inside the dilapidated building, raced up the three flights of stairs, and finally came to a halt in front of the fortune teller's apartment. Before she could even knock to demand entrance, the door swung open to receive her. "I must see you right now, Mannat *auntie*," she begged. "It's about Avinash. I made a terrible mistake. Please let me take my wish back. I have to save my son."

Wordlessly, Mannat ushered her client inside and then led her through the apartment, past the consultation room and the vitrine of souvenirs.

"Where are you taking me?" Rhea asked. They stepped out onto the balcony, awash now in sunshine and bright with rose blossoms. The monsoons were over at last. Mannat gestured toward a teary-eyed Karuna sitting on the bench.

"I believe the two of you know each other."

Mithaiwala

Life is divided into three terms—that which was, which is,
and which will be. Let us learn from the past to profit
by the present, and from the present, to live better in
the future.

–William Wordsworth

"Arranged marriages in this day and age? Unbelievable!" Julie
Preston handed Veer the day's *Atlanta Journal-Constitution*
and pointed to the article about Indian couples in their
city who had been set up by their parents. "Have you read
this?" she asked, scrunching her angular face in disapproval.

"No, I have not. I have more pressing matters on my
mind," Veer responded, staring fixedly at his laptop. He
was busy preparing for a design charette later in the day.
As one of the lead architects for Preston Design Group,
a prestigious architectural firm in midtown Atlanta, Veer
had no time to spare.

"I know you and Elizabeth did not have an arranged
marriage, but what about your sister back in India?" Julie

pressed on, intruding yet again into his personal life. Had she not been the president of the firm, and the daughter of the owner, Veer would have told her off. He was a private man; his family was his business and his alone. Besides, Veer was an outlier among Atlanta's community of Indian expats; subscribing to time-worn traditions was not his thing. That included not just his marriage partner but his choice of career as well. The memory of his father made a sudden entrance in Veer's mind. *If I had adhered to the blueprint that Papa laid out for me, I would have settled for becoming a* mithaiwala *selling Indian desserts*—laddoos, gulab jamuns, jalebis, kaju katlis—*for a living.*

"Yes, my sister had an arranged marriage. And she has been happily married for years," Veer answered Julie, and he waited for the barrage of question he knew she would pose next. He purposely withheld the juicy details he knew she craved—the specifics of his father's arduous hunt for the perfect groom—the kind one would conduct if searching for a pearl in a box full of white buttons—and how Laksha, his little sister, had willingly married a man she had met only twice, each time before an audience composed of well-meaning parents and restless siblings.

"Wow! That is incredible," said Julie. "So tell me, did your parents have to twist the poor girl's arm?" she asked, laughing a humourless laugh, her unnaturally plump lips shaped into a practiced smile. The woman spent more time at her dermatologist's clinic than she did in her own office. *She probably self-injects Botox with breakfast every morning,* Veer thought to himself, repulsed by her synthetic beauty.

"No. They did not coerce my sister into marriage," he said dryly.

He told the meddlesome woman nothing about his own bewilderment. Laksha's acquiescence to the life-binding dictate of marriage without the faintest murmur of dissent had confounded Veer. In his mind, he revisited his conversation with his sister from years ago.

"You do not even know this man, Laksha! Don't you want to fall in love with somebody, and then think about marriage?" he had asked, perplexed by her prenuptial enthusiasm.

"I trust Papa's decision, Veer. And I am just so happy to be getting married," she had responded, her voice rich with inexplicable joy. In Veer's opinion, arranged marriages robbed people of valuable life experiences in the name of planned happiness.

But he shared none of this with Julie.

"You do realise this contract is really important for the company, Julie. The presentation has to be flawless. There is no room for error." It annoyed Veer no end that the woman had been handed the reins to the firm even though she had neither the acumen nor the experience to run a successful business of this scale. She had quite simply inherited the enterprise. *The Gods who rule us have a strange sense of humour*, Veer reflected. *This incompetent woman is handed a major architectural firm. And what was I bequeathed? A little mithai shop.*

"Yes, I know this is an important contract, but you don't need to get so wound up, Veer," Julie cooed softly, closing the distance between them with one long stride on her extraordinarily high heels. She pushed aside the stack of files on Veer's desk and eased her narrow hips on the glass top, allowing the ends of her wraparound dress to separate just so. "But you know, you look so darn handsome when you are serious." She leaned forward and traced the side of Veer's stern face with a long, delicate finger. He caught a whiff of her floral perfume, and with it, an eyeful of her recently augmented breasts.

Fourteen years and 80 pounds ago Veer had been practically invisible to the opposite sex. But that was then, when he habitually gorged on *mithais*. And now? Julie Preston, desirable to most men with her contrived sexiness, was in his face, proffering herself to him.

"Seriously, Julie. Cut it out. I have work to do." Veer refused to be distracted one more second by the show of insincere coquetry.

He ignored her advances in the same way he had taught himself to disregard the insults hurled at him in boarding school. "*Motu Mithaiwala!*" the kids called after him. "Got anything good for us, you fat sweet seller?" Eventually, as the years went by, Veer learned to muzzle his reactions, for engaging with the offenders often left him with little more than an assortment of colourful bruises—dark purplish brown patches that looked like mouldy *gulab jamuns*.

~

"Take it easy, man!"
"Sorry. I didn't mean to hit that hard."
"Bad day at work, eh?"
"Yeah, something like that."

"We've all had one of those. Hold this up," the trainer said, lifting the punching bag Veer had inadvertently knocked down. "I'll hook it back on." Veer took off his boxing gloves and held up the bag as the agile man hopped up on a stool and grabbed the chains. "Done. You can go at it again. You know, I've never met a brown dude who can hit as hard as you!" he said with a laugh.

On any other day, Veer would have taken no note of the innocuous comment, but today was different. The word *brown* stung him like a bee. "I think I am done for the day," he said, and tossed his gloves in his gym bag.

"Yeah, you look pretty beat. Get some rest. Guess I'll see you tomorrow."

"I don't know about tomorrow. Not sure if I'll be back," Veer said, unravelling his hand wraps despondently. *I'm going to miss this gym,* he thought to himself, taking one last look at the poster of Muhammad Ali mounted on the wall behind the punching bag. The gym, his office across the street, his livelihood—he was going to miss it all.

What the hell am I going to do?

Earlier that evening, Veer had quit his job at the Preston Design Group. It had been an impulsive decision. And Veer was not an impulsive man. Rather, he was methodical, structured. He planned every move in precise detail. And yet here he was, in the middle of a crowded gym, halfway through his regular workout regimen, unsure of where and how to spend the next hour, let alone the next day, or month, or year.

All because the conservative white client had wanted him off the project that he had designed. "I do not want some brown-ass fellow from a third-world country working on my building. We don't need those monkey-God-loving labourers. This is a pure-bred American dream," he had said, thumping the conference table with his beefy fist. When Julie capitulated to his demands, Veer quit. Just like that.

"I thought I might catch you here." Julie's high-pitched voice bored into his head like a brad point drill bit. To Veer's dismay, Julie was a member of the gym as well. Though he was careful never to work out with her, it was inevitable that they would often run into each other here on their free time. "I'm sorry about how things turned out today. I would have found a way to put you back on the team eventually. But you did not even give me a chance. You just flew off the handle."

Liar.

"No Julie," Veer countered, mouthing unedited thoughts, "I think you would have made me work on the project because you need me. It is, after all, my design, my vision, and it is brilliant. But you would have kept the truth from that bigot. I would have been invisible."

"Maybe so, but our work would have been celebrated. Isn't that all that matters?"

"No, it is not. I will be seen for who I really am—not some diminutive Indian guy, but a man who designs lofty, magnificent buildings." At five-feet-six-inches, Veer revelled in erecting tall structures, making up in brick and mortar what he lacked in physical stature.

"Oh Veer, don't be so difficult," she purred. Julie placed her palms on his sweat-sodden T-shirt and looked into his intense brown eyes. "You know we can be great together.

Daddy thinks you are very talented; after all, you were fresh out of design school when he hired you. He has grand plans for you. For us. I need you by my side."

"No." Veer peeled her perfectly manicured hands off his chest.

"Come on, let's get a drink and talk things over," Julie insisted. "Let's have some fun tonight, and I'll fix everything." She moved closer, squeezing out the last few inches of personal space between them.

"No," he repeated firmly.

"Don't do this Veer. I really care about you."

"No you don't, Julie. You don't give a shit about me, about who I am."

"Yes, I do care, and of course I know who you are."

"Is that so?" Veer felt the reigns of his emotions slipping away from his grasp.

"Yes."

"Then tell me, Miss Preston, what is my full name?"

"What kind of question is that?"

"Answer me."

"Fine. Veer Kumar."

"Raghuveer. My name is Raghuveer Kumar. Named after Lord Rama. I was born and raised in India."

"I knew that," she said calmly.

"And yet you did nothing when that bigot insulted me and my people?"

"Frankly Veer, I am a bit confused by your sudden love for India. In all the years that I have known you, you never liked talking about anything Indian. Gosh, I don't think you even have any Indian friends. You carry this chip on your shoulder, like you are better than the rest of them. So why this...this fuss about 'my people'?"

"Just because I choose to keep my distance does not mean that I do not care about them," Veer said, taking a stance like a boxer in the ring poised for a fight.

"Well then, if you love your people so damn much, why did you leave them and come to this country?" Julie hissed.

He wanted to hit her. He could knock her out with a left hook. He would have too, had he not remembered his mother's admonishment, "Raghuveer, you may never, ever hit a girl."

My life is none of your business, Veer wanted to scream at Julie. He did not need to explain to anybody why he left his land, his home, his mother, when he should have stayed by her side, or why he chose never to go back. Rather than give expression to his anguish and outrage, he did as his mother had taught him—he loosened his fists and walked away from the annoying woman.

Veer drove off in the direction of his home without the intent of actually getting there.

No, I cannot go home just yet. Not like this.

For the first time, he was grateful for the deluge of vehicles and pedestrians on North Highland Avenue. The eclectic Virginia Highlands neighbourhood in Atlanta is a hotspot for restaurant-seekers. Waiting for a mother with two petulant toddlers to cross the street, Veer noticed boutique windows outfitted for Christmas, though Halloween was barely over. Diwali, the festival of lights, could not be far off, he reckoned, but he had not checked on the exact date. On the Hindu calendar, festivals fall on different days every year, which made it difficult to keep up with tradition. It was a feeble excuse for the tragic neglect of a rich cultural heritage that in fact used to mean a great deal to him. His actions today evidenced that forgotten sentiment.

Veer powered down the windows of his Audi and inhaled the sweet autumn air.

It does not smell like Diwali, he thought. There were no traces of smoke from smouldering firecrackers, no aroma of delicious dinners waiting to be feasted upon after *Lakshmi puja.* And not a whiff of *mithai.*

Fourteen years had sped past since Veer had truly celebrated Diwali. It was at his home, in a small town cradled in the hills of northern India.

As the sun melted into the cerulean sky, fireworks illuminated that Diwali night, usurping the limelight from the stars for just that once. The homes of the entire neighbourhood, even the most modest, twinkled with electric lights and oil lamps. The origin of the festival lay in the felicitous return of Lord Rama after a 14-year exile from his kingdom. And now every flame, every bulb, was a beacon of light vanquishing darkness.

In the sharp focus of his memory, Veer's house stood out as especially bright and colourful, a majestic peak rising high above the foothills. From the variegated lights pulsating along the edges of their roof—each a *laddoo*-sized beating heart—to the beautifully displayed *thali* of colourful sweetmeats, Diwali was everywhere.

He remembered his mother and Laksha looking beautiful in their saris, especially Mama, draped in maroon silk with a smattering of gold flowers. Together, the trio created a beautiful circular *rangoli* pattern in the foyer. "It will welcome Lakshmi into our home," Mama explained, stressing the importance of such blessings from the Goddess of wealth. Instead of using a variety of grains and lentils, as they did the previous year, Mama chose an assortment of flowers—yellow and orange marigolds, red and pink roses, and fragrant white *rajnigandhas*. It was the most splendid *rangoli* they had ever constructed. Even Papa noticed how grand it was. "It's like the *kalachakra!*" he exclaimed. That was high praise indeed. All knew that the giant wheel of time traversing eternity was something vast and beautiful and balanced in its perfection, ever staying the course of its preordained purpose.

Unlike Veer.

It was that very night that Veer took a detour from a life charted for him by his father—a trajectory that set him on a path thousands of miles away from his family.

I left Mama, and now Mama is gone forever.

Veer pulled into the parking lot of the neighbourhood grocery store. He needed to think, to take stock of the day, to sift through the emotions churning in his head like pods of cardamom swirling in a pot of bubbling milk.

Sitting perfectly still behind the wheel and reflecting, he suddenly noticed an oilcloth sign next to the grocery store—*Grand Opening—Bombay Bazaar*. Veer stepped out of his car and stared at the sign. He was surprised to see a south Asian store in his neck of the woods—an all-white neighbourhood. The closest Indian store was in Decatur, nine miles away. Veer knew this, because the day he received the news of his mother's passing, he had run the entire distance to buy a box of *kaju katli*. The diamond-shaped pieces of congealed cashew nut paste and sugar were his absolute favourite.

And Mama's too.

He had not eaten them. In a corner of his backyard, Veer had set the box on fire, as if he were cremating the body of his mother, so far away.

Curious, Veer walked up to the shop and peeked inside. There were countless arrays of what appeared to be spices in clear glass jars. The far wall was lined with books and music CDs. Rolls of brightly coloured yoga mats stood tall in a wicker basket.

Veer detected the scent of cardamom by the door. His eyes lit up.

Perhaps they have mithai....

Not that he intended to eat any, of course. As the son of a sweet-vendor, he had fallen early in life into a remarkably intense but thoroughly predictable love affair with sugar. To the young boy, it was the panacea for all of life's ills and difficulties.

His family home abutted the *mithai* shop established by his grandfather. As a child, in the days preceding his boarding school years, Veer would rush through his homework and spend much of his free time at the shop. A consistent recipient of stellar grades, he was spared the after-school tutoring that his friends endured. And he almost always turned down their rare invitations to play cricket, preferring to stir cardamom-infused milk with a paddle-sized spatula to wielding a cricket bat.

Shankar *kaka*, a veteran cook at the shop, taught him all the family recipes as though they were precious life lessons. On sweltering afternoons, Veer would make his way to the air-condition section of the shop, and his father allowed him to sit behind the counter to play with his wooden blocks and toy cars. The cold white marble floor was transformed in his imagination into snowy tracks where hot wheels skidded and screeched. Tall buildings erupted suddenly from the floor, as if by magic, challenging the cars to navigate treacherous chicanes and execute daring aerial jumps.

Before long, Shankar *kaka* would bring Veer a *kulfi*. He had a special fondness for the boy, and so he was careful to select Veer's favourite flavour—saffron pistachio. Using his sharpest knife, Shankar *kaka* cut the frozen *kesar pista kulfi* into small cubes, just the way Veer liked. Sucking on each piece before letting his teeth crush into the *kulfi*, the boy feasted unhurriedly. Finally, he brought the plate to his lips, drinking up the last of the melted flavourful liquid with all its nutty remains.

On days when India beat Pakistan at cricket, Papa invited Veer to sit beside him at the cashier's desk. Sometimes he even indulged in conversation and inquired about school with genuine interest. But when the Indian team "played like girls"—which happened astonishingly often—Papa would recede into his hard shell and become stern and silent, except to reprimand him without cause. "Save your naughtiness for home, Raghuveer, this is no place for fun."

Maintaining a perfect front before the customers was paramount. The day a customer slipped on a rogue car that had escaped Veer's plump fingers, sending a dozen *besan laddoos* flying into the air, was his last at the shop.

The powdery mess of disintegrated gram flour balls on the floor resembled frost-covered horse turds. Amused by that incongruous analogy, he forgot to apologise to the irate customer, evoking his father's fury in an open-handed spanking. Shankar *kaka* rescued him from an encore and walked him home, feeding him a fresh saffron *peda* along the way to take his mind off the pain.

At night, Veer's mother nursed his wounded spirit with an unguent of soothing words and warm embraces.

"Papa means well; he loves you very much," she reassured him, stroking his forehead. "You know, he is like a *jalebi*—fiery orange and crisp on the outside, but soft and gooey on the inside."

Veer had sampled his father's love—measured doses of affection awarded for absolute obedience—and it was neither tender nor bountiful. Motherly instincts detected a rebellion simmering; she attempted to douse the sparks with soothing words as she held him close, but Veer slipped away from her grasp and into a world of his own making.

The syrupy scent of cardamom that clung to his mother seeped into Veer's dreams. His deliciously bizarre nocturnal adventures consisted of constructing gigantic buildings with blocks of *mithai*.

I was living the dream, wasn't I—building incredible structures. And in America, no less!

Veer pushed his memories of India out of mind, stepped away from the door of the *Bombay Bazaar*, and headed home.

~

He pulled into the driveway of his custom-designed home, almost running over the tall green garbage bin on the curb. Veer had torn down the unremarkable one-storey ranch and erected a contemporary concrete-and-glass marvel in its place. It had been featured in several magazines, including a recent issue of *Southern Living*.

Six-year-old Rahul collided headlong into Veer as he walked in through the kitchen door. It was a customary greeting that always made him laugh, but today it knocked the wind out of him.

"Papa! How was boxing? Please please, can I wear your gloves?"

"Not 'can I', but 'may I'."

"Okay, okay. May I please wear your boxing gloves, Papa?"

Rahul tugged open the gym bag on Veer's shoulder with all his might and began rummaging through its foul-smelling contents. Tiny hands slipped into big red gloves. Rahul looked at his father, hands under his chin, signalling preparedness. Jab-cross-jab-hook. Rahul responded on cue, punching into Veer's palms with a zen-like focus. Elizabeth watched father and son trade punches, her thin pink lips stretched into an indulgent smile.

"Good," Veer said dryly, his voice devoid of its usual playfulness.

"More! More!"

"No Rahul, not today. I am very tired."

Elizabeth walked over and kissed Veer on the cheek. "You look exhausted. Did the presentation go well?" she inquired.

"Yeah. It was okay."

"Mommy, I'm hungry," Rahul hollered.

"No dinner for stinky boys," she said, smiling. "Off to the shower." She wrapped her arms around Veer's neck and winked. "You too, handsome."

~

Elizabeth set the salmon next to the platter of grilled vegetables and stood back to admire the table setting. She could never have imagined eating Brussels sprouts with gusto—she grew up on fried chicken and mashed potatoes—but having been with Veer for seven years, over time her palate had adjusted to her husband's more austere tastes. Elizabeth figured they consumed more greens in a week than the average American does in an entire month.

Over dinner, she suggested some ideas for the forthcoming weekend—the weather forecast promised ample sunshine. Rahul voted to go cycling along the Chattahoochee River.

"Only if you put your plate away," Elizabeth prompted, pointing toward the kitchen.

Cautiously, Rahul did as instructed, placing the plate on the counter—his arms still too short to meet the bottom of the sink.

"I did it Mommy, I did it. Can we get ice-cream today?"

Veer intervened before Elizabeth could respond.

"Rahul, you know that sugar is not good for you. You just had ice-cream a few days ago. Eat some grapes or strawberries instead."

"Papa, that was six days ago. I counted! Why are you so unfair?"

"There is no need for a tantrum, Rahul. Sugar will make you fat and then...."

"Veer! Stop!" Elizabeth hollered.

"I hate you Papa." Rahul folded his arms across his chest, puffed up his face and walked away, taking his tears with him like a raincloud ready to burst.

"That was a bit much, don't you think?" Elizabeth said, clearing the table, a grim expression on her soft, heart-shaped face. "What's eating you today?"

"Nothing. I'm fine," he said, avoiding her probing gaze. "Did you bring the mail in?" Veer inquired, changing the subject. He had no strength for another altercation.

"Oh yes, I almost forgot. Laksha sent pictures of the shop." she handed Veer a thick envelope that had already been ripped open. "Look," she said pointing to a picture of the renovated interiors.

After Papa died, Laksha had taken over the *mithai* shop and, since then, she had turned the small-scale enterprise into a lucrative business. Her first order of business was to pay off the street vendor—a *kebabwala*—to relocate his pushcart that partially blocked the entrance to the shop. More recently, she had bought out the clothing store next door to increase the footprint of *Doon Mithais*, making it the largest sweet shop in the city. Veer looked at the picture, amazed at the transformations—hard wood floors, recessed lighting, abstract art on the walls, temperature-controlled enclosures for the *mithais*.

"Wow! Laksha's done a fantastic job," Veer said, his troubles forgotten, the designer in him marvelling at the minimalist interiors.

"Laksha says the organic, low-fat sweets are very popular. I wish I could try some. Perhaps we'll make a trip to India someday soon?" Elizabeth suggested tentatively. It was a contentious subject—talking about India—but she brought it up every once in a while in the hopes that someday her husband would open that boarded up section of his heart.

"Oh, don't start with that now," Veer said, giving her a look that said "no trespassing."

"But why, Veer? Don't you ever feel like visiting your home?"

"This is my home."

"You know what I mean."

"Yes, I do, and I am asking you to stop."

"You know, if I ever moved to another country, I would still want to visit my home. It is okay to miss your roots. That is why cities have places like Little Italy, Chinatown, the Barrio, where people still nurture their roots. Don't you think it is important for Rahul to know *his* heritage?"

Veer did not respond. He loved Elizabeth, and had she kept her feelings from him, hidden them like dirty little secrets; he would have prodded just the same.

"Look at this," Elizabeth said, handing Veer a flyer for an upcoming Diwali *mela* at the Gwinnett Community Center. "An Indian girl in Rahul's class gave it to him today. We should at least go to this fair."

"I've been to one of these. I am not going again. Forget it. Just buy him a book about Diwali."

Years ago, when Veer had just moved to Atlanta, he had heard about the sizeable Indian community in the suburbs. A deep longing for a faraway home spurred him to attend one such fair, but the experience left him feeling tragically uprooted.

"'appy Diwali!" the man at the entrance had greeted him cheerfully. He, like all the other men in Veer's line of vision, was dressed in the traditional garb of a *kurta-pajama*. Since his arrival in the United States, Veer had never seen so many Indians congregated in one place. The Diwali *mela* at the Gwinnett Community Centre was in full swing. Bollywood songs were blaring over the loud speaker, and people were thronging to food stalls selling everything from *papri chaat* to *tandoori* chicken, and even hot *jalebis*—pretzel-shaped twists of deep-fried batter dunked in sugar syrup. Everybody looked happy, as though they had walked into a snow globe and were experiencing the splendour of falling snow. It seemed to satisfy them—this manufactured microcosm in an alien world.

Hesitantly, Veer waded into the crowd. Personal space had evaporated, leaving behind a condensed, homogenous mass of bodies. His skin was once again rendered colourless. He could dissolve into them, like grains of sugar in hot syrup. Several strangers smiled at Veer, acknowledging him, accepting him as one of their own. Veer had no family in this adopted country of his—no distant cousin, no *chacha* or *taiya* to visit—and here was a community ready to take him into the fold. Yet something held him back, as if the very existence of his kind reminded him of the absence of his own people, and of the loss of his mother.

On an impulse, Veer asked a book vendor where he could purchase fireworks. After all, one cannot properly celebrate Diwali without *patakhas*.

"*Patakhas!* No, no, sir; that is not allowed in Georgia. You will have to wait for the 4th of July!"

"Diwali without fireworks! Do they celebrate Christmas without a Christmas tree?"

"It is like this only sir. We can't have everything, *na*," he said, smiling.

Veer and the vendor were distracted by a sudden flurry of activity at the henna tattoo booth next door. Two ladies were fawning over a white woman.

"She is a district commissioner," the bookseller told Veer proudly. "It is good to have such important white people at our *mela*."

Veer could have stayed, made the most of all that was available. Instead, he turned around and walked out the entranceway, accidentally stepping on the *rangoli* on the floor. He kneeled down to rearrange the labyrinthine mosaic of fine, varicoloured powder, but the damage was irremediable.

"I did buy him a book," Elizabeth said, irritated with her husband's indifference. "It is a sorry explanation about such a fascinating festival. I'm sure you can do better than that."

"I'll find a book myself. Okay? Now let it go. I have a lot on my mind today."

Elizabeth reached across the table and took Veer's hand in her own. "You know, I've never eaten a *mithai*. I have no idea what it tastes like," she said gently.

"What is a *mithai*?" Rahul peeked from the corner. Like an ephemeral thunderstorm, his anger had passed quickly.

~

"*Oye, motu mithaiwala!*" The burly boy, two years his senior, caught up with Veer just after lunch. "You better bring some *laddoos* to my dorm tomorrow, or you are dead meat. Got that?"

"I'm not a *mithaiwala*," Veer retorted, silently wishing that the *motu* part was also untrue.

"Talking back, are you fatty? Time to teach you a lesson." The boy pushed Veer to the ground and dragged him by the collar of his school shirt, all the way behind the cafeteria.

Veer awoke with a start.

God, I must be really messed up in the head. I have not dreamt about boarding school in years.

He rolled over onto his stomach and pinched his eyes shut, trying to no avail to stop his mind from wandering back to the night before his father packed him off to boarding school.

"Must we send Veer away?" For the last time, his mother voiced her objection over dinner. Serving her husband hot *chapattis* dabbed with *desi ghee*, she spoke with restraint, reining in her words from the headlong gallop they might have taken to a controlled trot.

Both Veer and Laksha sensed the contrived cordiality in her tone. They braced for their father's response, momentarily forgetting to chew their food.

"His grandfather and I both attended that school. Veer will do the same. It is my decision," he said, chewing his food as he spoke.

Still shackled by tradition, Veer did not dare question his father's apparent lack of respect for his mother's opinion. Instead, as he often did, Veer reached for a sweet treat to extinguish the flames of unrest with a salvo of sugar. From the platter of *mithais* his mother served as dessert, Veer selected a *malai barfi*–a heavenly combination of milk and sugar with a hint of cardamoms cooked on a slow fire and cooled till the gooey mix held together. Caustic words caught in his throat were washed away in a nectareous tide.

At the threshold of puberty, in sixth grade, when the school accepted students, most children did not entirely comprehend or endorse their parents' motives. They were told something about receiving a good education, and becoming men, ideals that held little or no allure for young boys. On matriculation day, those with alum parents and siblings entered the grounds of the school with a swagger, signalling their lofty status. Veer, on the other hand, dug his feet firmly into the ground, refusing to join the herd of new students.

When sundry threats failed to propel Veer forward, his father softened his tone, recounting his yet unsurpassed batting average on the school cricket team and his grandfather's stellar academic achievements decades ago.

"So what? Both of you are still just *mithaiwalas*, like Shankar *kaka*," Veer replied stubbornly.

For a moment he thought his father was going to strike him again. Neither Mama nor Shankar *kaka* were there to save him this time. But what he saw in Papa's eyes was not rage. It was hurt, as though Veer had struck him instead. Unwilling to compound his angst with the added burden of guilt, he dragged his hold-all down the pebbled path. His father followed a few steps behind, covering the tracks Veer had inadvertently etched into the ground.

In the sparsely lit dormitory, Veer sat on the bare bed allotted to him. The dull white walls and the clinical smell of phenol reminded him of the hospital where his grandfather had died not long ago.

Lost in a haze of anger and confusion, he could not understand why parents would want their children to live like orphans. What good could come of denying him his mother's love? Was it not enough that he stood first in class year after year? Veer had never been more afraid, and there was no one to turn to for comfort. He felt abandoned, utterly lonely in this new, unfamiliar world into which he had been thrust.

Wrapping his arms around himself, he attempted to recreate the warmth of his mother's embrace. She had not come to see him off; Papa had forbidden her and saved himself the embarrassment of the tears she was sure to shed.

Acutely aware of his strange surroundings, Veer forced himself to undo the leather straps of his hold-all and roll out the cotton mattress like the other boys. Between the sheets and towels, wrapped in cellophane, was a box of *mithais*, with the words *Doon Mithais–Happiness in a Box* printed on the cover. A letter taped to the lid smelt of cardamoms; it was from Mama. Fresh tears clouded his vision.

"I love you, my son," the note read. "I know this is difficult for you as it is for me. Think of me as you enjoy these *mithais*. And remember to share and make new friends. Shankar *kaka's* son just got a job as a cook in your school kitchen—he will keep bringing you sweets from home, I promise. Let this be our secret. Now wipe those tears away—or you'll make the *mithai* salty!"

The food at the school mess took some getting used to. Veer had to learn to chew twice as thoroughly or risk choking until someone casually thumped his back. Unlike the soft *chapattis* at home, the rip-resistant bread (fittingly called "elephant ears" by the other boys) made his jaw ache. Naturally, any easily edible food was precious commodity, and *mithai* ranked right up there with chocolate and chips. Shankar *kaka*'s son kept him provisioned with a steady supply of *besan laddoos* and *kaju katlis*; and Raghuveer, the rotund boy with ruddy cheeks, came to be known as "*motu mithaiwala*."

"Damn it," Veer said under his breath and slipped out of bed. He went down to the kitchen, where he poured himself a tall glass of water.

If I were at school right now, I would have reached into my stash of mithais. Heck, I would have become motu mithaiwala *forever had I not written that one-sentence essay.*

In 11th grade, the headmaster had asked the students to write a paper about where they envisioned themselves five years into the future. One by one, everybody was summoned to the headmaster's office to discuss at length the ambition each student had disclosed and the practical tools necessary to achieve those results.

Raghuveer Kumar had been moved out of the alphabetical order all the way past Umeed Uniyal. Given that Veer had submitted his assignment consisting solely of the words "Anything but a *mithaiwala*," he was not surprised. The headmaster's response, however, was no scholarly tirade. Assessing the chasm between youthful aspiration and cultural edict, he pointed Veer in an unexpected direction.

"Your grades are outstanding, Veer," the headmaster said. "If you like, I can help you apply for a full scholarship for an undergraduate programme in America. Study whatever catches your fancy my boy, and then select a path that excites you. You may realise your dreams there, or you may discover that your pot of gold lies right here, in every box of *mithai*."

Veer withheld the news from his parents until that Diwali night, hoping the festive spirit would work in his favour. But Papa's refusal came as no surprise.

"Boys who leave home never come back," he said. "Your responsibilities are here with us, Raghuveer. You are lucky you have a flourishing family business waiting for you."

"Papa, have you ever considered that I may not want to become a *mithaiwala*?"

From the corner of his eye, Veer saw the *rangoli* on the floor. For a moment he wished the wheel of time would roll in reverse, throwing him back under Mama's protection. Taking a stand against Papa was nothing if not scary.

"Why? What is so bloody wrong with being a *mithaiwala*, huh? Is it beneath you?" The cool evening air failed to arrest the blister-like eruptions of sweat on Papa's forehead. "You know, I wanted to be a cricketer—and I would have been a bloody good one—but I put aside my aspirations and did the right thing."

Like all fathers of his generation, and the one before, and the one before that, Papa portrayed his life as a template for success. He expected Veer to use the same metrics, and to that end he offered his only son what was, in his mind, a generous offer.

"Look, son," he said, bridging the physical gulf between them with a gentle hand on Veer's shoulder, "I am not asking you to go to some C grade college in this small town. Go to Delhi University. Have fun. I will pay for everything. People may think of us as some lowly *mithaiwalas*, but you know I make an honest living. Isn't that worth something?"

Veer took a few steps away from his father. Refusal displayed itself on Veer's face, in the clenched jaw and the dark, angry eyes. *I'll be damned if I end up as just another* wala.

Recognising defeat, Papa flared up like an *anaar* bursting into sparkling flames. What a spectacular display of anger, Veer thought to himself, smiling sarcastically, as defiant teenagers often do when they are too proud to acknowledge their fears.

His father stared right at him. *Is he really going to hit me?* Veer wondered. *On Diwali, no less?*

"At least think about your mother. How can you leave her when—" his father's voice was no louder than a whisper, a hissing *anaar* drawing on the last traces of gunpowder.

"When what, Papa?" Veer probed, losing the attitude and dropping his hands from his hips to his sides. He took a step closer. "When what?" he repeated urgently.

An eternity escaped before Papa responded. He raised his hands above his head, shaking them as if he was trying to decipher the contents of mysterious package. "Damn the woman, she made me promise not to tell you and Laksha anything. Go. Go tell your mother about your plans. She will set you right."

Veer found his mother in the kitchen, garnishing the sumptuous meal she had laboured over for days. She looked tired, but that did not surprise him, given that she was always on her feet, cooking both at the shop and at home every single day.

Without waiting for her to look up, Veer blurted everything out to her—first about the scholarship to a university in Georgia and ending with the row with Papa.

"He insinuated there might be something wrong with you. He said that to dissuade me, right? You aren't sick—are you, Mama?" It was a feeble, fearful inquiry.

"Listen to me, Raghuveer. You must go and live your life to the fullest." Contrary to her husband's expectations, Veer's mother did not compel him to hew to tradition. Instead, she pushed him away from it all. All the way to a country where, she had been told, sugar looks like salt.

"But he will never forgive you Mama. Maybe I should stay—I don't want you to suffer because of me. Besides, you don't look very well. Please tell me what is wrong? What was Papa talking about?" Veer stopped pacing the kitchen and paused momentarily by his mother's side, searching her deep brown eyes for answers he was not sure he wanted to hear.

"Papa will not say anything to me, because this is my dying wish." Gently, she told him about the tumour that was devouring her insides. "I've eaten so much *kaju katli* in my life, I am sure I am the tastiest body cancer has ever eaten into!" she joked.

The thrill of impending freedom collided with the agony of loss like the shifting plates of the earth beneath his feet. Veer started at his mother, immobile, frozen in place.

"I cannot leave you Mama," Veer cried, unashamed of the tears falling freely.

"Oh, but you must. Even Lord Rama had to leave his beloved kingdom." Not a single tear betrayed his mother's pain. "It is the right path for you," she said. Then she hugged him, for that was her way of setting him free. Then she took a piece of *kaju katli* from the freshly set tray and offered it to him. "May your life be filled with sweetness."

I should have never abandoned you, Mama. I had a choice.

Veer poured himself another glass of water and drained it in one long gulp. The clock on the wall read 3:20 A.M. He reached for the phone and dialled his sister's number in India, remembering to punch in "1" before dialling the country and city code. He never forgot how he had accidentally dialled 911 the first time he called home after arriving in the United States.

"What is your emergency?" the operator had asked him.

"I am just trying to call India," he had responded, confused and embarrassed.

Veer dialled the number to *Doon Mithais*. Laksha answered almost immediately.

"Veer! What a surprise! What time is it there? Why are you up at this ungodly hour? Is everything okay?"

"Everything is fine. Don't worry," Veer said in a soothing voice.

"I bet you have been up working. It's not good for you, you know."

"Hey, I am the older one. I should be giving you advice, not the other way around."

"Yes, you are the older one, but I've always liked taking care of you."

"Like the time you beat up that boy who lived across the street when he called me *motu*."

"Ha ha, you still remember that? It was years ago! But it looks like you don't need help in that department anymore. You look so slim and strong in the photographs Elizabeth sent."

"Yeah, I've been boxing for a long time now. Having my little sister stand up for me was embarrassing enough."

"So, how are things?"

"Things are fine at my end. I saw the pictures of the shop. I love what you've done with the place."

"Yes, the shop is looking great. And the business is fantastic."

"All your hard work is paying off, Laksha."

"Yes it is. But you know half of everything is yours."

"I'm never coming back, Laksha. The shop is yours."

"No, Veer. That would not be right. The shop was supposed to be yours, not mine. Let me at least send you your share. I can wire the money to you."

"I don't know, Laksha. I don't deserve that money."

"Yes you do. Mama and Papa would want you to have your share. Think of it as a cumulated Diwali gift!"

~

"Veer! It is almost eight o'clock! Don't you have to be at work?"

"I'm taking the day off," Veer said, pulling the covers over his head.

"Are you feeling all right?" Elizabeth felt his forehead with the back of her hand.

"I'm fine. I just need to rest, that's all. Go!"

"Okay," she said reluctantly, "I'll try and come back early from work."

"Please don't do that. I will be fine. I'll call if I need anything."

"Promise?"

"Promise."

"Okay. Rahul has chess after school today. I'll pick him up at 3:30 and then make a quick stop for groceries. We should be home by 4:15."

~

"Ta-da!"

Dressed in a frilly red apron, Veer greeted Rahul and Elizabeth with a pyramid of *kaju katli*.

"Wow! What is this, Papa?"

"It is a building made from *mithais*, Rahul."

"The sweet Indian stuff?" The child's eyes sparkled like fireworks in the night sky. Veer took a piece from the very top and handed it to Rahul.

"Can I eat it?" Rahul looked incredulously at his father. Gone was the stern expression from the night before.

"Yes, you *may*."

"Yummy! Did you make this, Papa?" Rahul bit into the treat, savouring it slowly, as Veer looked on. He was reminded of himself decades ago, lost in a world of irresistible sweets.

"Yes, my son, I did. I am a *mithaiwala*, you know."

Just as Shankar *kaka* had once sat him down on the counter, Veer propped Rahul up next to a pot crusted with sticky white goo and told him all about the heavenly combination of milk, sugar, *ghee*, and cashew nuts. He told his son about *Doon Mithais*, about his grandfather and great grandfather. About Mama and Shankar *kaka*. About being a '*mithaiwala*' himself.

Elizabeth walked into the kitchen carrying two large grocery bags. She looked at the mess all around her.

"Veer, what is going on?"

"Here, have a piece of *mithai*, and I'll tell you everything."

Veer filled her in on the events of the previous day, and his plans for the future.

"I am going to start my own firm. We have money saved up, and Laksha is sending the rest."

"Here Papa, have one," Rahul gave Veer a piece of *mithai*. He bit into it very slowly.

"Be careful Papa. Your tears will make the *mithai* salty!"

~

"Rahul, come here right now. We have to finish homework before Mommy gets home, or we'll be in the dog house." Veer unzipped Rahul's backpack, thankful for its limited contents. His own schoolbag had weighed him down as a child. Rahul bounded into the room, deliberately bumping into him.

"Don't worry, Papa, I know what to do. I have to write a competition on what I want to be when I grow up."

"You mean c-o-m-p-o-s-i-t-i-o-n. So, what do you want to be?" Veer smiled, expecting the usual answer. Rahul wanted to be Bob the Builder.

"I want to make people happy. And eating *mithai* always makes me happy. So I think I am going to be a *mithaiwala*."

Glossary

Readers may not be familiar with all the Indian place names, cultural allusions, Hindi words, and other expressions mentioned in the stories. The list below provides explicit definitions and explanations for these terms.

–ji	honorific suffix in languages of the Indian subcontinent, denoting respect.
–wala; –wali	male and female forms, respectively, of the adjectival suffix appended to a noun to indicate that the person engages in some type of activity or profession, e.g., *fruitwala* (a man who sells fruit) or *kaamwali* (a maidservant).
aam janta	common people; used in a derogatory sense, it means the masses or hoi polloi.
accha	Hindi word indicating agreement, such as 'Okay,' 'Good,' 'I understand,' etc. *Accha ji* is a slightly more polite way of saying 'Okay.'
Ajit	stage name of Hamid Ali Khan (1922–1998), a Hindi movie actor who made a career out of playing the villain in many Bollywood films.

aloo paratha	popular Indian breakfast meal consisting of unleavened dough stuffed with mashed potatoes and spices.
angrakshak	bodyguard
apsara	in Hindu mythology, a beautiful female spirit of the clouds; a nymph or celestial maiden.
asana	a pose or posture in yoga practice.
autorickshaw	three-wheeled, motorised means of transportation, often used as a vehicle for hire.
Avinash	Hindi male name meaning 'indestructible.'
ayah	nanny
ayree	sound that someone makes to express disapproval or caution.
ayurvedic	system of traditional medicine in the Indian subcontinent.
baba	term of respect or endearment toward an older male, such as one's father or a swami (religious teacher).
bael	*Aegle marmelos*, or Bengal quince; a species of fruit tree native to India and considered sacred in Hinduism.
bahut samay pehle	'A long time ago' in Hindi. Fairy tales and children's stories often begin with this phrase, which is comparable to "Once upon a time" in English.
baksheesh	tip, alms or bribe
bakwas	bullshit, nonsense
banarasi	*saris* made in the Indian city of Varanasi that are considered among the finest in India and renowned for the intricacy of their designs.
beedi	slim, inexpensive cigarette with tobacco rolled in a *tendu* leaf instead of paper.

besan ladoo	popular, ball-shaped Indian sweet made with gram flour.
bhajan	devotional song that expresses love for the divine.
bhakt	devotee
bhel (bhelpuri)	popular Mumbai street food made from puffed rice and vegetables.
bhelwala (m)	snack vendor who sells *bhelpuri*.
bibiji	term of address meaning 'respected ma'am.'
bindi	round dot, traditionally red (to signify honour, love, and prosperity), that Indian women apply to the middle of the forehead as a decoration.
biryani	in Asian cuisine, a spicy rice-based dish made with vegetables and/or meat such as lamb or chicken.
boondi prasad	sweet, deep-fried gram flour balls.
bun samosa	bread bun with a spiced filling (such as potatoes, onions, etc.), often sold by street vendors in India as a cheap, savoury snack.
cablewala	cable television operator.
chai	spiced milk tea
chaiwala (m)	tea seller
Chanda Maama Door Ke	title of a popular lullaby which, loosely translated, means 'Moon uncle so far away.' The song, from the 1955 Bollywood film *Vachan*, is based on a much older traditional song and is comparable to 'Twinkle, Twinkle, Little Star.'
chanderi (sari)	traditionally woven *sari* from Chanderi, a town in the state of Madhya Pradesh.
chapatti	unleavened flatbread, a common staple of south Asian cuisine.

Chaudhvin Ka Chand Ho	title of a popular Hindi song from the 1960 Bollywood feature film of the same name; the phrase translates as "Are you the full moon?"
chokra	derogatory term for a boy; callow youth.
churel	hideous female ghost that feeds on human blood; a witch or ghoul.
chut	coarse Hindi expletive denoting the female genitalia.
chutiya	term of derision denoting a fool, idiot, bastard, fucker.
dal	stew made from lentils.
dalal	broker, go-between
darshan	visitation by a God, a vision of the divine, a blessing, or the bestowal of grace.
desi ghee	clarified butter
dhakai jamdani	richly woven muslin textile from Dhaka, Bangladesh, used in the production of luxurious saris.
dharma	In Hinduism, Buddhism, and other Eastern religions, *dharma* is a key concept with no single equivalent in Western languages. In Hinduism, it signifies behaviours that proceed from and are related to duty, law, virtue, and good conduct.
dhoti	traditional men's garment, similar to a skirt, consisting of a rectangular piece of cloth wrapped around the legs and knotted at the waist.
dhyan	deep meditation
dhyan se	expression meaning 'Be careful!'

dhyana mudra	in yogic practice and Buddhist iconography, the hand gesture of meditation with open palms facing upward on the lap, four fingers of each hand fully extended and overlapping, and the thumbs touching each other diagonally to form a triangle.
Diwali	Indian festival of lights
dost	friend, pal, buddy
dupatta	long scarf worn by a women, usually as an integral part of her outfit.
Dussehra	Hindu festival day, usually taking place in October at the end of the nine-day Navratri festival, celebrating Goddess Durga and commemorating the victory of Lord Rama against the 10-headed demon-king Ravana, as recounted in the epic Ramayana.
firang	general term in India for a foreigner, especially a white-skinned foreigner; occasionally used with a slightly derogatory connotation.
fruitwala (m)	fruit seller
Ganesh	elephant-headed God of the Hindu pantheon, widely revered as a patron of the arts and sciences and as the 'remover of obstacles'.
ganja	marijuana
gharwali	housewife
ghat	flight of steps leading down to any body of water, especially a sacred river (such as the Ganges).
gulab jamun	Deep-fried balls of dough dunked in flavoured sugar syrup.
gulmohar	*Delonix regia*, or flame tree; a species of flowering plant with fern-like leaves and colourful flowers.

Hanuman Chalisa	long devotional hymn, consisting of 40 verses, addressed to the Hindu God Hanuman.
Hanuman puja	traditional worship of the Hindu deity Hanuman.
haramzada (m), *haramzadi* (f)	bastard
harijan	untouchable
haveli	mansion
hing	asafoetida
hogaya	common colloquialism indicating that something is finished. The phrase *'Theek hai, hogaya'* means 'Okay, we're done.'
ikat	type of woven cloth dyed with a pattern.
is bechare ko mauth aa jaye to acha hoga	'It would be best for him to die.'
jaanu	sweetheart
jadu tona	black magic, sorcery
jaldi	fast, quickly; exclamation meaning 'Hurry!'
jalebi	deep-fried batter in circular shapes, dunked in flavoured sugar syrup.
jai Ganesh deva	opening lines of a prayer to the elephant God, Ganesh.
jyotishi	astrologer
kaamwali	maidservant
kafal	*Myrica esculenta*, or box myrtle; a small tree native to the hills of Nepal and northern India.
kaju katli	cashew nut based dessert often coated with a thin layer of edible metallic leaf.
kaka	term of endearment toward an older male.
kalachakra	wheel of time

kameez	long shirt or tunic
kanjivaram (sari)	traditionally woven *sari* made by weavers from the town of Kanchipuram in the state of Tamil Nadu in southern India.
kebabwala (m)	kebab seller
kesar pista	saffron pistachio
khatri	caste of people from the Punjab region of India, typically engaged in mercantile pursuits.
kheer	rice pudding
kismetwali	woman blessed with good fortune. Used in the literal sense in the story of the same name, it refers to one who deals in fate or destiny; a clairvoyant.
koel	type of cuckoo bird of Asia with a loud, distinctive call.
kudewali	woman garbage collector
kulfi	type of frozen dairy dessert in India, similar to ice cream.
kundalini	in Eastern tradition, the primordial physical and spiritual force, latent in all humans, often described as a snake or serpent lying coiled at the base of the spine, only waiting to be awakened through spiritual practice leading to enlightenment.
kurta	loose, collarless shirt
kurta-pajama	outfit of clothing consisting of a loose, collarless shirt and baggy, straight-legged pants.
kurti	long blouse
kutiya	derogatory term for a woman; bitch
kutta	dog
Lakshman	brother of the Hindu God Lord Rama.

Lakshmi	wife of Vishnu (supreme God of Hinduism) and the Goddess of wealth, prosperity, good fortune, and beauty.
laddoo	ball-shaped Indian sweet.
lassi	traditional yoghurt or buttermilk-based drink, flavoured with spices and served chilled as a warm-weather beverage.
loo	hot, dry afternoon wind that blows over western region of north India in the months of May and June.
maa	mother; often attached as an honorific title to the names of Hindu Goddesses.
maal	stuff, often connoting cash as well as drugs or other illegal merchandise.
madarchod	motherfucker
mahal	palace
maharaja	Sanskrit term meaning 'great king.'
maharani	Sanskrit term meaning 'great queen.'
mahila	woman
maidan	open space in a town, such as a square, park, or playground.
mala	garland, necklace, or bracelet
malai barfi	popular Indian sweet made with milk solids.
mali	gardener
malika	queen
malishwali	masseuse
Mannat	Hindi female name meaning 'wish' or 'desire.'
masala chai	south Asian tea flavoured with spices.
masi	maternal aunt
matka	type of gambling that originated in Mumbai, India; literally 'large pot.'

mauli	sacred cotton thread, dyed red and sometimes also yellow, used in Hindu prayer ceremonies.
mela	fair
memsahib	polite form of address in the Indian subcontinent, used toward a woman; equivalent to 'Madam' or 'Ma'am.'
Mere Sapno Ki Rani	title of a Hindi song from the 1969 hit Bollywood film *Aradhana*; translates as 'Queen of My Dreams.'
malai	cream. The skin that forms over milk cooked on a stove is almost pure cream and is collected to be used for making desserts, *ghee*, etc.
mithai	any type of sweet or confection in India.
Mithaiwala (m)	vendor of sweets
mogra	species of jasmine
motu	(slang) fat
namaste	literally, 'salutations to you;' customary respectful term of greeting or valediction among Indians.
NIVH	National Institute for the Visually Handicapped, located in the city of Dehradun, Uttarakhand, India.
oye	exclamation used in India and Pakistan, equivalent to saying 'Hey!'
paan	preparation of betel leaf (combined with tobacco or other fillings) with mild psychoactive properties; used by south Asian people as a digestif or to freshen the breath. It is chewed and then spat out (or swallowed).
pagal aurat	crazy woman
paisa walas	wealthy folk
pandit	Hindu scholar, typically also a practicing priest.

papri chaat	popular Indian street food
patakha	firecracker
Parvati	gentle manifestation of the Goddess Shakti (wife of Shiva), and mother of Lord Ganesh.
patola	expensive double-ikat silk sari produced in the Gujarat region of western India.
phool	flower
phoolwali (f)	flower seller
phool jharu	type of broom, similar to a feather duster, with a bushy head made from bamboo grass.
phulkari	literally 'flower working,' a type of embroidery from the Punjab region of India, typically used in headscarves, shawls, and *dupattas* (long scarves worn around the neck).
pittu garam	game of Seven Stones, played between two teams, the object of which is to build a small tower of stones without getting hit by a tennis ball thrown by the opposing team.
policewala	cop
poori aloo	potato-based breakfast dish, popular in northern India.
Pratap	Hindu ruler (1540–1597) who exemplified the manly virtues of bravery and chivalry.
puja	prayer ritual
Pyaasa	title of a 1957 Indian film; the Hindi word means 'thirsty'.
raj	period of British Rule in India (1858–1947)
rajnigandha	tuberose
rakshasa	humanoid monster or evil spirit in Hindu mythology.

Ramlila	dramatic re-enactment, staged over 10 nights during the Navratri festival, commemorating the 10-day battle between Lord Rama and the demon-king Ravana, as told in the Hindu epic *Ramayana*, and culminating (in many parts of India) in the burning of a giant effigy of the demon.
sabziwala	vegetable seller
sahib	polite form of address in the Indian subcontinent, used toward a man; equivalent to 'mister' or 'sir'.
sala (m); *sali* (f)	commonly heard swear word, used as a mild term of abuse.
sali kuti	'fucking bitch'
sali randi	'fucking whore'
salwar	loose-fitted, pajama-like trousers.
salwar kameez	traditional apparel, worn primarily by women in India, consisting of pajama-like trousers and a long shirt or tunic.
safaiwali	cleaning lady
sari	traditional wrap-around garment worn by women.
savari	vehicle or ride
savasana	'corpse pose' in yoga practice.
seekh	skewer, as used to prepare kebabs on a grill.
seekh kebab	kebab prepared with ground meat and grilled on skewers in a *tandoor* (type of oven) or grill.
seenghwala	peanut seller
shakti	wife of Lord Shiva, and the divine personification of feminine energy in the universe.
shavewala (m)	barber

Shiv puja	traditional worship of the Hindu deity Shiva.
Shivji	honorific name for Shiva.
Shivling	representation of Lord Shiva, with a generally phallic shape, used for worship in homes and temples.
shukriya	thank you
sindoor	red or orange cosmetic powder, traditionally applied by married women along the parting of the hair.
tamasha	traditional form of theatre in the state of Maharashtra. It has come to denote any sort of pointless commotion; a tempest in a teacup.
tandava	ecstatic divine dance of bliss performed by the Lord Shiva by which he brings about the destruction and rebirth *of the universe.*
tandoori	any food item cooked in a tandoor (a cylindrical clay oven). Also refers to a blend of Indian spices.
tawa	flat griddle
tendu	*Diospyros melanoxylon,* or East Indian Ebony; a species of flowering tree native to India. Leaves from this tree are wrapped around tobacco to form a *beedi* (type of inexpensive south Asian cigarette).
thali	plate, or a meal composed of small servings of several dishes.
tharra	cheap, usually illegal, locally brewed alcoholic drink made from sugarcane or wheat and consumed in north India; a kind of moonshine similar to rum.
theek hai	common colloquialism meaning 'okay' or 'that's fine.' The phrase *'Theek hai, hogaya'* means 'Okay, we're done.'

tikka masala   spiced dish made of roasted chunks of meat, usually chicken, in an orange-coloured cream sauce.

taxiwala (m)   cab driver

ujjai   literally, 'victorious breath,' this diaphragmatic breathing technique is used in some yoga practices; also called 'ocean breath' because of the sound made when breathing in this manner.

upma   south Indian breakfast food made from semolina, similar to porridge.

Vaishno Devi   Vaishno Devi Mandir is a famous Hindu shrine located in the Trikuta Mountains of northern India and dedicated to the Goddess Shakti.

wah-wah   praise

yaar   (slang) for 'man' or 'dude.' Colloquially, 'Oh *yaar*' is the equivalent of 'Oh man.'

Yamdoot   messenger of death

Yeh Duniya Agar Mil Bhi Jaye Toh Kya Hai   song title from the 1957 film *Pyaasa*, meaning 'Even if I could have it, what is this world to me?'

Yeh to hota hai   Hindi phrase expressing resignation, meaning 'Oh well, it happens, what can you do?'

zamindar   Land-owning aristocrat, similar to a lord or baron, who collects taxes or rents from the tenants and peasant farmers who live on his property.